HOW
TO
WRITE A
ROM-COM

HOW TO WRITE A ROM-COM

CRISTINA WOLF

An Aria Book

First published in the UK in 2025 by Head of Zeus,
part of Bloomsbury Publishing Plc

Copyright © Cristina Wolf, 2025

The moral right of Cristina Wolf to be identified
as the author of this work has been asserted in accordance with
the Copyright, Designs and Patents Act of 1988.

All rights reserved. No part of this publication may be: i) reproduced or transmitted in any form, electronic or mechanical, including photocopying, recording or by means of any information storage or retrieval system without prior permission in writing from the publishers; or ii) used or reproduced in any way for the training, development or operation of artificial intelligence (AI) technologies, including generative AI technologies. The rights holders expressly reserve this publication from the text and data mining exception as per Article 4(3) of the Digital Single Market Directive (EU) 2019/790.

This is a work of fiction. All characters, organizations, and events
portrayed in this novel are either products of the author's
imagination or are used fictitiously.

9 7 5 3 1 2 4 6 8

A catalogue record for this book is available from the British Library.

ISBN (PB): 9781035915347
ISBN (eBook): 9781035915309; ISBN (ePub): 9781035915323

Cover design: Gemma Gorton
Typeset by Siliconchips Services Ltd UK

Printed and bound in Great Britain by
CPI Group (UK) Ltd, Croydon CR0 4YY

Bloomsbury Publishing Plc
50 Bedford Square, London, WC1B 3DP, UK
Bloomsbury Publishing Ireland Limited,
29 Earlsfort Terrace, Dublin 2, D02 AY28, Ireland

HEAD OF ZEUS LTD
5–8 Hardwick Street
London EC1R 4RG

To find out more about our authors and books visit www.headofzeus.com
For product safety related questions contact productsafety@bloomsbury.com

For anyone who is waiting for their happily ever after.

May you live happily ever now.

Forever is composed of nows. – Emily Dickinson

PROLOGUE

There are a few things that should pop into one's head after one face plants into the asphalt outside of Radio City Music Hall.

1. Shit, I'm going to get hit by a car.
2. Ew, this ground is so gross.
3. Ouch.

I thought none of those things.

My thoughts went to *The Wedding Planner*. Awesome and completely underrated mid-2000s rom-com with Matthew McConaughey and Jennifer Lopez. Jenny gets her heel stuck in a grate and McConaughey has to save her from a runaway dumpster. As far as "meet-cutes" go, it's pretty iconic.

That is *not* what happened to me.

Let's be honest, it's New York. So, did I really expect anyone to stop and help me up? No. I've lived in Manhattan for years now. Unless there is a real threat, we New Yorkers rarely even shudder.

But in my line of work, that is, happily-ever-afters, my mind is constantly on the search for my knight in shining armor. While I may work in romance, love itself has eluded me, well–forever. So, there I was, walking in front of one of the most iconic Manhattan landmarks, totally wiped out, and I was wondering one single thing:

Where. The. Hell. Is. *He*?

The "he" in question being that tall, dark, handsome, mysterious stranger who comes to my aid. My McConaughey. The unsuspecting, dashing, man of my dreams who falls in love with me the moment he sees me splayed out on the pavement without a hair out of place. Was he *busy* today or something?

Don't get me wrong, I'm a feminist, a "damsel-can-handle-her-distress" supporter, but I'm also a romance editor. And we live for this shit.

When I stood up, grunting at the one person who asked "Are you okay?" as they continued to pass by at the speed of a gazelle and dusting off my knees, I finally saw him.

I caught a glimpse as I readjusted my backpack on my shoulders—a dash of blonde curls on the opposite side of Sixth Avenue. The moment couldn't have been longer than a few seconds, but my eyes locked onto him from across the speeding traffic. From a distance, I could tell that he was coming to help me... or was at least concerned about the fact that I fell in the middle of a busy intersection. I was too far away, but I'm sure his eyebrows were furrowed. They had to be.

He took a step toward me. Then another.

And then his attention was taken by a child beside

him, and a honking bus sped by. By the time I made it to the sidewalk and looked back across the avenue, he was gone.

Fucking rom-coms. Fucking Matthew McConaughey. You're the reason I have unrealistic expectations of men, Matthew.

And yet, as I fell asleep last night—with an ice pack on my knee because I'm twenty-eight and tripping on the street can be the cause of major injury now—the image of a stranger with crystal blue eyes seemed etched in my brain, fogging my vision, like a lens I couldn't quite clear.

ONE

This isn't the way my life is supposed to go.

My life is supposed to be glamorous—real *Sex and the City* type shit. I should have men showing up at my apartment door because they just had to have me right then and there. I should be walking to work in Jimmy Choos and having lunch in Bryant Park with potential clients and spending exorbitant amounts of money on the cocktails I have with my friends every night.

Yeah, no, this can't be right.

Cleaning the floor at the Starbucks on the first floor of our office building with a stack of brown napkins that couldn't soak up a drip of water is *so not* where I thought I'd be right now.

"I'm so sorry, again, but I really need that coffee. I have a meeting in ten minutes," I say, my brain spitting out words faster than my mouth can handle. I throw the stack of napkins in the trash and look at the barista helplessly.

"Then maybe you shouldn't have spilled it," a sassy Gen

Z-er snaps back at me, flipping her sleek blue hair behind her as she refills a machine with milk.

"Okay, well *that* attitude is not helping," I reply forcefully, laying my hands on the counter.

"Lucy—" Elle warns behind me.

"Brindy, can I call you Brindy?" I say, barely glancing at the girl's name tag.

"Since my name is Brenda, probably not," she replies, not even glancing in my direction.

Damn dyslexia.

"Bren, listen. I am sorry I spilled that beautiful caramel macchiato that you just made. And I will come here every day and offer you penance in exchange for the blessing of my immortal soul, but at this very moment, my boss is probably standing next to my desk, tapping her foot—a foot which is most likely in a pair of Louboutins that cost more than my last two pay checks—wondering where her coffee and her assistant are," I say, forcing a broad smile on my face. "So please, in the name of our good Lord who on this day really wants your girl here not to lose her job, can I pretty please with whipped cream on top, have another caramel macchiato… with whipped cream on top?"

"Wow, that was a lot," Elle mutters. I shoot her a menacing look out of the corner of my eye.

Brenda glares at me, and I'm sure the word "murder" is somewhere in her thoughts.

"Have you seen *The Devil Wears Prada*?"

"I've met your boss, she's nothing like Miranda Priestly," Brenda deadpans.

Okay, points to the snooty barista. Didn't peg her as a connoisseur of classic Anne Hathaway movies.

I see Elle nod. I elbow her in the side.

"Have I told you about the time she threatened me within an inch of my life with a stapler?"

"Lucy, she was in labor!" Elle squeals, gently hitting me on the arm.

"And that makes it *okay*?"

"Oh my God, fine! Anything to get you out of my face!" Brindy/Brenda whines, slamming a jug of milk on the counter so hard that some shoots out the top. I quickly grab another handful of napkins and reach across the counter to wipe it up. "But the next time you come in here, I swear you better not make a mess."

"Bren, I promise. This will never happen again," I plead, pressing my hands together.

"You said that last time," Elle mutters.

"Whose side are you on?" I snap at her, whipping my head around so fast that my hair hits me in the face.

"The side that gets me to this meeting on time," she mumbles.

"Exactly, so *zip it*," I say, motioning for her to lock her lips with my hand.

Brenda hands me the hot drink without putting a cardboard sleeve on it, so my hand is absolutely scorched when I touch it. Well played, Brindy. Well played.

"Oh, for fuck's sake," I mutter as Elle types in our floor number into the elevator keypad. I move the cup of coffee from one hand to another to distribute the pain.

"Will you chill out? Everything is going to be fine. Anne

is never ready to start these meetings on time anyway," Elle says. "Why so *sassy* today?" she adds.

I love Elle. She is the best friend and roommate I could ever ask for. Sometimes, I envy her. She's able to put on a positive, upbeat face, even when she feels the complete opposite on the inside. She can match my cynicism punch-for-punch, but she can also be optimistic in a way that I struggle to be. She is the sunshine in my day, always looking for the bright side, always there to challenge my occasional (read: usual) bitterness. I envy so much about her, down to her long eyelashes that accent her brilliantly big eyes and her long blonde curls.

I wish I could look as effortlessly beautiful as Elle does on a daily basis. In the time it takes me to curl my (what I view as) boring chestnut brown hair, Elle can shower, throw some curling product in her perfect blonde hair, and be ready for work. So, most days, my hair ends up in a messy bun at the top of my head, because I just can't be bothered with it. Today, I was going for beachy waves, but said waves are quickly getting on my nerves. Plus, it's May in New York, which means the trip from the Upper West Side to Rockefeller Center was a steamy one.

I grunt. "I don't know. Everything just seems to be such a struggle lately," I mumble, pushing some of my hair out of my face.

"What do you mean?" Elle asks as the elevator dings past another floor.

"Ugh, it's just—," I mutter. "You know I had an agent lunch last week and she was pitching a book that I would kill to acquire, you know, if I actually had that ability."

"So, I'll acquire it," Elle says with a smile.

"That's not the point," I respond with a huff. "I need a raise. I need a change of pace. I've been getting coffee for two years, so long that I'm on a semi-first name basis with the barista." I let out a long breath, annoyed at myself for dumping all of this on Elle. "I don't know. I just… I want to remember why I'm in this industry, you know?"

"You're here because you love books, you goose," Elle says as we watch the digital numbers on the wall in front of us approach our floor. "And you love books about love. We all do."

"I just don't know if that's enough anymore," I mumble. Elle puts a hand on my shoulder and pouts. "It's hard to be passionate about books about love when you haven't felt it in so long."

"You mean you weren't in love with that Uber driver you went out with last month?"

"Is that *never speaking about him again*?" I snap, pressing my hand against my forehead. I shudder at the thought. Elle laughs.

"Maybe my standards are too high, but I don't think it's too much to ask to swipe through these stupid apps and find someone who A) knows how old they are, B) isn't trying to sell me marijuana, and C) isn't holding a dead fish. But no, I'm met with '23, not 29! 420 friendly!' And mutilated Nemos with every tap."

Romance books don't prepare you for these problems.

"Well, I guess that's the plight of the single romance editor," Elle says, referencing her own single status. "This was never a storyline in *Younger*, I'm not sure how we're supposed to deal with it."

"Maybe we should write our own book about our sad love

lives. *Lonely romance editor finds love after years of vagina drought*," I say as if I'm reading the headline of a newspaper. Elle and I giggle as the two middle-aged men in suits in the elevator with us give us the dirtiest look of all time.

"A bestseller for sure," Elle whispers as the men exit the elevator. Our howling laughter follows them down the hall.

I follow Elle to our desks at the back of the floor. Heartwarming, the romance imprint we work for, is seen by some as the black sheep of the fiction division. They hide us away in the dark corner. Heaven forbid we get in the way of the "serious stuff" with our talk of orgasms and happily-ever-afters. I wish someone would write a book about how underappreciated the romance genre is, how important romance can be for people. People like me.

I think back to that thirteen-year-old girl reading *Twilight* under her desk in class and deflate a little bit. Back then, I thought the romance I read about was the rule, not the exception. But the longer I work in romance, the more I'm starting to think that maybe that dream isn't for everyone.

That girl was so unaware of the *lack* of love that adulthood had waiting for her.

Somewhere in my mind, maybe I thought the closer I got to romance books, the more I immersed myself in them, the closer I would get to finding my own happily ever after. And yet, at twenty-eight years old, I still haven't found a man that I can make it through a dinner with, let alone date long term.

Adulting is hard. Dating is hard. Love is hard. They should really put that on the advertisement for this growing up shit.

That day in front of Radio City, the iconic landmark I

was supposed to count myself lucky for being able to work next to every day, became a symbol for all of the "should" in my life. I *should* be happy that I'm "living my dream" and not constantly be asking for more—and yet, I still found myself yearning for something, or at least *someone*, to share this dream with.

Elle and I rush past our company's new open-plan setup and quickly drop our bags on our desks. My cubicle is right next to Anne's, so I feel her eyes boring holes in me before I make it around the small cork wall that separates us to hand her the coffee.

"Did you trip and spill the coffee again?" Anne asks, taking the cup from me. I wrap the cup in a napkin I picked up at the kitchenette on our floor on our way in, so Anne doesn't have the same burnt palms that I do.

When she finishes clicking her mouse more times than is necessary to open her email, she raises her eyebrows and pushes her large clear glasses to the end of her nose, so she can look at me in a knowing way.

Wow, she really looks like Miranda Priestly when she does that. I wish I could take a picture to compare.

"I have no idea what you're talking about," I mutter, ostentatiously rolling my eyes toward the ceiling to avoid her gaze.

"Lucy Bowen, what do I keep telling you?" Anne says, spinning around in her chair so fast that her short black curls swing around her face and bounce with a level of enthusiasm that I wish I had this early in the morning. "You need to—"

"Work on my core, I know," I finish for her, returning to my side of the cubicle wall.

"It will really help with your balance," Anne says with only a hint of condescension in her tone. Anne is tall and thin, with a sunken face that she hides behind glasses that are too big for her face. She can be menacing when she wants to be, but also appear friendly with authors at the same time.

"Oh, by the way!" Anne says a little too loudly. "Lucy, do you have those sales numbers I asked for—?" Her voice halts when she sees my hand already outstretched containing said files. She eyes me with a smirk. "You're so good."

"I keep telling you that," I quip. As much as I complain about Anne's frantic and disorganized work style, I am lucky to have such a friendly relationship with my boss. I know other assistants who are not so lucky, which is why I'm comfortable making comments like this. I've made it no secret to Anne that it's time for a promotion, but as with anything in publishing, that process has been going about as fast as a train would go through molasses.

When Anne clicks her tongue, I take my cue, ambling after her toward the conference room. The others soon trickle in, mumbling by way of greeting. Anne kicks things off by discussing news in the industry, bestsellers, and any upcoming projects of interest.

"What do you think about the historical romance you mentioned last week, Nicole?" Anne asks. She's in her signature meeting position—legs crossed, curly hair bouncing in tandem with her leg, glasses sliding down the tip of her nose. She always seems like she is thinking of something else when she is talking to you, which can be frustrating at times. But she's there when it counts, and in my case, I'm hoping that means she'll be there for me at my annual review in July.

"The writing is really strong, but it takes place in colonial Florida. Just makes me think of how when *Outlander* went to America, everyone jumped ship," Nicole explains.

"That's a bummer," Anne responds. And just like that, the book is out of the running. It may seem heartless, but there is so much more to being published than good writing. An editor might fall in love with a book, but if it doesn't have its own place in the market, or if it's too similar to another book, it's out.

"I have a promising own-voices rom-com," Terri adds. Anne immediately sits up and scribbles something in her notebook.

"It's enemies-to-lovers, with an Indian-American heroine trying to avoid an arranged marriage by pretending to be in a relationship with her co-worker," Terri explains.

"So fake-dating, own voices, and workplace romance?" Anne asks, eyebrows raised.

Tropes are one of my favorite parts of the romance genre. There's something I love about plugging characters into their own boxes. I can only hope that one day, I'll find a box—or a trope—that I fit into.

"Yep," Terri says. Terri has been at Heartwarming almost as long as Anne and is our only senior editor.

"Okay, send it to me," Anne responds, shuffling papers around in front of her. "There's one last important thing we need to talk about." Her face is serious, even for her. We all look at each other, slightly bemused.

"Ruby Jones is threatening to dump us."

TWO

The silence in the room stretches on for what feels like an hour.

"Ruby Jones, as in *the* Ruby Jones, the biggest earner on our list?" Terri repeats, as if we all don't know who Ruby is.

"*What?*" The disbelief in Elle's voice speaks for everyone in the room.

I do my best to conceal my surprise, and the subsequent disappointment, that Anne withheld this monumental development from me. I know basically all about every author and book on our list, but most definitely everything about all of Anne's authors. Why didn't she tell me?

"Maybe that wouldn't be the worst thing. Ruby has always been a little off her rocker," Nicole adds cautiously.

"Well, while that may be true, she sells books, so we need to get her *back* on her rocker," Anne quips, her boss-voice in full effect. We exchange a look.

I'm more than familiar with Ruby's eccentricities. She's an older woman who lives in Oklahoma and writes trope-driven romantic comedies. She's done cowboys, enemies, friends, co-workers, neighbors, best friends of older brothers—the list goes on.

"What is her problem this time?" Terri asks.

"According to her, we've been treating her like a 'backlist author,'" Anne explains, using air quotes.

"Her last two books have been instant *USA Today* bestsellers. How is that treating her like a backlist?" Elle snaps. I'm glad Elle said that, because that was my exact thinking. But I'm still a little too shocked by the news that one of our biggest authors—one who quite literally keeps some of the lights on in this place—is threatening to leave, to say anything.

"She says she doesn't feel *creatively* supported. Her sales have been slowly dropping over the course of her last four publications, and apparently, we're not doing enough to 'vary her brand in the ever-changing marketplace,'" Anne continues, once again, employing air quotes.

"Jesus," Terri says with a groan. Nadine rolls her eyes. They've dealt with Ruby a bit longer than Elle and me, so they can have those types of reactions. My brain goes right to problem-solving mode.

"I'm really hitting a wall with her, and we need to come up with something new, something fresh, or we're going to lose her."

"Isn't it kind of the author's job to come up with the ideas?" Elle asks, a hesitant tone in her voice.

"It's Ruby. We *all* have to be willing to compromise," Anne says. "So, I have some small-town ideas lined up, but we really need to focus on the specifics. Ruby's not giving me much to work with here. She basically wants us to outline the book for her." Anne rolls her eyes so hard I'm surprised she doesn't get dizzy. "Any thoughts?" she asks the group.

Small-town romances are usually set on whimsical streets like Blueberry Lane or Chestnut Creek. They're mostly PG and form the inspiration for almost every Hallmark Christmas movie ever produced. They've never been my favorite subgenre of romance. Well, that's putting it nicely. They're my *least* favorite. I grew up in a small town in Pennsylvania, right on the border of New Jersey. It wasn't so small that I had cows as neighbors, but it was small enough that there was one high school with a graduating class of about a hundred students.

My parents are small-town people, even if they don't like to admit it. They raised their family—well, *me*—there, and always talked about how much they hated it. No good restaurants, no diversity, and no potential for upward movement. *Sameness*—that's the word my father always used.

"*You're the generation that is going to make a difference out there Lucy Loo,*" my mother always said. "*And you're not going to do that here.*"

"Strong female friendships," Terri offers.

"Restoring a house or an inn, returning home, maybe second-chance love story," Nicole suggests, listing the plot for basically every small-town romance we've ever sold.

"The market is already full of those stories. What about something else?" At first, I don't believe it's me speaking out loud. I never offer opinions. Rarely, if at all. That's not what I'm here for. I'm here to make sure the whole team doesn't fall apart and blend into the wall while doing it.

"Such as?" Anne asks, clearly as surprised as I am that I'm speaking up.

That's a great question. At that moment, with half a

dozen sets of eyes staring at me, I have no choice but to go with the line of thought that drove me to open my mouth in the first place.

I have a terrible problem with keeping my mouth shut. My mother calls it "foot-in-mouth syndrome." I've been working on it, I *really* have. But sometimes, when something pops into my head, it just comes out of my mouth.

"Well," I say, waving my hands to buy myself some time, "what about a spin on the small-town romance? Instead of the heroine embracing her life in the small town, she hates it."

"Why would she hate it?" Terri asks.

"Plenty of reasons. Maybe she inherits the house from an estranged relative," I start, referencing a common inciting incident in the genre. "But she's a big-city lawyer who doesn't have time to fix it up. Maybe she's bitter and the last thing she's looking for is a small-town romance."

"Hmm, sounds like someone else who is bitter and needs a little love in her life," Elle adds, winking at me. I make a face that implies that I will be murdering her with a stapler after this meeting.

"Are *you* bitter?" Anne asks me, all heads at the table again turned in my direction.

I stare Elle down through the side of my eyes. She giggles. I take a deep breath.

"Just because I'd like to swipe through Tinder and think something other than '*yikes*' doesn't mean I'm bitter." The group chuckles.

"So, what would you do, if you had to live in a small town?" Anne asks, leaning forward in her chair.

"Turn back around," I say jokingly.

"Be serious, I'm curious about something," Anne says. I squint my eyes at her, wondering where she's going with this.

"Anne, I grew up in a small town, remember? I left for a reason." I shift uncomfortably in my seat.

"I know, I know, but you have no desire to ever go back?" she presses.

I shrug my shoulders. "The change of pace might be nice for a few days, but then I'd probably end up complaining about the lack of restaurants—or the fact that there isn't a Starbucks within ten miles."

"What if there was a dashing young gentleman?" Elle adds, looking as giddy about this scenario as Anne.

"There wouldn't be," I reply flatly.

"Why not?" Anne asks.

"Because that's not real life." Elle knows how much I want to believe in those sorts of notions. Unlike me, she's always believed in happily ever after. But it's just been so long since anyone has been genuinely interested in me, that I'm starting to think that the whole idea is a trap.

"What if it was?" Anne shoots back, a mischievous grin on her face. I scrunch my brows. I genuinely cannot make out where she is going with this.

"What if *what* was?" I ask.

"What if it was *your* real life?"

"Wait, what are you talking about?"

"What if I sent you to a small town?"

I give her my best "*have you gone mental?*" look and assess the rest of the room's reactions. They look as confused as me—except for Elle. Elle looks entertained.

"Don't say no right away," Anne starts.

"No."

"Lucy!" Elle scolds. I widen my eyes at her.

Anne leans her elbows on the table and sets her pen down for the first time since we entered the room. "I just think that the character of a burnt-out, big-city girl moving back to a small town could be a solution to the Ruby issue," says Anne, smiling.

"I'm not burnt-out," I protest, crossing my arms. "Just because I want to live in a place where I can get a Diet Snapple, same-day delivery, and a bagel that isn't sold in a plastic bag in the grocery store, does not mean I'm burnt out." *But being overworked and underpaid in the most expensive city in the country might*, I add in my head.

"I'd say it's called having standards," Callie pipes up, nodding at me. I shrug in her direction.

"So, let me get this straight. You want to ship me off to a small town?" I ask, turning back to Anne.

Anne purses her lips. "Well, I'm just saying that I'd like to see the end result of an editor going to a small town to believe in love again." I let her reference to me as an editor rather than an assistant slide. Maybe my promotion isn't so far back in her mind after all.

"I believe in love. I get paid to believe in love."

"That's the spirit," Elle says sarcastically. I stick my tongue out at her.

"So, Lucy goes to a small town? To do what, *exactly*?" Terri asks.

"Why are we assuming that I would have to be the one to go? Maybe we should focus our attention on Elle," I offer.

"I'm not as *bitter* as you," Elle replies, scrunching her

perfect button nose. I scratch my temple with my middle finger.

"Plus, Elle is not as much of a strong-armed city girl," Anne rebuts, winking.

"I'm not disagreeing with you, but I did elbow a guy in the gut on the subway yesterday," Elle interjects, raising her finger like she's making a valid point.

"Yeah, alright, settle down over there, Rocky," Anne mocks. She turns her gaze back to me. "I'm more interested in the idea of a bitter—"

"Hey!" I whine.

"Sorry—*allegedly* bitter, hardcore city girl going to a small town."

"And what would that actually entail?" I ask skeptically.

"Getting to know the locals, scoping out the romance scene, appreciating nature, all that shit," Anne adds.

"And you're somehow going to turn that into a romance novel?" I ask.

"Well, I'm *hoping*, Miss Tinder-Never-After, *you're* going to turn it into a small-town rom-com. You might be inspired by the scenery, or some charming townies," she muses. "And from there, you'll have a whole universe to base a series around."

"Maybe there will even be a single, handsome local who will lure you away from the big city for good," Elle muses.

"I'm sure there won't be," I say seriously.

"So, you'll do it?" Anne practically jumps out of her chair.

"Do what? This is all hypothetical!"

"Listen, my in-laws have a house upstate. They rent it out most of the year. Let's say you go up there and work remotely from—" Anne pauses for a moment, glancing down at the calendar in her notebook. "Memorial Day to July 4th. See what you can come up with."

I look at her like she has seventeen heads. "Let me get this straight," I say taking a deep breath. "You want to pay me to spend a month at your in-laws' lake house?" Anne grins. I look around at the rest of the team. All eyes are on me. "No one else thinks this is crazy?"

"Frankly I'm bummed that I don't qualify for this work trip. I sure didn't get an offer like that when I was an assistant," Nicole mumbles.

"Ditto," Elle adds.

"Lucy, you still have quite a few vacation days to use," Anne reminds me. I mentally grumble about how far it's gotten me. "You can roll them in with the trip, take some time for yourself. And anyway, we need to demonstrate that we're doing everything we can to get Ruby her next bestseller. It's going to take a big gesture of commitment, and this might be it."

"And what would you do without an assistant for a month?" I ask Anne, tilting my head knowingly.

"I did work in the industry for a number of years before you came along, Lucy," Anne says with a sassy tone.

"You can't even use the printer," I deadpan.

"*Irrelevant*," she scoffs. "And I'm not suggesting that I wouldn't have an assistant. You would be working remotely."

"I think a break from the city would be good for you," Elle says, probably thinking about our conversation from this morning. "And I would happily do any printing for Anne while you're gone." Elle and I lock eyes and it is so clear how excited she is for me. It almost doesn't make me mad at her for supporting this idea and making me the center of attention at this meeting. She knows how much I hate that.

"We'll iron out all the details before you go, but the summer is slow for us. The timing is perfect." I turn my head back to Anne and try to think of some way to respond. "Just promise me you'll think about it."

I'm not sure what to say. A month alone in a lakeside cabin? Anne has shown me pictures of her and her wife Penny at her parents' place, and it's cute, but I haven't spent time at a lake well—ever. The last boat I went on was a Carnival cruise.

I take a beat to consider this. Anne wants to pay me to basically work from vacation? Has she completely forgotten all the unspoken rules of publishing?

I continue sitting there, speechless, while everyone begins filing out. Elle is the last to leave, winking at me as she disappears from view. I shake my head. I think this team has all collectively gone to the zoo today.

"The only way I would do something like this is if there was a promotion at the end of it."

It happened again. My mouth acted as a completely separate entity from my brain. I never say things like this. I'm not the one who says what she wants, I'm not upfront and brutally honest, I leave all those qualities to Elle. When I say something like that, it comes off as judgmental or harsh.

My mouth opens to retract my statement, but I quickly close it. What if I *was* that type of person? Someone who had the courage to ask for what I wanted?

Ironically, my lack of a filter has just answered that question for me.

"You must *really* want a promotion, huh?" Anne says, crossing her arms.

"Well, yeah, I thought it was fairly obvious," I say, my voice trailing off. I feel a drop of sweat trail down my temple and I try to subtly wipe my forehead. A knot has formed in my throat and I curse myself for not bringing any water into the meeting.

Anne sits back in her chair and crosses her arms. "You've worked here for three years, of course, it is obvious," she says bluntly. She tilts her head at me, putting her tongue against her cheek before she continues, "Shall we negotiate?"

I let out a quiet breath. I can do this. I like Anne. She's not *that* intimidating, right? I can make the best of this situation.

This is the opportunity I've been waiting for. Sure, I never expected it to materialize like this, but this can be my chance to prove to Anne that she should have promoted me a long time ago. I can outline a book. I can find inspiration for Ruby and convince her to stay at Heartwarming. If there was ever an assignment that was perfect for me—besides the fact that it involves going to a small town where the closest sign of civilization is a Walmart—this is it.

"I can see your brain spiraling. Don't overthink this," she warns.

Clearly she's never met me.

"Anne... I don't even have a car," I blurt out.

Anne studies me for a moment before responding. "Penny and I have two cars. You can drive mine upstate. I'm taking some time off between Memorial Day and July 4th so really Penny and I can share."

"You trust me to drive your car?" I ask bluntly.

"Are you a bad driver?" Anne probes, one perfectly-shaped eyebrow raised.

"Not at all, but—"

"Then there you go. Next?"

I blink furiously trying to regain my composure and decipher the alien that has clearly inhabited the woman who used to be my boss. "Right," I say, clearing my throat. "How—how would we consider this trip a success?" I ask awkwardly.

Anne nods. "Good question. Let's say by the time you leave you'll have fleshed out two love interests and maybe five supporting characters. And that includes an outline of your fictitious town—what it looks like and what brings the locals together. You should also recommend ideas for dates or meet-cutes, Ruby will love that," Anne says. "Also, I wouldn't tell anyone why you're there—they might shun you. When people ask, just say you're on sabbatical." When I finish scribbling notes in my book, I find Anne looking at me expectantly. "So, you'll do it?" she asks.

I take a deep breath. "Well," I say hesitantly. I wipe my sweaty palms on my pants and try to regain my nerve. Anne nods to urge me on. "If these criteria are met and I find inspiration for a new series, Ruby approved, of course, there would be an opportunity for advancement upon my return?"

Anne takes a deep breath. After a few awkward, painful, *soul-crushingly* silent moments, she finally speaks.

"Sure. Yes."

Sure? Did she really just say sure?

"If you manage a successful outline, then yes, I'll see what I can do on the promotion front. But this isn't a vacation, Lucy. I know I don't have to explain to you how catastrophic it would be for us to lose Ruby."

I swallow hard. "Understood."

"Wonderful!" Anne exclaims, clapping her hands together.

"Yes, wonderful," I echo.

Small Town U.S.A. here I come.

THREE

Operation Small Town, Day 1

Hudson Hollow, New York. Population 1,500.

So... *this* is happening.

After three hours on the New York State Thruway, I was elated when I saw the exit for Hudson Hollow. I thought I might stop in Starbucks on my way to the house, refuel, grab some snacks, etc. Except the last Starbucks I saw was at a rest stop 80 miles ago.

There are a few people moseying up and down the main street, and almost all of them don't try to be subtle about gawking at me in Anne's BMW. As I drive through at the mundane speed of 20 mph, I see a sign for a library, a corner convenience store, the post office, and a restaurant called Liz's. So far, Hudson Hollow doesn't have me feeling so good.

I take a few deep breaths and continue driving. The mindful breaths serve two purposes.

1. To remind myself that I'm here to do a job. Unless the

photos Anne showed me of the house were fake, it looks really nice. I'm trying really hard not to judge the book by its cover, or the town by its three storefronts.
2. If I don't take deep breaths, this road may make me hurl.

Finally, the winding road ends and I follow Siri's instructions into a more residential area. I turn onto Joan Street and pull up to the second house on the right. I immediately spot the lake, which is right smack behind the house. And boy, is it some view. Even from my seat in the car, I can see mountains in the distance. Like... *actual* mountains. At that moment, I realize that I may have never seen a mountain before in my life. Shit, Anne was right, I am the only viable candidate for this trip.

I quickly text my mom to tell her I've arrived and that I will call her once I've settled. Saying the phone call with my mother explaining this assignment didn't go well would be putting it mildly. I had to refuse to give her the exact address because she would not stop saying she was coming with me.

"*I don't see how this is getting you a promotion,*" my mother had said, her tone irritated on the other end of the phone. "*I don't see how you can prove yourself out in the boonies.*"

"*Mom, you live in the boonies,*" I reminded her matter-of-factly.

"*And I always wanted more for you!*"

"*Mom, will you relax? I'm not going to step foot in a small town and turn into a pumpkin.*"

"*That reference doesn't even make sense.*" I rolled my eyes at how quick-witted my mother was.

"*You work hard, I just want your boss to see that.*"

I could hear the worn-out sigh in her voice when she said that. My mom is tough, tougher than I'll ever be. She's a small Italian woman, with a Pixie cut and glasses that take up half of her face—a middle-aged Rita Moreno who went gray early. She is small and she is fierce, no buts about it. She doesn't take anyone's shit, and she's fiercely protective.

When I was diagnosed with dyslexia, she told me things might be hard for me, not just in life, but in school. I would have to be the student who worked twice as hard as everyone else. I would have to use the tools my teachers gave me and make them work to my advantage. And if I worked hard, I could have the same opportunities as everyone else. After all, for her, a second-generation immigrant who was the first in her family to go to college, education was everything.

My mother never wanted my dyslexia to prevent me from being successful. So, to her, working in Manhattan was the kind of success she and my father didn't have. And she was so proud of it. Of me.

"*Anne knows I work hard, Mom. And with this trip, maybe she'll realize just how much she needs me*," I reassured her.

"*She better. Because you haven't worked this hard just to wind up in another small town.*"

God Forbid, I thought to myself. But I wouldn't dare say it out loud.

I pull down a gravel road and stop when the navigation announces that my destination is on the right. I get out and try to shake the feeling of anxiety that has suddenly crept up in my chest, accompanied by my mother's foreboding voice.

I can do this.

Anne's in-laws' house is a small ranch style. It sits on the side of a steep hill that leads down to the lake. The front of the house is lined with horizontal logs, and a beautiful wood door is framed by two tree trunk-looking columns. If I really *was* a character in a small-town rom-com, I might call it inviting, quaint, adorable. Definitely different from what the houses looked like in the town I grew up in. Maybe I should tell my mother that not all small towns are the same.

I jump when I hear crunching gravel behind me. I quickly turn around to see what everyone might expect me to find at this point in a romance novel: the most gorgeous man I've ever seen in real life.

I put my hand over my forehead to block the sun. Nope, I haven't fallen out of my car and smacked my head open. There is actually a real-life small-town version of a romance heartthrob standing in front of me.

Shit, maybe this whole thing has been a dream. Maybe I finally got hit by that bus on Sixth Avenue and I'm in a coma. And since my job is my life, my coma dream is some alternate version of reality where a book that I'm working on comes true. That's the only explanation for this guy standing in front of me right now.

"Um, hello," his deep voice snaps me out of it. He's not Australian. That must mean this is real life. If I was having a coma dream, my love interest would most *definitely* have an accent.

"Hi," I say in a shaky voice. Through squinted eyes, I make out shaggy blonde hair and a lean, tall frame. He's a blonde, beautiful boy, there's no doubt about it. He's broad-shouldered and good-looking in a way that suggests he is also charming as all hell.

The thing that strikes me the most about *this* man, though, is the strange look on his face. He's looking at me... like I'm... *crazy?* As if I have something offensive written on my forehead? I attempt to inconspicuously run my hand through my hair to make sure it's not too dishevelled from the car ride. His eyes are piercing, serious, and intent on me, and his gaze starts to make me squirm. I feel heat rising on my neck, and I take a step backward because—I don't know why—it seems like the right choice. This guy is either about to tell me I have something in my teeth... or murder me.

"I'm sorry," he says, his voice breaking. "You look very familiar, er, you remind me of someone." He takes a step back as well, trying to collect himself. I let out a small exhale, accepting that I probably won't die on this cul-de-sac. Thank goodness this beautiful man isn't a serial killer. That would have been so disappointing.

"Sorry," he chuckles. "Is this your first time in Hudson Hollow?"

I let out something between a laugh and a scoff. "It is, yes, I'm more of a city dweller. Small towns make me somewhat claustrophobic."

He scrunches his face for a moment, and I realize that might have been insulting. "Erm, not that this town isn't beautiful. It is! From what I've seen, anyway." Why am I rambling? *Stop talking, Bowen.* I quite literally smack my hand on my forehead, wishing I could redo the last two minutes of my life.

"Well, hopefully, Hudson Hollow will change your mind about small towns." *I doubt it*, I answer in my head. Good job not opening your mouth on that one, Luce. "Anyway, I'm Liam. Liam Miller. That's me, just across the way." He gestures to the two-story cottage that sits on the other side of the road. Unlike my accommodation, his place looks statelier, with rustic wooden siding and accents of color on the shutters and doors.

Maybe he's a plant. Maybe Anne planted him here to give me inspiration and mess with my head. It seems extreme, but that's what makes it even more likely. It also seems extreme to threaten to staple someone's hands to a wall, but she threatened to do that once as well.

And no, being in labor was not an excuse.

"I'm Lucy," I say at last, offering him my hand. Liam and Lucy. I could gag right here and now.

"Al and Mella mentioned a new renter would arrive this week. Although—" he stops himself. I raise my brows, curious about what the rest of that statement might be. "It's just—I wasn't expecting someone like you."

"Someone like *me*?"

"I don't mean it like that," he says, the words rushing out of his mouth. He raises his hands in defense. "I just mean, most of the renters around here are fifty-year-old fishing enthusiasts. They don't look like they just stepped out of a magazine."

I look down at myself. I'm wearing Vans sneakers, yoga pants, and an off-the-shoulder light sweatshirt. Grocery store chic, as Elle would say.

"What kind of magazines do you read?" I ask, narrowing my eyes at him suspiciously.

"You just look very Manhattan, that's all," he says. "Not that that's a bad thing."

I let out an awkward laugh. "Well, you're not wrong, I

am from Manhattan. And clearly I look very out of my element here. Which I am."

"Right," he says, a subtle smile playing at his lips. "So, what brings you to town?"

"Oh, just a little vacation. Taking some time away from the city." Anne's voice echoes in my head. *Stay as close to the truth as possible without revealing too much.*

Anne and the team prepared me for weeks before I left. They insisted that no one in the town know why I was really here. I thought it was a bit silly, but I'm determined to be successful on this project and give Anne no reason not to promote me. I'm realizing now that I maybe should have taken more notes.

"Nice. Well, welcome. I'm just across the way if you need anything. And I work at the café in town as well."

"The café in town?"

"Yep, we just have the one. Well, unless you count Stewart's. But they're mostly good for root beer and ice cream."

"You work at the café?"

"Yes ma'am. Well, I own it." His cheeks flush as he says this.

"Of course you do," I grumble.

"Sorry?" He frowns.

"Let me ask you: Are you also a single dad? Did you marry your high school sweetheart but something went wrong? Does the name Anne Turner ring any bells?"

Liam looks at me like I have gone mad. He opens his lips as if he wants to speak, but quickly decides against it.

I may have misread this situation.

When several seconds of awkward silence pass, he says, "I really don't know what to do with that." He laughs.

"I am *so* sorry," I mumble, covering my face with my hands. "I have this habit of not thinking before I speak. Or more accurately, my thoughts and words form at the same time. It's hard to separate them sometimes." I'm babbling so fast that I'm sure this will go down as one of the worst meet-cutes in history. "I'm working on it," I finally say.

Liam smiles. Only one corner of his mouth picks up but his whole face changes. It makes me smile as well.

"That's all right. To answer your question, no, no ex-wife, no kids. No criminal history. Excellent chef. Best in town."

"Very humble too, I see."

"Ha ha!" He laughs loudly. The sound reverberates in my chest. "I have to get back to work, but it was a pleasure to meet you, Lucy…"

"Bowen."

"Lucy Bowen." He repeats with a somewhat bigger smile. "I'll see you around."

As he begins to walk away, he puts two fingers between his lips and whistles. I follow his gaze to his house. A large black and brown German Shepherd emerges from the backyard and, in three long strides, runs to Liam's side.

"And who's this?" I ask, smiling at the dog.

"This is Blue," Liam says, patting the dog's side.

"Friendly?"

"Massively. He's a big goofball."

I take a few steps and squat down to the dog's level. I outstretch my hand and let him give it a proper sniff. When he gently bumps it with his nose, I pet him under his neck and he licks my face.

"Oh, sorry!" Liam says, reaching for Blue.

"Don't be," I say, standing up. "I love dogs. I wish I could have one, but it doesn't really mesh with city living, you know?"

He studies me for a moment, and the look on his face transforms again. His eyes look... *concerned*? Like he's trying to place me? I wonder if I have the same look of suspicion on my face.

But how can I look at Liam and not think, *really*? This is the first guy I meet on this small-town adventure? The literal poster child for what a small-town romance protagonist should look like?

Serendipity like that doesn't just happen to me.

And this isn't actually a small-town rom-com.

Liam snaps at Blue and the dog quickly ditches my pets and looks at his owner. "Up, up," he commands, pointing to the car. Blue smoothly jumps into the passenger side of the truck.

"See you around," I say.

I wave as he jumps into his white Jeep Wrangler and takes off down the road. Way to make a first impression, Lucy.

FOUR

Just as I make it to the front door, my phone rings. It's Elle.

"Are you with Anne right now?" I answer the phone with a snap.

"Well, hello to you too. And no. It's Memorial Day. I like my job, but not enough to spend a day off with my boss."

"Oh right," I mumble. I toss the house keys onto a small table in the front entrance and drag my suitcase in as I nestle the phone between my shoulder and my ear.

"What's the matter?"

"*What's the matter*? Well, I'll tell you! Our boss is a sociopath, that's what."

"What did she do now?"

"She has me so paranoid about this book idea that I just accosted her in-laws' neighbor!"

"I have to say, that sounds more like *your* fault than Anne's. Why did you accost said neighbor?"

"Because he's my love interest. Right there, directly across the street. How convenient is that?"

"Hmm, so he's cute?"

"Fucking gorgeous." I sigh.

"Richard Madden cute?"

"His eyes are bluer."

"Idris Elba gorgeous?"

"*Absolutely*."

"God, it's like Anne planted him there."

"That's what I said! So, I basically accused him of that."

"Lucy!"

"It was fine. I rolled with it. He might think I'm nuts, but it's not like he's my *actual* love interest. I'm meant to be outlining a romance, not starring in one!"

"I wouldn't be so sure," Elle murmurs, her voice teasing, but I do my best to ignore her comment. I'm here to do a job, and the blue eyes of the man across the street are not going to distract me from that.

If preparing for this trip the past few weeks has taught me anything, it's that the idea of love is a dream. It's something we chase because fairy tales and movies and books push us to look for it in our daily lives. Isn't that why I love romance novels so much? Because they're an escape? They take me away from the ordinary and let me live in the world of *extraordinary* for a little while—a world where Prince Charming exists, or at the very least a charming neighbor in a small town. But despite the situation I find myself in, that's not real. That's why it's called fiction.

"Tell me about the house!" Elle pleads in my ear.

"I just walked in," I reply, closing the door behind me and taking in the impressive foyer. "I'll call you later and we'll FaceTime."

When I hang up with Elle, I decide I need to make a plan.

Arriving has me feeling a bit overwhelmed, and so I press my hand to my heart to try to steady it. I'm alone. I try to remember the last time I was *truly* alone. Maybe at the gym in the early morning, but only for a few minutes before other people trickled in? Maybe when Elle visited her mom for Christmas before I headed to my parents' place? But that wasn't for more than a few hours.

This is crazy!

Would it be more exciting if I was renting a penthouse apartment on the Upper East Side with a view of the park and the entire city as my domain? Yes. But for now, Main Street U.S.A. will have to do.

When I finally make it more than two steps through the doorway, I realize I can see straight through to the back of the house, which is lined with floor-to-ceiling windows providing a gorgeous view of the lake. The kitchen is a small, galley-style with retro blue appliances. The countertop is a taupe linoleum, and a small bar top opens up to the living area. While the house clearly hasn't been updated since the seventies, it has a unique charm and vintage vibe that feels incredibly inviting.

I step outside to the raised back deck with a long staircase that leads down to the lake. There's a rickety dock at the bottom of the hill, and a swing hanging from a large tree on the downward slope.

I close my eyes and take a deep breath. And just like that, I feel peaceful. Five minutes in the country and I already feel rejuvenated. Not least of all because when I close my eyes, I hear nothing. Perhaps in the distance a child is screeching with excitement or a boat's motor is running, but other than the soft hum of the wind through the trees, I'm alone with my breath.

I take a photo of the view and forgo the filter before I quickly post it to my Instagram.

> Away from the city for a few weeks doing something super exciting for @HeartwarmingRomance. More info to come, but a more pressing question: Do we think the merman of my dreams will emerge from this gorgeous lake any minute? I'll keep you posted!

I started posting about books when I first came to the city and was trying to "explore" or whatnot, as opposed to being curled up in my apartment with a book. So, I wandered around taking photos of what I was reading. It was a great accompaniment for my hopeful publishing career, and even caught the attention of my now-employer. Since then, I've kept posting about Heartwarming books along with others. I've reached about five thousand followers and counting as @lucyloveslove.

Back inside the house, I find a small bedroom and bathroom off the foyer. Behind the kitchen is the master suite, with a large king-size bed and a bathroom with a soaker tub. That's my evening sorted. But first, snacks. I Google the closest supermarket and find that the small convenience store I passed earlier is my best bet.

So back down the Highway to Hurling I go.

The main street of Hudson Hollow is quainter than I originally gave it credit for. I'd say the storefronts run about the same length as eight city blocks, and they are all covered in beautiful red brick. The name of each establishment matches one another in muted gold lettering. It looks like a scene from a catalogue.

Or an episode of *Virgin River*.

The only sign that sticks out is the one for Liz's, which I now assume to be hunky Liam's place. Hudson Hollow's very own Jack Sheridan. I can't pinpoint the exact scent coming from its open door, but it smells like a mixture of maple syrup and French fries. Maybe he *is* an excellent chef after all.

Lucia Brothers Fine Foods looks more like a deli you might find on a corner in Manhattan, but when I see a sign promoting fresh coffee, my nose perks up.

The store is small but has most of the staples—water, bread, milk, eggs, and wine—so I stock up. I don't find many of the ready prepared meals I'm used to eating, so I try to recreate them from the meat selection that they have. I quickly realize that this may be a terrible plan because even though my mother is a fantastic cook, I haven't inherited her skills.

My mind immediately thinks of Liz's, and I wonder if I've embarrassed myself too much to step foot in there. I evaluate my cart of mac and cheese and bagged lettuce and consider that my pride may lose out to my stomach pretty quickly.

As I'm evaluating the differences between two instant brownie mixes, I notice someone has gotten uncomfortably close to me—New Yorkers usually make it a point not to stare. We tend to keep our heads down and our earphones in and avoid direct eye contact.

Not my new companion.

I turn my head to find a little boy sitting on the bumpout shelf of the produce wall behind me. I estimate him to be about three or four. Of course, that could be completely inaccurate. I've never really been around kids. I have no siblings and only one cousin who is a year older than me. For all intents and purposes, I have always been the baby of the family. *What do four-year-olds look like these days?*

I smile weakly at him and return to browsing. But his stare does not waver. His eyes are brown and beady, hidden just barely behind a curtain of straight blonde hair. I can feel his eyes on the back of my neck. Where is the adult to go with this small person? Don't they usually come in a package deal?

I turn around and smile again, subtly looking around to see if there is a blonde woman or man who might match this child's fair complexion.

"Your mom ever tell you that it's rude to stare?" I say, raising my brow at him. He scrunches his face in one motion, his eyebrows meeting his eyelids, and his lips touching the base of his nose. Even I have to admit, it's cute.

"Robbie!" The boy's head snaps up at what I assume to be the sound of his name. I follow his gaze to a woman standing at the bottom of the aisle. She looks to be somewhere about my age, maybe a few years older. Her platinum blonde hair is a mess of pin-curls and her blue eyes stick out like gems on her face. Yep, she goes with this kid.

"Sorry about him," she says with a smile.

"You're fine," I say, batting a hand.

I refocus my attention on the shelf when she says, "You must be from out of town." I tilt my head, somewhat surprised she's still speaking to me. Wow, maybe I really need to get out of the city more often. Manhattan has turned me into a robot.

"Guilty," I say. "I'm renting a lake house for a few

weeks," I reply, tossing both of the brownie mixes into my cart.

"Oh, how nice! You must be up at Al and Mella's place."

"That's me," I say. I love that everyone can spot the newbie in town, and that they also happen to know exactly where I'm staying. Awesome. I'll be having nightmares about being slashed in my sleep tonight.

Maybe I watch too many scary movies.

"You may have met my brother, Liam, he lives across the street."

Of course he does.

"Ah, yes, we met this morning."

"He's the friendly type," she says with a laugh. "You have to try his cooking, it's just the place next door," she gestures. "Best food in town," she says.

"He said as much himself, actually," I say. She laughs, and a lightness touches her eyes.

"Sounds like our Liam. Anyway, sorry, so rude of me! I'm Jillian, and this is Robbie," she says, squeezing the little boy to her side.

I smile at him. "We've also met. Nice to meet you formally, Robbie. I'm Lucy." Jillian gives him a nudge and he steps forward, begrudgingly.

"Nice to meet you, Lucy," he mutters.

"We won't keep you, but I hope you have a great time in Hudson Hollow. I'm sure I'll see you around," she says with a wave.

"Thanks," *complete stranger in the store*, I finish in my mind.

When I go to check out, I choose to ignore the raised eyebrows over my five family-size boxes of mac and cheese.

"Having a party tonight?" the man behind the register asks, smiling as he scans the boxes.

I give him the same smile I gave Jillian. Maybe fake smiling should have been part of my small-town training. "Nope, just me."

"You must be Al's and Mella's guest," he says, his bushy gray mustache bouncing up and down as he speaks. I confirm that I am and have the same conversation for the third time today. "Well, welcome!" he exclaims.

"Thank you, it is certainly a *welcoming* place," I reply, trying to mask the sarcastic tone in my voice.

"I'm Maximus Lucia, pleasure to meet you," he says, sticking out a large, calloused hand. I shake it with a smile. He's an older man, short and plump, with a bald head everywhere but above his ears and around the back. His most defining features are his aforementioned mustache and James Earl Jones-like voice.

"Maximus? Wow, that's quite a name," I blurt, quickly regretting it. I close my eyes and scold myself. "Er, I mean, I've never met someone with such a *prestigious* name before."

"*Prestigious*? Well, that's a first!" he says with a big belly laugh. He goes back to scanning my items.

"I'm Lucy," I offer. Maximus hands me my bags with a grin.

"I hope to see you around, Miss Lucy."

Even though I was slightly anxious about being the new girl, I feel more confident having met Maximus, Jillian, and Robbie. Anne said I needed two characters with lead potential and maybe five prominent side characters—I think I may have just met a few of them.

I mentally scold myself for not bringing my notebook with me on this expedition into town, so I could jot all of this down. I bought a new notebook just for this trip and I am low-key fangirling over it. Aunt Josie always used to tell me that one way to spot a writer was their love of a new notebook. Whereas my mother drilled me in schoolwork, Josie loved to encourage my writing. And I loved her for that.

As I drive back up to the house, I reflect on my day so far and mentally draft my email to Anne. Day One Summary: met two townies, embarrassed myself in front of an actual small-town romance hero, and pumped gas at the creepy gas station without being murdered.

I'd call that a success.

FIVE

Operation Small Town, Day 2

"Small towns aren't the enemy, babe," Aunt Josie says, her face barely visible on the screen of my phone.

"Nobody said they are. I just said I prefer the city," I reply, leaning my phone against the napkin holder on the kitchen table.

"The coffee doesn't define a place. The people do," she states, her large brown eyes coming into view on the screen.

"If you ever tried a pumpkin spice latte, like I've *told* you to, you wouldn't be saying that," I rebut, pulling my bagel out of the toaster. I scowl at this piece of cardboard that is being marketed as a bagel. I feel bad for people who don't know what New York bagels taste like. Life without real bagels is no life at all.

Aunt Josie is in Europe somewhere, on assignment for her job as a reporter for a glamorous fashion magazine. Josie couldn't be more of an oxymoron. She lectures me on not taking small towns for granted but spends most of her life gallivanting from Paris to Milan to Barcelona.

When she finally sits down and actually focuses on the screen, I can tell she is in the living room of her rental in London. She's been stationed there for a few months, but she'll be on her way to Paris soon for Men's Fashion Week. She pushes her short hair back with her glasses and puts on another pair so she can see me on the screen. I discreetly laugh at the image of her with two pairs of glasses on her head. If there was a picture next to the word "scatterbrained" in the dictionary, Aunt Josie and her multiple pairs of spectacles would be it.

"And as I've told you before, there is more to life than Starbucks. Don't be one of those *basic bitches*, Lucy. Be an original," she says. I always felt that Aunt Josie would have thrived in the 1930s or 1940s, with a cigarette between her fingers, her hair done even if she's just sitting around the house for a day—not that she does that very often. Her voice is the combination of Phoebe Buffay and a decades-long chain smoker.

"Please don't use the phrase *basic bitches*," I groan, plugging my laptop into an outlet behind the kitchen table. I sit down on what may be the most uncomfortable wooden dining chair in existence and immediately question my "work from home" seating choice. I miss my office chair already.

"Darling, I have to be off," she says, and I can tell her attention is already elsewhere. It's hard to keep Aunt Josie's mind in one place for very long. I wish I could bottle her up and keep her contained, like my own personal genie, that way I'd always have her with me.

"Yes, you're always telling me," I grumble, rolling my

eyes. She exchanges the glasses on her head for the ones on her face and grimaces at me.

"Listen buttercup, don't make your mind up yet. You might find you surprise even yourself." I glare at the phone and Josie grimaces at me. She hangs up before I even have a chance to say goodbye. Classic.

I check the time. I bring up Anne's name in my phone and press call. It rings twice before she picks up.

"Hello," she chimes in a harmonic voice.

"Hello, this is Lucy calling from bumblefuck nowhere," I start.

"Ha! It's not bumblefuck nowhere," she scoffs. "How's it going?"

"Well, I've been trying to connect to the internet for five minutes so I'm not optimistic," I quip.

"Well, the Wi-Fi might not be the strongest out there, I'll give you that," she says with a laugh.

"So," I say, clearing my throat, "Here's my plan: I'm going to get some work done in the morning, and then go and scope out the town in the afternoon. I've already met three locals who were *super* welcoming," I say, finally seeing my inbox load.

"That's great. Listen, the new Donna Martins manuscript just came in. Edit that for me over the next week and we'll go from there."

"Okay, great. I'm going to send you daily reports with all my notes."

"I can practically hear the steam coming out of your ears as your brain is working," Anne says sarcastically.

"You know me so well."

"And you know you don't need to send daily reports.

I trust you," Anne says, and I just imagine the look on her face. Her glasses are at the end of her nose, her arms and legs are crossed, and she's looking up from beneath her brows.

"And you know I would give them to you anyway," I reply. "I also have a whole list of small-town rom-coms I'm currently making my way through."

"Fabulous. And what have you learned?"

"Well, it's simple, really. The small-town stories are really all about the people. So, I just have to explore enough to study them."

When I did my deep dive into the subgenre, I realized that every book has a happy ever after or happy for now, a brooding hero, or a heroine on the run from her past, but while some of these factors might change from book to book, there is one aspect that remains the same: the town and its people are the hub that allows the spokes of the romance wheel to turn. The heroine always has a strong support system in the town and the events there drive the plot of the story. So, as much as I hate to admit it, I have to explore. And in order to get enough inspiration to outline this book, I have to become one with the locals.

"You sound like a wildlife photographer on assignment," Anne teases.

"I don't mean it like that," I say, shaking away the visual that remark conjured. "Exploring means I'll learn where all the good hangout spots are, and find out what makes this town special, what makes the people tick. It's beautiful here. If the romance story doesn't work out, we can just use the pictures from my phone to make a coffee table book," I jest.

"Well, I'm not sure a coffee table book will cut it, lovely as it sounds. If we don't give Ruby some guidelines for this new series, I'm concerned she will actually leave—God knows she's threatened it enough over the years."

"Don't worry, I won't let you down, Anne," I say, with the same confidence of twelve-year-old Lucy writing an essay on *The Hatchet*.

I hang up with Anne and try to shake the feeling that I'm doing something wrong. I feel like I can't trust my mind when it comes to my guilt gauge. *Am* I doing something wrong? Or am I just doing something for myself? I'm here to conduct research. There's no harm in that.

I try to hold on to that mindset as I begin my work for the day. Since my workspace has undergone a massive upgrade in the last week, I head outside to the picturesque porch swing. I have a few emails to send out in preparation for next month's sales and promotions, so I go through those and finalize some reports for Anne.

With the help of text-to-speech and a pair of earbuds, I edit the first few chapters of Donna's manuscript before my stomach starts rumbling for lunch. For a moment, I consider wandering into the kitchen and making a salad, but then my conversation with Anne about exploring convinces me otherwise. After a quick change into a flowy tie-dye sundress, I toss my hair into a bun and head into town.

I have to admit that I am somewhat embarrassed walking in to the real-life Luke's Diner in my very own Stars Hollow, considering my last interaction with Liam was… bizarre. I'm going to need to apologize, and hopefully I can still make an ally out of my neighbor. He may be gorgeous, and he's probably, most definitely *taken*, but he could also be a good resource.

When I step inside, I'm surprised by how crowded the restaurant is. The pictures I had in my head pale by comparison. Much like the exterior of Liam's house, this place could be in a magazine. To the left of the entrance is a long bar with metal stools and shiplap beneath the counter. The right side is lined with a long booth and snug tables with more metal seating. I take an empty seat at the bar just as Liam emerges from the kitchen juggling two plates of food. He doesn't notice me at first, which gives me a chance to observe him. I don't think I've ever seen someone move so intentionally. He is aware of everything around him, and moves with such grace, like he has been doing this for a thousand years.

I'm not going to lie and say I don't admire the muscles in his forearms as he grips the heavy tray. He's wearing a black T-shirt with the word "Liz's" written in script across the front. I love a man in a black T-shirt. Elle and I often fight about which is superior: a hero in a Henley or one in a black T-shirt. We both stand firm on either side. What can I say? We romance readers like to pick our battles.

When he finally sees me, I catch a range of emotions cross his face. None of them scream "Happy to see me." Could I have ruined my chance at polite acquaintanceship with him? He hesitates, like he's not sure whether to walk toward me or run in the opposite direction. I can see the trepidation in his eyes, and I try to coax him in my direction with an awkward wave. He doesn't wave back, but he presses his lips into a firm line, somewhat resembling a smirk.

When he finally decides to approach me, my stomach clenches, and I'm suddenly aware of my body's reaction to him. He's extremely attractive, that's a no brainer, but I am surprised by just *how* attractive I find him. Quickened pulse, slight light-headedness.

Snap out of it!

"Hi," he stutters, avoiding eye contact. "Here's a menu." He tries to turn away quickly, but I call out "Hey!" in a completely awkward, way too loud voice that makes it seem like I'm hailing a taxi instead of trying to get his attention.

He turns around and raises a brow at me. "Sorry, I just," I say, readjusting myself on the barstool. "I just wanted to apologize again, you know, for yesterday."

"No need to apologize," he says in a low voice. He avoids my gaze.

"Well, admittedly, I acted a little weird, and I'm sorry. It's the Manhattan in me," I offer, aiming for civility.

"It's really fine," he says, his back already partially turned. "Let me know what I can get you."

I look down at the menu quickly and pick the first thing I see. "I'll have the B.L.T."

"Be right back with that," he says over his shoulder.

The lunch crowd is made up of a diverse group. I'd expected Hudson Hollow to be an old-folk town, but to my surprise, it's not. The booth lining the opposite wall is lined with middle-aged women, some younger with kids, and some older. A couple of men in dress pants appear to be on their lunch break at the end of the bar, and a few teenagers are giggling in the corner. All in all, Hudson Hollow seems like a smaller version of the suburban town I grew up in, only with much bigger houses, and much more space in between them.

It's certainly charming, I have to give it that. The matching brick storefronts, and the pristine asphalt streets lined with clean white sidewalks—it is reminiscent of a coastal town in Montauk or the Jersey Shore. Everything is a small business, and I'm sure the owner of each store on this strip has an interesting backstory. I can't wait to explore each and every one.

I pull out my notebook and sketch out a map of Hudson Hollow as I know it so far. I can't help but smile as I draw the lake, like I'm drawing my own version of the Hundred Acre Wood. I barely notice when Liam slides a plate across the bar at me until he subtly clears his throat.

"Thank you," I mumble, quickly snapping my notebook shut.

"You know they have maps on the internet now? You probably even have one on that rectangular electronic device you have there," he says sarcastically, motioning to my phone.

When I look up, he lifts the side of his mouth up in a sideways smile. Yep, that was my heart dropping to my stomach for a moment. Holy moly, those dimples.

"Ingenious," I mutter, pursing my lips at him.

"Are you an artist or something?" I can sense a tone of skepticism in Liam's voice. I don't know him, so I don't know how he acts around new people, but he seems wary of me. Maybe he's just slow to warm to people.

I clear my throat so I can quickly think of an excuse for why I was just drawing a map of the town like a creeper. "No, just a creative mind." *Now change the subject.* I crane my neck. "You need a bigger place; it's packed in here. Is it like this every day?"

"Not always. But it was a three-day weekend, so we have a higher volume of people passing through."

"Makes sense," I say, nodding. I swirl around in my chair, watching him stack some empty plates on the bar. "Have you always lived here?" I ask. Divulge your information, Liam Miller. I need to know more about the contemplative thoughts that make your brows furrow so. If you are going to look like the perfect small-town hero, at least give me something to work with, man.

He puts the plates down and leans against the back of the bar. "Yep. Born and raised. I went downstate for college, to the CIA."

"The CIA?"

"Culinary Institute of America," he explains.

"Oh, so you're like a serious chef?" I say, and immediately regret it. I silently kick myself. "Not to say there are non-serious chefs. I just mean—"

"That maybe you should think before you speak?" he finishes, tilting his head. My cheeks flush under his knowing gaze. Maybe my comment about small towns *did* bother him yesterday.

"Exactly," I say, hiding my face behind my hands. I'm not equipped to handle undercover work. I am *not* cool, calm, and collected. I am flustered, neurotic, and flaky. Elle would be so much better at this.

"So, what is it exactly you do? Apart from insulting everyone you meet, that is," he asks. He does his best to hide a smirk.

"I'm in publishing," I say, shrugging, hoping to move the conversation along. When he just blinks, I add, "I'm a book editor."

"Cool. What sort of books do you edit?"

I'm not ashamed of what I do, but I don't always like to admit what kind of books I work on. There's a taboo around romance books that I wish didn't exist, and people really don't understand how important they are to the industry as a whole, and to our readers. Once, a guy I went on a date with assumed that I edited porn books for a living. That was a fun dinner.

But maybe Liam is different. Maybe I should let him draw his own conclusions.

"Romance books," I say confidently. Let him form his own opinion about it. Let him make a joke. Maybe I don't care what people think.

"Ah, like the Hallmark movies?" he asks, not a line of expression on his face.

"Kind of," I say, surprised. "You know about those?" Not to stereotype, but in my history with buff, good-looking guys, I haven't come across one who knows a thing about Hallmark movies.

"They wanted to film one here once. I talked to one of the director's assistants," he says, trying to hide the smile on his lips.

"Talked to?" I ask, raising my eyebrows.

"Okay, maybe more than talked to," he admits with a shrug.

"Does that mean you don't have a small-town high school sweetheart like the plot of every great Hallmark movie?" Liam grunts in reply.

I find myself strangely interested in Liam's dating history. But if I ask more about it now, when I've known him for less than a day, it would come across as super creepy and

I've already done enough damage in the few conversations we've had. But I'm wondering if he's the perfect inspiration for my small-town hero. If so, I need to know more about him. At least, that's the reason I'm sticking with for my sudden fascination with him...

"Do you remember the name of it?" I ask.

"Umm," he says, groaning. "Something on Serenity Something?"

"*Summer on Serenity Lake*. That's so funny, that's one of our books! I think they ended up filming it in Canada."

Affirmative grunt. His gaze returns to the glass he is drying with the dish towel he removed from his shoulder. I watch as his fingers make circles with the rag, becoming mesmerized by the movements of his hands.

"Miller!" I hear a deep voice call from the back of the restaurant. I turn to find a tall man around my age wander in with a large cardboard box in his hands. "Where do you want this?"

Liam shifts his gaze and instantly his face softens.

"Hey, man, thanks," he says, "kitchen, please."

"You got it," he beams, brushing past us. He's a bit shorter than Liam, with a close buzz cut and arms that belong to a bodybuilder. Where Liam's looks scream small-town homeboy, this guy has the look of the city about him. When he remerges, box free, he flashes me a supersized grin.

"Well hello there," he says to me, sliding into the seat next to me. "Who do we have here?" he asks Liam.

"Brett, this is Lucy. Lucy, this is Brett. He hangs around the restaurant scavenging for food. Harder to get rid of than a fungus," Liam teases.

"Also known as Liam's best friend since middle school, put

'er there." Brett smiles, extending his hand to me. I admire his hard jawline which is dappled with faint stubble.

"Nice to meet you," I say, trying not to wince from the sheer strength of his firm grip around my hand.

"Lucy is renting Al and Mella's place for a few weeks," Liam explains.

"Oh right," Brett says. "You're the new girl Liam mentioned." There's an awkward pause between us while Brett nods enthusiastically. "Well, I'm off," he says at last. "We still fishing on Sunday?" he asks Liam. Liam nods.

"Indeed, and thanks for the delivery, appreciate it."

"Happy to put my muscles to good use," Brett says, winking at me. "Nice to meet you, Lucy." I watch him walk out before turning my attention back to Liam.

I try not to overthink the fact that this town has so many good-looking men. *This is not a romance novel. This is not a romance novel.* Some things can just be a coincidence. *Right?*

"So how come you're renting up here for so long? Saved-up vacation days or something?" he asks.

"Yeah," I say, pausing to think of my next words. A first for me. "I needed a break from it all. I—I just got out of a really bad relationship." Solid lie, Lucy.

"Oh, well, er, I'm sorry to hear that," he says, suddenly flustered.

"Yeah, that… Mike… Vikrim," I start.

"*Vikrim?*" He narrows his eyes at me.

Shit, maybe he's one of those one-in-a-million guys who actually likes *Friends*.

"—*inski*. Vikriminski. He was from Sweden. Just up and left."

Good God, I am the worst liar in the history of the world.

Liam presses his lips together as if to stop himself from laughing.

"Well, that Mike Vikrim–*inski* must have been an idiot," he says in a placating voice.

I smile at the compliment, completely unsure of its nature. "Thanks," I mumble.

"And why Hudson Hollow?" Liam asks.

"Sorry?"

"As your destination," he explains, and again, the threat of a smile pulls at his lips. "You must be big into kayaking. Or wait, let me guess, hiking? You're here for the trails?"

"Hah!"

Oh shit.

I quickly clear my throat, trying to cover up the fact that I literally just laughed out loud. "Sorry," I say with a chuckle. "No, I am not big into those things actually."

Liam twists his face in a way that suggest he thinks that I'm crazy. Honestly, I feel crazy. I didn't realize how much lying to peoples' faces was going to be involved in this trip. It doesn't make me feel good.

"So?" he prods.

"It came highly recommended," I lie. "I was looking for somewhere affordable where I could sit outside and read all day."

Good save, Lucy. Good save.

"Ah, well, Hudson Hollow is good for that too, I suppose," Liam replies, still appearing uneasy about my answer. Or maybe he's disappointed, I can't quite tell.

"Tell me, what's the takeout situation around here?" I ask. I'm not going to lie, I chose my college based on its proximity to good Chinese takeout. But I think if I ask what the Chinese food is like, I may sound a bit too much like Marisa Tomei in *My Cousin Vinny*.

"You're looking at it," Liam muses.

"Oh," I say, trying to wipe the shocked look off my face. "So, people don't eat like… anywhere else?"

Liam rubs his fingers on his jaw. "Uh, there's a Chinese restaurant in Catskill, but that's about thirty minutes away."

"Huh." How do people live like this? I take another inconspicuous glance at Liam, trying to understand this person whose life is the polar opposite of mine. How do people survive on one restaurant? They cook the rest of the time? I can't fathom that.

"Well, thank you for lunch and for the chat," I say, hopping off the barstool. "See you around?"

Subtle nod in reply.

Once I'm out on the sidewalk I realize I've been sweating. Geez, it felt like an interrogation room there.

Oh, but *Liam*. When I first met him, I thought he was gorgeous (obviously), but I never thought he would be so intriguing as well. I'm desperate to know his story. Why open a restaurant in the town you grew up in? Wouldn't you want to escape after college? And why Liz's?

That boy is a book that needs his pages sniffed and devoured and I think I am the perfect person to do it.

SIX

Operation Small Town, Day 5

The library in Hudson Hollow may be my new favorite place in town. No, scratch that. The world.

When I first passed the library, and I mean *passed* it, because there was no sign for it, I didn't give it a second glance. When I finally doubled back and realized I was in the right place, the nondescript building didn't particularly excite me.

Boy, was I wrong. I know I'm not supposed to judge a book by its cover, but let's be honest, I work in publishing, and we judge covers all day long.

Readers and publishing people understand the excitement one finds when stepping into a room full of books. We all first felt truly understood when the Beast revealed his library to Belle. Right then and there, having a library fit for a ladder on wheels became our dreams.

I feel a bit like Belle when she enters the Beast's library. The library is *huge*. There are two floors lining the outside walls, with a magnificent, tiled ceiling towering above. The circulation desk sits in the middle, surrounded by mismatched tables and chairs where a scarce number of people sit. How are there not more people here? How is this not a *tourist* destination? Look at all the *books*!

Okay, I might be overreacting. But libraries have always been my happy places. I lived in the library throughout middle school and high school, and I chose my college for its library. It had four floors—I never wanted to leave.

I make my way to the circulation desk and have to pause for a moment to decide how I'm going to approach this. I can't exactly go up to this person and say, "I'm using this town for a book, can you tell me everything about it?" That would not only be blowing my cover, but I don't think the locals would take too kindly to it.

"Are you lost?"

My head snaps up when the woman behind the counter speaks in a rough, loud voice. Suddenly, all eyes in the room are on me. Cool.

I clear my throat and race to get my story straight. I can do this. Calm. Confident. Be one with the locals.

"Hi," I say quietly, leaning against the desk. I'm hoping if I keep a quiet tone, the rest of the people will go back to their books. I take a quick glance at my surroundings and realize that is not going to happen. There's an older man sitting at a nearby table staring directly at me. A mother and her son are in the children's section at the far side of the room, using their position in the raised platform to lean over a banister to get a better look at me, and a few kids are giggling in the computer section behind me. Not exactly the warm welcome I've received from everyone else in this town.

"I'm visiting for a few weeks," I say in a more confident whisper. The woman behind the counter finally looks up from her desk. She's on the older side, with short, thinning hair, and a cardigan that looks like it was handmade. Her glasses are on the edge of her nose and she looks up at me from behind them, like I'm inconveniencing her in a major way.

"Are you looking for a *book*?"

Well, this is a library.

I inhale subtly and put on my best fake smile. "I was actually looking for some information on the town's history. Would you be able to point me in the right direction? Some archives, perhaps?" In my mind, this was the part where she gets excited that an out-of-towner has shown some interest in this historic town and she offers to tell me all about its Native American history.

That's not what happens. Instead, she shrugs her shoulders and huffs at me.

This library experience is really not going as expected.

"We don't have much. Anything we do have would be down that aisle over there," she says, pointing behind me.

"Oh," I say, disappointed.

Where is the old, crotchety historian who will become my mentor while I go on my journey to self-discovery?

Anne is *not* going to be happy about this.

"Hey, Beth." My head snaps up at the sound of a familiar voice. I find him like a magnet. Liam is in his usual jeans and T-shirt look as he strides up to the welcome desk. He gives me a quick look in his peripheral vision, and then strides right past me toward the librarian. "Here's your sandwich," he tells Beth, placing a white paper bag on her desk.

Beth gets a sandwich. I don't even get a "hello," but Beth gets a sandwich.

"I am capable of walking across the street, you know," Beth replies sassily.

"A simple thank you will do," Liam answers, leaning against the desk. "Not everyone gets my special door-to-door service, you know."

Charm. Beth gets a sandwich *and* charm. What the fuck?

"Thank you, Liam," Beth says.

Liam seems to finally notice my presence—either that or he was pretending not to notice me this entire time—I'm not really sure which. He turns slightly so our forearms gently graze one another and I see goosebumps rise on his skin. I look up and he barely meets my gaze.

"Hey, neighbor," I say in a weak voice. I pair it with an awkward wave. "Although I'm not sure I can call you that when I'll only be your neighbor for a month."

Liam gives me a firm smile, and looks down at the floor quickly, before finally accepting that he has to make eye contact with me eventually. Once he does, his eyes take hold of mine and I can see there are more words in his mind that don't make their way out. Beth rolls her eyes at us. In an instant, Liam's attitude seems to change. His shoulders lift, almost visibly shaking off the façade he was just wearing.

"Sorry, can I ask you something?" I say, fully aware that I am, in fact, asking him something.

"Go ahead," he mumbles.

"Do I... *bother* you? Or make you uncomfortable? Because if I do, I really apologize, but I'm not really sure what it is that I'm doing—" We start meandering down an aisle of books, heading toward the door.

Liam uprights himself. "Stop. It's not you, it's me," he says. "Look, I—I don't take to newcomers very well, we're a close-knit community, you understand? It's basically ingrained in my DNA to be wary of people from the city."

"Wait. Let me get this straight. You don't like me because I live in the city? Not because I acted slightly manic when we first met—which I have apologized for."

"You wouldn't understand," Liam starts, hurriedly pushing some rogue blonde locks out of his face. "The last time someone came to Hudson Hollow from Manhattan, with their posh outfits and fancy cars and fast talking, they came to build a resort on the lake, looking to demolish hundreds of homes in the process."

I open my mouth to speak but take a beat.

"There's so much to unpack there I'm really not sure where to start," I finally say. "Do I look like a property developer to you?" Suddenly, Beth appears from behind one of the large columns and shushes us. Like she literally puts her finger to her lips and goes *Shhh!*—I've never seen a real-life librarian actually do that.

When she disappears again, I turn back to Liam, whose arms, whose *very* muscular arms, are now crossed in front of him. Stay focused, Lucy. Don't compare them to the forearms described in every single freaking romance book you've ever read.

Liam sighs. "Historically speaking, when people visit from Manhattan, families notwithstanding, their intentions are usually to build a resort, or luxury condominiums that price out the locals. They're only concerned with what the town can do for them. And I guess I was worried that you were more of the same," he sighs, shrugging. "I'm sorry. I shouldn't have been so quick to judge you and your intentions."

Um.

Well.

Fuck.

You might be a bit on the nose there, Mr. Miller.

Okay, but this isn't actually the plot of a Hallmark movie. I'm not here to demolish his town or franchise his business. I'm just here for the *experience*. I'm not stealing anything. I'm not taking anything away from the townspeople. I'm just seeing what it has to offer.

"I hope you realize that not everyone from the city is evil," I say, brushing it off. "And not everyone from the city drives fancy cars. Most of us can't even afford cars. The car I'm driving is a friend's car. It would literally take me ten years at my current salary to even be able to finance that car." *Man, that is so depressing to say out loud.*

Liam exhales and the tension in his shoulders visibly softens.

"I don't think *all* people from the city are evil," he says. "I just don't trust them."

"Well, there are about three million of us that live on that island, so maybe you should open your mind a little bit," I suggest. I put my thumb and pointer finger together, making a "just a little bit" gesture with my hand. Liam finally breaks a smile.

"I guess that's reasonable," he says.

Well, this scouting mission has been a little bit of a bust. Beth the Bitchy Librarian gave me zero insight into a happy-go-lucky townie who could own a used bookstore, and now Liam, the self-proclaimed Officer Against the Infiltration of

Urban Outsiders, is continuing to treat me like an enemy of the state. How am I ever going to write an outline for this book when I can't even find one inspirational character?

I start to turn for the door when Liam speaks again. "Lucy, wait," he says, catching me up. "I'm sorry, really. I just—can we try this again?"

"Try what again?"

"This," he gestures between us. He stands up straight and quietly clears his throat. "So, Lucy, nice to see you again," he says in a British-sounding voice.

"Jury is still out on that one," I reply, raising a brow.

Liam ignores me. "I see you've chosen to spend a beautiful summer's day in an old dusty library, what's that about?" he asks, still in character.

Shit, he's eerily intuitive. Or maybe it just stems from him being chronically suspicious. How do I lie to him when I can clearly see that he's trying to make the best out of this strange situation?

"I'm an editor, I go where the books are," I say with ease. Okay, there are worse things I could have said. That wasn't too bad.

"Sure, but what are you *really* doing here?"

"What?" My cheeks go red as I consider the real meaning behind his question. Does he think everything I've said to him has been a lie? Is he asking me what I'm doing in Hudson Hollow? Have I only been on the job one week and already my cover is blown? I would suck on *Law & Order*. "I didn't realize you doubled as the library security," I quip, trying to divert attention away from Liam's question. I turn and walk toward a stack of books, trying to end our conversation. He follows me.

"Or it's just a curious mind wondering what kind of publishing company allows their employees to take a month's long vacation."

"Are you familiar with the HR policies of publishing houses?"

"I could be if I set my mind to it," he replies quickly. I narrow my eyes at him. He does the same to me.

I feel myself wavering. *Stay as close to the truth as possible*, Anne's voice echoes in my head. "Well," I start, unsure of what I'm actually going to say. "If you *were* familiar with our policies, you would know that employees are entitled to a four-week sabbatical after working at the company for five years." He doesn't need to know that the rule actually applies to people who have been there ten years and it's an eight-week sabbatical.

"Is that so?"

"Yep, so here I am."

"Hmm," he grunts. He quickly checks his phone. "I have to get back. And I am sorry, for being judgmental," he adds.

"Sure you are," I shake my head.

"See you, Lucy," he winks. He walks away before I can respond.

A wink.

A wink that felt dangerously flirtatious. Was it? And why did it make my stomach flip?

I try not to let the feeling of excitement in my belly have too much of an affect. I am here to do a job. I'm not here to fraternize with the good-looking chef from across the street. That's what the main character in a Hallmark movie would do. I won't be distracted from my goal. Heartwarming's next editor cannot get distracted by small-town life. She must stay focused.

So, she will.

SEVEN

Operation Small Town, Day 9

"This is how we do ittttt!" I sing, moving my hips to the beat of the music.

Living alone is *amazing*.

Bless Anne for sending me on this trip.

I pour myself half a glass of rosé and shake my head so that my messy top knot bounces around. I have the occasional cocktail when I'm out to dinner, usually something fruity that I drink for the taste. And the maraschino cherry. Okay, *mostly* for the maraschino cherry. But since coming to Hudson Hollow and being on my own for the first time ever, I feel emboldened. I want to dance in my underwear and drink too much wine. Because I can.

"I'm kind of buzzed and it's all because… this is how we do it!" I'm a terrible dancer. There's a lot of arm and hip jerking, very Chandler Bing-esque. But who cares? No one is here to see it, except maybe the inhabitants of the house across the lake, because I do have all the blinds open.

Just as that thought crosses my mind, the doorbell rings.

I check the clock on the T.V. It's after nine. I doubt a robber would ring the doorbell, but I've never lived in a house by myself before, so maybe it's customary for burglars to see if someone is home before breaking in.

I'm giving this way too much thought.

I put my wine glass down and do my best *Risky Business* slide to the front door. I'm wearing fuzzy socks and a long sweatshirt, so I may actually resemble Tom Cruise from an external view. I peek out the windows that line the side of the front door and see Liam standing on the porch. He has a V-neck white T-shirt and jeans on and is holding something in his hands. I gasp and his gaze moves to the window where I'm standing. Shit.

I jump back and unlock the door. Before I open it, I tighten my bun and brush my long bangs out of my eyes. I take a deep breath and open the door.

"Hey!" I say, too enthusiastically. Was that my second glass of wine or my third? Pull it together, Bowen.

"Hey," he says with that smile I'm starting to love. "Having a party?" he asks, his eyebrows gesturing to the music blasting from the house's stereo.

"Ha! A party of one," I say nonchalantly. "Unless you're a robber, then there's definitely a mob of muscular football players in the back."

"And what exactly am I coming to rob?" he says, starting to catch on to my currently impaired mental state.

"Well," I sigh, pressing my hand against my face. "My

mouth just says things sometimes, especially after I've had several-ish glasses of wine."

"Several-ish?"

"Yup, it's a scientific term." He laughs. "Special delivery?" I ask, noticing the tin foil-covered plate in his hand.

He glances down at it. "Well, my dessert supplier accidentally delivered a double order. Do you like chocolate?"

"Liam Miller, you're a dream," I say leaning against the doorframe.

"Huh?"

"Yeah, I mean, you look like, well *you*," I say, waving my hands up and down his body, "and you've brought cake. Pretty dreamy," I say matter-of-factly. Am I flirting with Liam Miller? I think I might be.

"Er... okay, sure..." he says with a sheepish smile. Liam doesn't seem to know how to react to me right now. The wine is lowering my guard a bit, but his seems to still be firmly in place.

"Anyway, come in—" I say, but stop when I see an uncertain look on his face. "What?" He takes a step toward me and leans his arm against the doorframe above me. My heart stops but the muscles in between my thighs kick into overdrive.

"It's just... I'm not sure if you're aware, but you're not wearing any pants." He grins.

My jaw drops. I quickly close my lips with a *pop* and peek down at my legs.

Fuuuuck!

Liam's eyes give me the once over, his smirk growing wider with every inch that his gaze rakes over me. I feel heat rush to my cheeks as I say, "Well, would you like to come in while I put on some pants, then?" I try to shake some sense into myself, but the wine is making me particularly confident.

"Is putting on pants a condition of me coming in? If so, I'd rather not," he says. I can't quite tell if he's making fun of me or flirting back. I haven't seen this side of Liam before. I haven't seen this side of *myself* before. I feel… *playful*.

"Ha ha, very funny. I'll be right back," I say, scampering into the bedroom. I hear Liam's laughter and the door closing behind me. When I reach the bedroom, I pull out the first pair of pants I find. I catch sight of myself in the bathroom mirror. I have no makeup on, but that ship has sailed. He might notice if I throw on some eyeliner now. At least my hair has a sexy, disheveled thing going on. I take off my sweatshirt—because it has suddenly gotten *very* warm in here—and throw on a comfortable bra and my favorite Fall Out Boy T-shirt. It's gray and loose-fitting, but it's the best I can come up with in a pinch. I roll my eyes at how much I suddenly care about what Liam thinks of my appearance.

I take a deep breath and make my way into the kitchen. Liam is fiddling with the stereo under the T.V., turning down the volume. His back is turned to me and he is bent down reaching for the speakers. The bottom of his T-shirt pulls up, exposing his lower back. Is the lower back particularly sexy on a man? Not usually, I don't think, but for some reason, this makes me blush.

"Would you like a glass of wine?" I ask, taking a sip of mine. I need to calm down. My glass is practically shaking as I raise it to my lips. I'm usually not this nervous around men, especially when I've had a drink or two. But something about Liam is different. There's this tension between us that has my body on high alert.

Liam does one of his head-to-toe gazes at me, and for a second, I feel like he's judging me for my hip-hop boozy dance party.

"Rosé isn't my drink of choice, if I'm honest," he says, his voice deep.

"Me either," I admit, fiddling with the stem of my glass.

"But tonight," he starts, a curious tone to his voice.

"Tonight, I'm enjoying my vacation," I say, a satisfied grin on my face. I can just barely make out the small lift of a smile on the corner of his mouth.

"Very well," he says. I grab a glass and pour out the remainder of the bottle.

Okay, I've definitely had three glasses.

I exhale as I hand him the glass, our fingers brushing for the briefest of moments. I bite my lip and move to the window, where I stare up at the moon. It's brilliantly white tonight, casting a warm glow on the black lake below.

"A bit different from the view in the city, huh?" Liam says. I turn around to find him resting his elbow on the counter, his long legs stretched out in front of him.

"A lot different," I say, taking another glance out the window. "My aunt—we're very close—she travels a lot. She would always tell me that no matter how far away she was, we were always seeing the same moon," I explain, smiling at the memory. "As I got older, I would tease her for that, because she totally stole it from a Nicholas Sparks book."

"Or *The Outsiders*," Liam adds.

"*The Outsiders?*" I repeat, trying to understand what

he is saying. I'm embarrassed by the second it takes me to catch up. "Oh, I loved that book! I read it in middle school."

"Me too," Liam says, a smug grin on his face. "You should ask your aunt if she can see the sunset real good from the west side and see if she gets that reference."

I smile widely. Liam Miller just referenced *The Outsiders*. Holy shit. I don't know what to make of this man.

For a moment, neither of us says anything, and we just stay where we are, watching each other. I don't know what is going on in Liam's head. Does he really dislike me for being from the city? I think about explaining to him that I'm from a small town too, and maybe that would make him trust me a bit more. But on the other hand, I am proud of where I am in my life. And I don't like that he questions me because of it.

But, I think, there's also a part of him that is genuinely curious about me. If he decided not to like me because I'm some sort of uptown girl, then he wouldn't have apologized for the other day. And he certainly wouldn't be here right now, bringing me cake.

I find the most awkward way to break the silence by blurting, "So... cake?"

Liam's shoulders jump a little bit at my outburst. I shuffle over to the plate he laid on the counter and unwrap it. I'm immediately bombarded by the smell of decadent chocolate frosting. "Oh my God," I say, tilting my head back and closing my eyes. "That smells so good."

When I turn my focus to finding a knife to cut it, I notice that Liam's eyes are glued to me. I'm so glad I lost the sweatshirt because his gaze is like a heat lamp on my back.

"Do you want some?" I ask, thinking that maybe I should have waited until he left to dive into this. Shoveling cake in my mouth probably isn't the most attractive thing. Then again, it would be rude not to have a piece.

Liam shakes his head. "I'm on frosting overload today. I've got five more cakes just like it back at the café and a few in my car to give to my sister tomorrow."

"Oh, I met her actually, in the store the other day. Jillian, right?"

"Jill. I'm not surprised you've met," he chuckles. "She can't resist accosting any new person she meets. But she means well. Most of the time."

"And your nephew, Robbie. We bonded in the produce aisle." Liam lets out an understanding laugh.

"He has personal boundary issues sometimes," Liam explains fondly.

"Seems kind of common around here," I say, immediately regretting it. "I didn't mean that in a bad way, I swear," I rush to explain. "It's just very different from what I'm used to. Maybe I've been living in the city too long, but if someone snuck up on me in Whole Foods, I'd probably deck them."

"Deck them, eh?" He smirks. "The city sounds like a very violent place."

"It can be a fearful place sometimes, I guess," I say, putting my fork down. "But the people do have good hearts. You've heard the adage, I'm sure, us New Yorkers stick together, and all that."

He studies me for a moment, perhaps thinking the same thing I am. We are so different, despite living mere hours apart. Liam sees this town as a family, he literally puts food on their tables. And then there's me. The city girl who, according to him, only looks out for herself.

"Anyway, Robbie is sweet, despite his intense staring," he says, breaking the silence. I smile weakly at his comment. "He's got a twin sister too, Mia. I might dote on her a bit too much." I melt just a little over this. I'm about to reply when a dog barks outside.

"That's Blue. He probably saw me come over here and wants his dinner," Liam says, standing up. "He gets cranky when I go places without him."

"Even at the restaurant?"

Liam looks around as if someone could hear our conversation. "Well, don't tell anyone, but most days, he's hanging around my office."

"It's a small town, I'm sure everyone knows your secret," I say.

"At least no one's turned me into the Health Department yet."

"Well, he sounds hangry. You should probably get over there," I say. "Thanks so much for the cake."

Liam makes his way toward the door. "My pleasure. Thanks for the wine." He stops and flashes me a grin. "And enjoy your party."

As soon as the door shuts behind him, I consider what the hero of Ruby's new series would look like. Something like tonight's events would be a great way to get the two main characters to bond. I grab my notebook and start jotting down notes about a potential love interest. How might the hero and heroine meet? What would his job be? Would he be blonde, like Liam? Muscular or lean? Maybe the hero could be the town librarian because Lord knows Hudson Hollow's library is beautiful enough for the whole book to be set there.

I spend the next hour hashing out some plot points and writing a very sloppy outline. When I'm exhausted and almost out of ink, I'm proud of everything I've come up with, and I know Anne will be pleased too. For all the work I've done, the secret writer in me can't help but wish I could write this book myself.

EIGHT

Operation Small Town, Day 15

I don't venture into town for a few days after that.

It's not often that I put myself in the position to feel embarrassed—I try very hard to keep myself poised at all times. Which is why I don't drink much. Call me a control freak. And now I know that two (fine, *several*) glasses of wine mixed with a hunky dose of Liam Miller definitely makes me feel out of control.

Hence why I'm avoiding him. Super mature, I know, but I don't need the distraction.

I spend a few days holed up in the house, alternating between working at the dining room table, managing Anne's panic about Ruby, and attending virtual meetings.

I'm having more fun than I expected putting this idea together for Ruby. With extra time on my hands away from the office, my creativity has been flowing, and sketching ideas for this book has given me a much-needed confidence boost. Being dyslexic has often made me self-conscious, especially in a career centered on reading and writing. Yet, just as I once used speech-to-text in school to craft stories that earned my teacher's praise, I've been able to push my storytelling skills further on this project.

A dyslexic with a knack for writing, I remember a teacher saying once. I smile at the memory. Who would have thought?

In the city, I'm at the office until at least 7 pm every night, so by the time I get home and eat dinner, it's all I can take to not fall asleep on the couch before I can make it to the bed. Here, I get to enjoy lounging. I've already made it through three of the small-town books Elle sent me. I'm officially a small-town aficionado.

> Just finished Love It or Like It by Bailey Bishop and I have officially hit my small-town groove. Two weeks in mountain paradise and I have to admit I have love on the brain (and not just because it's my job). Lately, I've been in a love/hate relationship with love. Anyone who has been on a dating app recently can probably relate. I love romance novels because I love the portrayal of love, but I'm having the hardest time believing in the real thing. Do you know a couple whose story could be the inspiration for a romance novel? Tell me about it in the comments!

Posts like this always get the most comments on my page. People tend to relate to my cynicism, even though they are romance readers like me. It can sometimes feel reassuring, but I also have a hard time believing that other people are really going through what I am going through.

This is how it happens for me: I start talking to a guy, usually on an app because no one meets in person anymore, and I get my hopes up. I start picturing how our romance novel-life would unfold. I'm convinced that most people do the same thing, even if they don't work in romance. Given that my day job involves happily-ever-afters, it's not such a stretch that I can't help but picture my own.

Usually, my hopes are squashed by the guy not answering my messages, bailing on plans to meet up, or never texting again after we have. It's demoralizing. I really try to give men the benefit of the doubt, but I don't understand why they make it so hard. We're all looking for the same thing, right? Someone to spend time with? Have fun, make a connection, and fill up some of that loneliness that we all feel? If that's true, then why am I still stuck in this cycle? Have the books I adore set an unrealistic expectation for me?

I'm sitting on the deck one morning, editing, when my phone vibrates, the sound startling me. It's *so* quiet here.

Elle: Help!

Lucy: Yes?

Elle: You know the scene in *Friends*, like waaaayy in the first season, when Monica dates that guy Allan that everyone loves?

Lucy: Of course.

Elle: You know how they say that the size of a man's whozawhatsa is the same as the length from his pointer finger to his thumb?

Elle—the woman who edits erotica but also uses terms like whozawhatsa.

> Lucy: I'm so excited to see where this is going.
>
> Elle: Well, I have an author who wants to use that theory but I'm not sure if it's true.
>
> Lucy: Ask one of our male colleagues.
>
> Lucy: Oh wait, we work in publishing. The only man there is the CEO.
>
> Elle: Bitterness not helping, Lucy.
>
> Lucy: Google it? I personally do not have any experience to prove that theory.
>
> Elle: Damn.

I chuckle and put my phone down on the table beside me, turning as I hear a voice coming from the side of the yard.

"Mia, get back over here!"

I hold my hand over my eyes to shade the glare from the sun, just as a small child appears on the gravel path next to the deck. She can't be more than four or five and has pin-straight blonde hair and a familiar face. It doesn't take long for me to realize why her face is so familiar. I've seen those blue eyes before. I saw them in my dreams last night.

"Mia, you cannot run away from me like that!" Jill

rounds the corner of the house, a large bag slung over her shoulder, sunglasses falling off her face, her hair blowing in her eyes from the breeze off the lake. The troublemaker in question, Mia, shows no remorse, and instead smiles when she sees me on the deck. I stand up and make my way to the railing, apprehensive about interrupting the scolding Mia is about to get.

"Mia, when we get out of the car, you *must* hold my hand. That is a street, there could have been cars!" Jill puts her face very close to the little girl's, and the tension in her voice is palpable. I can tell this woman is having a day. And it's only ten in the morning.

Jill turns in my direction, pushing her hair back off her face and fixing her sunglasses on her nose. "I am so sorry, Lucy," she says, taking Mia's hand.

"No worries! Everything okay?" I ask, feeling a little bad for Jill. She is visibly stressed.

"Yeah, just kids, you know?" I don't, but I nod my head anyway. "This is Mia," she adds, gesturing to the little girl currently attached to her hip.

"Very nice to meet you," I say with a smile. "Are you guys doing something fun today?" I ask in my best talking-to-children voice.

"We're going on the boat," Mia replies, her voice high-pitched and squeaky. She sounds like Minnie Mouse.

"Wow, that's fun," I say.

"Hey, why don't you join us, Lucy?" Jill asks, readjusting her bag on her shoulder.

"Oh no, I wouldn't want to intrude."

"Nonsense. You have any plans?"

"Well, I—" *can't think of anything quickly enough*, I finish in my head.

"We're just going out for a bit. It will be fun. Meet us across the street in a few minutes," she instructs, dragging Mia away before I can reply.

Across the street. At her brother's house. To go on her brother's boat. The brother who saw me dancing around in my underwear the other night.

Great.

I consider calling after her and making up some excuse, but I decide it'll be good for me to do something outside my comfort zone. And really, I'd be lying to myself if I didn't want to see Liam again. Slippery slope, I know.

I throw a bathing suit on under my short set and walk over to Liam's house about ten minutes later. When I knock on the front door, I'm immediately met with barking. Deep, loud barking that makes me jump a little bit. I hear a muffled version of Liam's voice commanding the dog to sit and stay before he opens the door. When he sees me, his familiar skeptical scowl appears across his face.

"What did I tell you? She can't help but accost the new people," he says, referring to his sister.

"I heard that!" Jill calls from inside the house.

"Come on in," Liam says, stepping aside. I step into the foyer, which doesn't look all too different from the rental, apart for the staircase. Blue moseys over to me and puts his weight against my legs.

"Well, hello to you too," I coo, scratching behind his ears. When Blue and I have finished our greeting, we follow Liam into the house.

To the left of the staircase is a dining room and to

the right, a living room. From the front door, I can see all the way to the back of the house, which is lined with floor-to-ceiling windows. The décor is not all that different from his restaurant. It's a farmhouse style with white shiplap walls and bright wood floors. I follow Liam into the kitchen, which is breathtaking. The counters are white marble and stretch around every wall of the room. There is a gigantic island in the middle of the room with a large farmhouse sink. All the finishes are copper which makes the kitchen look so upscale. Well, that and the industrial stove and custom wood vent hood.

"I feel like I'm on an episode of *Fixer Upper*," I mumble, taking in every inch of the space. Liam snorts.

"I'm sure that's exactly what my sister was going for," he says.

"She designed this for you?"

"I did," Jill says confidently, rounding the corner from the kitchen to greet me.

"It's stunning," I say. Her smile brightens.

"Jill is a decorator," Liam explains. Jill eyes him. "Sorry, interior designer or some shit," Liam amends.

Jill rolls her eyes before turning and steering Robbie toward the bathroom. Liam shrugs. "Can I get you a drink, Lucy?" he asks.

"Sure. Water is fine." He moves swiftly through the kitchen, grabbing me a glass. I take the moment to look around the rest of the living room. There is a large, plush sectional and a stone fireplace that touches to the ceiling. The chunky wood mantle is lined with picture frames of Liam and Jill, the twins, and two older people who faintly resemble all four of them. Their parents, I assume. I can't help but notice how much Liam resembles his mother. I hear him humming as he strolls around the kitchen. I turn to meet him and take a moment to really study him. I've never noticed the freckle beneath his right eye, or the dimple that appears in his cheek when he lifts one side of his mouth up.

When I first saw Liam, I thought it was hilarious that there was actually a tall, blonde, handsome man living across the street from me, like there would be in an actual small-town romance book. But he's so much more than a trope. I'm ashamed that I let myself prejudge him based on his looks.

"This is unbelievable!" Jill screeches as she comes out of the bathroom. Robbie has been changed into a rash guard and adorable swim trunks. I catch a glimpse of Mia on the couch, already dressed in a Paw Patrol bathing suit.

"What's the matter?" Liam asks, handing me a glass of water. When our fingers touch there's a short twinge of static electricity between us. Liam stares at our hands for a moment, before turning his attention back to his sister, shaking his head.

"That was work. I have to run over there," she says, tapping away angrily on her phone.

Oh no.

Thank goodness I have the resolve not to say that out loud.

But seriously, *no*. No freaking way.

"I'm sorry, Liam, but can you watch the twins?" Jill asks, an air of disappointment in her voice. Part of me feels bad. Maybe she was looking forward to spending this time with her brother and kids. But then why did she drag me into it?

"Of course, Jill, but your job—"

"—seriously sucks, I know," Jill finishes, rolling her eyes. "Lucy, I'm so sorry I have to run, but please stay."

"Oh no, I couldn't possibly—"

"You could," Liam says, the deep tenor of his voice surprising.

Jill and I both stop to look at him. He shifts his gaze between us quickly and widens his eyes. "Stay, that is. You could stay and come out on the boat with us."

His voice is choppy and awkward, but astute in his desire. My stomach does a bit of a flip-flop at the way Liam looks at me, and while his eyes are scorching me, my heart quickens at the realization that Liam wants me here. *Wants* to spend time with me.

Jill apologizes again and explains to the kids that she'll be back in a few hours. Before we know it, she's out the door and I somehow find myself in Liam's kitchen, alone with him and two small children, wondering how I got here.

Man, this day took a turn.

"Are you Uncle Liam's girlfriend?" Mia asks, leaning against my legs. She clearly has the same personal boundary issues that her brother does.

"Well, I've only known him for a few days, so, no ma'am," I say, looking up at Liam.

"I have a boyfriend. His name is Kyle. We're going to get married," she explains, each of her words mumbled by the most adorable lisp.

"Congratulations. Don't rush into anything, though."

"He gives me his pudding every day at snack time. I *have* to marry him," she says, matter-of-factly.

"I completely understand," I say with a laugh. "Good for you. A girl with standards."

I turn around to see Liam piling things on the counter while Robbie patters his bare feet around the kitchen island, very much getting in his uncle's way. "What can I take?" I ask, trying to be useful instead of just watching these events unfold in front of me. I can already see this scene in the book. Maybe the hero will be an uncle, or a single dad. This would be a great moment for the reader to learn more about his backstory. Romance readers also love their heroes with kids, it's catnip.

"Can you take the twins' bag? Jill packs enough for them to stay a whole weekend, not a few hours," Liam says, gesturing to the bag on the couch.

"Sounds like a classic mom move," I joke, swinging the bag over my shoulder.

Liam quickly looks at his phone. "She just texted me to make sure I put sunscreen on them. I know the children need sunscreen, Jillian, I've been doing this for four years now," Liam says, aggravated.

"You sound like you could be their father," I say, and then cringe at myself. "That didn't come out right." Liam purses his lips and shakes his head.

"I'm getting used to that from you," he says, rolling his eyes.

"Is their dad not in the picture?" I can't help but ask. Liam makes sure the twins are on the deck before he answers.

"We haven't seen him since the twins were born," he says, emotionless, although I can sense the anger behind his eyes.

"I'm sorry. I didn't mean to pry."

"It's okay." Liam closes the last coolers and takes them off the counter. I follow him to the backdoor as he continues. "Jill has had a rough go of it, so me and the town, we kind of take care of her," he explains. I nod and Liam opens the sliding door to where the twins are waiting on the deck.

"Let's do it, people!" he yells, raising the coolers in the air. He's met with adorable screams. I laugh out loud at the cuteness in front of me.

Liam's yard backs up to a canal, like mine, except there are no houses on the other side of the shore. He has a clear view of a wooded area and overgrown seagrass. The mountains in the distance make the view resemble a screensaver.

Liam and his infectious laughter follow me. When I turn around, the air catches in my throat.

Liam is not wearing a shirt.

Sound the *freaking* alarm. Liam. Is. Not. Wearing. A. Shirt.

He's bent over, searching for something in a storage cabinet of the dock. On the side of his body closest to me, I see his obliques squeeze with every small movement. With every breath the large muscle that wraps around his back slides back and forth. When he turns closer to me, I have to swallow when I see his abs.

"What?" Liam asks, his brows furrowed in concern. I must have a shocked look on my face. My expressions are almost as incriminating as the words that sometimes blurt out of my mouth.

He stands upright and faces me. The sight of his defined pecs and flawless nipples nearly knocks me over. Wow, when did I become such a lightweight about hot guys? *Pull it together, Lucy*.

"The boat," I say, trying to recover. "It's really impressive."

Liam shrugs. "Nah, it's just a little speedboat. You'll see some nice ones once we get out on the water," he grins as he hands me a life jacket to put on Mia. I kneel down and slip Mia's small arms through the holes, and she plays with my braid as I buckle her in. I can't help but giggle in her presence.

"Let's go!" Mia squeals as I finish with her life jacket. As I turn around, I notice that Liam put one on both Robbie *and* Blue. Blue's jacket is camo and he looks at me like an embarrassed kid being tortured by his parent. The look in his eyes says, "*I am a cool dog. I have a reputation to maintain.*" I snap a quick photo of him in his seat at the front of the boat. I don't want to forget this moment. The hero in Ruby's book is definitely going to have an adorable dog, no question.

"Can he not swim?" I ask Liam.

"Of course he can," he scoffs, feigning insult. "But safety first." I'm better able to focus when he talks now, because he's replaced his previously bare torso with a long-sleeve shirt.

He takes my hand as I step onto the boat and sit in the seat next to him. The twins jump on the bench seats in the front of the boat. Mia plops herself right next to Blue and throws her arm around him. I like that kid.

Liam lets the boat idle as he leads us out of the canal. As we travel farther north (or south, or east, or west, it could really be any of the above), I notice that the houses on the shoreline become scarcer. Instead of docks and stairs leading up to cabins and multi-level homes, the houses become more spread apart before fading entirely. The number of boats in the water also decreases, and soon only a few anchored boats remain.

Liam's blonde hair whips in the wind, and I take this moment to admire his profile as he stands and looks over the windscreen.

"Are we there yet?" Mia asks, her bare feet pitter-pattering on the carpet floor.

"You bet," Liam says, shutting off the engine. "Who wants to go tubing?"

The twins shriek in unison.

"I think we have to let Lucy go first," he says, flashing me a coy smile.

"I'm sorry, what?" I ask, surprised to hear my name.

"Yeah! Lucy, go! Go!" I'm met with squeals of joy as little hands shake my legs.

I glare at Liam.

"You don't want to try it?" Liam asks.

"Oh, well, I don't know," I say hesitantly.

"Don't tell me Miss Big-City Girl is scared of a little lake water?" Liam accuses, the teasing tone of his voice too cute to be annoying.

"I never said I was scared," I quip.

"It's okay if you are. I happen to know a four-year-old who could show you how it's done." Liam flashes Robbie a devilish grin.

"Hey, who you calling *four*, mister?" Robbie yells. "I am four-and-a-half and you *know* it!" He points a chubby little finger at Liam.

"I am *so* sorry. Please forgive me," Liam responds in a serious tone, begging Robbie with his hands.

"Just this one time," Robbie says, climbing up on the captain's chair. "I forgive you," he says, patting a hand on each of this uncle's shoulders like he is knighting him.

"So, are you up for it?" Liam asks, turning his attention back to me.

"Well, if I want to save face in front of this harsh little rabble, then I guess so," I say, standing up.

Liam hands me a life jacket, and I hesitate before undressing into just my bikini. I'm not uncomfortable in my body, but I'm also not all about flaunting it either. I let my shorts drop down to the ground and feel even more uncomfortable with kids watching. Liam averts his gaze, turning around to fiddle with something on the boat's control panel. I opt to keep my tank top on, and quickly buckle the lifejacket Liam handed me.

"Where do you want me, Captain?" I ask, instantly regretting it.

Liam blinks and shakes his head like he cannot believe I just said that.

"There are so many answers to that question, it's so hard to pick just one," Liam says, a wicked grin splitting his face.

"Oh, come on," I say dismissively, both to Liam and to the butterflies wreaking havoc in my belly. I turn on my heel and carefully make my way to the back of the boat. Liam follows behind me. He grabs the tube that is lassoed to the side of the boat and props it against the edge, next to the engine. Then he holds his hand out to me.

"On you go."

The tube is more like a float, instead of a donut, so

I figure I might not look that ridiculous. I try to be optimistic as I grab Liam's large hand and hoist myself up on to the seat at the back of the boat.

"Lay down and hold on to those handles there, alright?" Robbie instructs, pointing to the float.

"Shouldn't I be in the water?" I ask, becoming more hesitant about this endeavor.

"I'll push the tube in once you're on it," Liam says amusedly. "Which I hope you manage to do sometime this year," he adds.

I glare at him and the side of his mouth picks up. "Shut up," I say with a laugh.

I lay down on the float and grab onto the handles. My feet dangle off the back and I'm suddenly nervous something might bite them.

"What lives in this water—*ahh*!" Liam gives the tube a firm shove and off it goes, thrusting me into the lake.

I squeal when the water flows onto the tube and pools around my body. I screech as I try to lift myself up to avoid the freezing water, but I quickly realize that is one surefire way to flip over.

"*Shit*!"

"Lucy!" Liam scolds. Mia giggles at his side.

"—*take* mushrooms!" I add, still squealing from the icy water pooling under my belly.

"Ready?" Mia calls in a sweet voice as I drift further away from the boat. I lift one arm away from the float and give her a thumbs up. Liam flashes one back at me and turns toward the controls, slowly increasing the boat's speed. He kindly starts off slow, so I smoothly follow the boat in a calm wake. Just as I'm getting into position to truly admire his backside from this angle, he picks up speed.

I hear giggling and clapping as the front of the tube is thrust into the air. I tighten my grip on the handles and shriek as water sprays in my face. Liam swings the boat right and left, creating a bumpier wake which my vessel bounces over. Every time I screech, I hear an echo of childish glee from the back of the boat. After a few moments, I adjust to the sensation and rapidly let go with one hand to push the hair and wipe the water from my face. Once I do, I feel a sense of adrenaline that I was not expecting.

"Woo!" I yell, feeling the wind against my face as Liam drives straight and goes even faster than before. In the calmer wake, I garner the courage to tuck my knees under me and kneel on the float, holding on to the handles on the side. I laugh at the distant sight of Mia and Robbie jumping with joy on the boat.

I am flying, I am soaring, I am free.

NINE

We're out on the boat for hours. The twins take turns on the tube, and even try to ride together one time, which ended with a near rescue mission to fetch Robbie, who somehow flew off the tube. We snacked on tuna fish sandwiches, which I mentioned was in very poor taste, considering the setting. That got me into the lovely position of explaining to Mia where tuna comes from. I'm pretty sure I scarred her for life.

Back at the house, we quickly get the twins—and Blue—washed off in Liam's outdoor shower. It's after 4 pm, and Jill should be back soon to pick them up so he can head to the restaurant. Once they're changed into dry clothes, Liam sets them up with *Finding Nemo* in the living room. I take the opportunity to go onto the deck and remove my wet tank top. Just as I wring it out over the balcony, I hear the sliding door open behind me.

"Here, take this," Liam says, handing me a black shirt.

"Oh, that's okay," I say, shaking out my sad, wrinkled tank top. Goosebumps appear on my arms from the breeze off the lake. I could run across the street and grab a new shirt, but of course, Liam's offer is much more enticing.

"It's fine. I have about a hundred of them." Liam opens the shirt, and I see it's the same "Liz's" T-shirt that the staff at the restaurant wear. I smile as I accept it.

"I'm making coffee, want some?" Liam asks.

"Yeah, that would be great."

"Two sugars and a splash of milk?" he adds as I follow him inside.

"How did you know that?" I don't even bother masking my surprise.

"Trick of the trade. I can tell a person's coffee order just by looking at them," he says with a wink.

"That's such a lie. You just guess and hope for the best." I shake my head.

"Well, you'll never really know, will you?"

I join the kids on the couch, who are both sprawled over Blue who lays in between them. Mia has her head on his shoulder and is using him like a pillow, while Robbie has his small legs thrown over Blue's back, dangling over Mia's head. It's quite a scene. Blue looks miserable, but I can tell he secretly loves it.

I hear the coffee machine whirring to life and can't help but think that Liam and I have made some serious progress today. He only grunted once or twice, I think because he couldn't hide behind his rigid façade in front of the kids. But I have only known him for a couple of weeks, so I'm trying not to push it. And as much as I loathe the idea of being part of a coincidental setup—I do believe Jill had to go to work—today gave me a chance to learn more about Liam. He is actually just a big goofball, especially with the kids. Part of me can't wait to get back to the house so I can jot down some notes for a potential hero for Ruby's book.

When Liam emerges from the kitchen with two mugs, he nods his head toward the back door. I open it for him and follow him outside.

"Blue is like the fun uncle who puts up with the kids just because he knows they're not staying for good," I say as I shut the door behind us.

"Ha!" Liam laughs, setting down two mugs on the table in the middle of two Adirondack chairs. "I'm the fun uncle, he's like the grumpy old granddad who denies he's had any fun but who loves those kids to death."

"He definitely does." I plop down in one of the chairs and take in the view. In the distance, behind the mountain peaks, the clouds are starting to gather. I think for a moment there's going to be a rainbow, but when I look again it's not purple I see on the edge of the clouds, it's a darker gray. The crescent moon sits just at the edge of the clouds, the edges of which are sticking out like the fingers on a hand. One part of the sky looks like a completely different world from the other—one side bright blue, the other getting darker by the second.

Or maybe it's just my imagination.

I take a quick photo of the landscape, trying to subdue my urge to type a note into my phone about the structure of the clouds. I must have writing on the brain; I haven't felt this inclined to write about nature in a while.

"View keeps getting better, huh?" Liam says, taking a sip of his coffee.

"That's an understatement," I say.

"Do you actually *like* living in the city?"

I pause, taking in Liam's question. I don't think anyone's

ever asked me that before. I try to recall my parents' reactions when I first moved, but nothing comes to mind.

"It comes with its challenges," I reply. I draw my legs up beneath me and rest my head in my hand. I can't help but admire Liam and his sun-kissed skin, sat against this dreamy backdrop of the lake and the sky.

"That was a very diplomatic answer," Liam says, a curious tone in his voice.

I sigh. Can he see right through me? Am I that much of an open book? I never thought my face was as revealing as the words that come out of my mouth, but Liam seems to be able to pick up on my every expression.

"It's very different from where I grew up, which I like. And it's where my job is," I add.

"And you love your job," Liam responds quickly, a hint of skepticism in his voice.

"Of course," I say with a nod. I'm caught off guard by Liam's question, a question that surprisingly strikes a nerve. Since coming here, I've realized that living in Manhattan puts me in a bubble. I'm so accustomed to having everything I need—or think I need—within a five-minute walk of my apartment that I've forgotten that there are other ways to live. Admittedly, I've been enjoying the slower pace of Hudson Hollow, the beautiful views, and the peace and quiet.

I keep my eyes on the lake to avoid Liam's intense gaze—this setting is entirely too romantic for me to be caught staring at him. As much as I hate to admit it to myself, I'm far too interested in him. And I shouldn't be, *can't* be. I'm only here for a short time, and I'm here to do a job. I can't let any *potential* feelings for Liam, or whatever this is, jeopardize that.

Research. Small town. Cast of characters. Stay focused, Lucy. Don't look directly into those perfect blue eyes.

"So, Jill's a single parent. That must be tough," I say, hoping he'll accept the change in subject.

Liam takes a sip of his coffee before he speaks. I tilt my head to read his expression and catch myself tracing the stubble along his jaw, wrapping around his lips. He's changed out of his boating attire and is back to his usual jeans and "Liz's" shirt look, only he's paired it with a collared plaid shirt. He looks like the lakeside version of a lumberjack, complete with the five o'clock shadow and the luscious hair that falls just below his ear.

"It is, but she works hard to hide how much she's struggling. For herself, for the family, for the twins."

"What about your parents? Do they get babysitting duty too?" I say with half a smile.

"My dad does what he can, but he's been in rough shape since my mom passed," Liam's voice tapers off at the end of his sentence. He turns and looks over the railing, his gaze fixed on something in the distance. We're silent for a few moments, long enough for a warm breeze to send the brush across the canal rustling like a wave.

"I'm so sorry," I start, my voice cracking. "I shouldn't have asked."

Liam puts his hand up and quickly pats his knee. "Don't be. How could you know?" He pauses. "She died last year, colon cancer." My heart drops. "By the time we knew something was wrong, it was too late. It was very quick."

"Liz was her name, wasn't it?" I ask, already knowing the answer by the look in Liam's eyes.

"Elizabeth, yeah," he replies with a soft smile.

I don't want to say "I'm sorry" again. I am sorry, of course, but I feel like that is the last thing people want to hear when they are grieving. I don't want to be generic, or come across as disingenuous. I want Liam to know that his pain is palpable, and that I truly feel for him.

"Do you think about her a lot?" I ask.

Liam is surprised by my question. He nods slowly, his eyes boring into me. "Every time I look at the lake," he says.

"I lost my grandparents in high school. I was really close with my grandfather. I looked for him everywhere too, just to find that one thing that would remind me of him every day. It makes missing him hurt just a little bit less."

Liam looks out over the water again. "She loved the lake. She loved Hudson Hollow, she never wanted to go anywhere else." A smile spreads across his face as he speaks, and I don't think he realizes how tender it is.

I take a deep breath before I say anything. "You hide it well," I say softly. "That you're suffering, I mean. I'm guessing you and Jill have that in common."

Liam nods and gives me a thin-lipped smile. "Today is a good day. I have bad ones too. But you... you made today easier."

I match Liam's intense gaze and restrain myself from reaching out to touch him. I think back to when I took his hand on the boat. It wasn't the usual touch and spark that I read about in my books. It was a warm comfort that fell over me like a cloud. The kind that made me think, *why have I never held this hand before now?*

Just as I'm about to respond, Liam's phone rings. He looks at it quickly. "That's Jill, she's on her way." I nod and we both stand up in unison. I turn and walk into the house before I pull a classic Lucy and make an awkward joke to cut the tension.

I help Liam get the kids packed up. Mia tells me that today was the "mostest" fun and she hopes it's not a "bajillion" years until she sees me again. She even gives me a hug before I leave. Robbie grunts at me when I say goodbye. Apples and trees.

That night, I'm curled up on the couch, wearing the T-shirt Liam gave me which I put back on after my shower. Even though it doesn't smell like him—this shirt smells like it just came out of a cardboard box—I still find myself wanting to wear it. It doesn't help with the feeling of guilt in the pit of my stomach as I speak the details of my day into my notes on my computer.

After an hour, I have a few lakeside meet-cute scenes sketched out, my favorite one is where the two love interests meet after a jet ski collision in the middle of the lake. I smile reading it over, but my smile quickly fades when I realize the hero I'm visualizing in my head has blonde hair that falls to his ears and a laugh that echoes from his chest.

I'm going to have to change that.

TEN

Operation Small Town, Day 17

"Anne, you have to calm down. You know I can't understand you when your Brooklyn comes out," I say in a quiet, hurried voice. I adjust my phone in my sweaty palm, and simultaneously feel a droplet of sweat roll down my back. Maybe today should have been a lounging on the deck day rather than a walking through town day. Too late for that, I think, looking up at the sun blaring down on me.

"Ruby is restless. I've told her that she's our top priority, and that we're working around the clock on her outline, but that woman is impossible to please," Anne rants. I can hear her running out of breath on the other end of the phone.

Maybe Ruby leaving Heartwarming wouldn't be the worst thing. It would certainly be good for Anne's blood pressure.

"Anne—" I start, but she quickly interrupts me.

"Lucy, I'm putting all my faith in you with this project.

If we can't get Ruby back on board, well—" Anne's voice drifts off, and I realize she's waiting on me to reassure her.

Which is what I'm great at.

"Anne, you don't have anything to worry about. I know how important this is," I say, stopping in my tracks and leaning against the window casing outside of Lucia's. I take a deep breath. I look around, making sure no one can overhear my conversation.

"This place is chock-full of inspiration." My stomach turns as the words come out. "I have pages of notes already, and several key scenes sketched out. It's all going according to plan," I say, hoping that my tone sounds more reassuring than it does guilty—which is how I feel right now. About Liam, about being here under false pretenses, about all of it.

Anne lets out an exaggerated sigh. "Thanks, Lucy, I know you're doing great work. Oh, gotta run!" She hangs up abruptly.

No pressure.

"Lucy!" I start at the sound of my name. I turn and find a woman I've never met waving in my direction.

She's on the older side, with gray hair cropped just above her ears. But age doesn't seem to be stopping her from power-walking toward me. Why do I have the feeling I'm about to be confronted by the Taylor Doose of this town?

"Hello," I say when she finally reaches me. "Apologies, have we met?"

"Ha!" She laughs with a big exhale, trying to catch her breath from her spurt of exertion. "I heard there was a new face in town, and when I saw you standing there, I took a chance."

I raise my eyebrows. "Oh, well, I must stick out like a sore thumb then."

Yep, definitely Taylor Doose.

"You do, but only because I know everyone in Hudson Hollow!" She smiles. "Anywho, I wanted to introduce myself. I'm May Lucia." We shake hands. "I'm one of the founding members of the town council, so it's my business to know everyone else's business in town, if you know what I mean," she explains with a wink. I can feel my eyes bugging out a little bit, but I try my best to control my face.

"Well, at least you're honest about it." I chuckle. "Lucia as in Lucia's?" I ask, gesturing to the store behind me.

"Indeed, it's my husband's place," she says proudly. She gestures inside the window, where Max is talking to a person at the register. His warm, soothing laugh echoes out onto the sidewalk. I think I'm developing a soft spot for Max.

"You busy on Saturday? The council is hosting a little soirée and you really must come! It's our annual charity softball game. We're raising funds for a new playground over at the elementary school."

"Oh, that sounds great," I say. My mind flashes back to almost *every* small-town romance I've read, and I have to keep myself from smiling. Every single one includes some sort of community event or function. This place is uncanny.

"Fab! I'll see you there?" she asks eagerly.

"Well, I'm not much of a softball player, if I'm honest," I say, thinking back to the time Elle forced me to play in Heartwarming's summer league. The memory makes me shudder.

"You don't have to play. We can use some fans! Just as

long as you're cheering for *my* team, that is," she says, and I can't tell if she's teasing me or not.

I laugh. "You got it. I'll be there." This is exactly what I need right now. Anne will eat this up. A town picnic? All the locals coming out together? It's the perfect opportunity to meet some more kooky characters—the one thing I'm really missing.

I follow the instructions May provided down to a sandy beach along the lake shore, where a small cabin and a patch of grass has been set up as a makeshift softball field. I spot Liam almost immediately, he's setup on the other side of the grass beneath a tent and a steaming grill. He's talking to Brett, who is dressed in a matching green T-shirt.

I make my way over and they both smile when they see me.

"Hey, new girl, you look nice," Brett says, his tone jovial. "Doesn't she look nice, Liam?" Brett nudges him and Liam's eyes meet mine. I quickly look down at the denim sundress and sandals Elle helped me pick out over FaceTime.

"She does, er, you do, Lucy," he says softly.

"Thank you." I feel heat flood my cheeks as I divert my gaze. I scan the nearby crowd and notice there are two distinct groups of people, some in green and others in red. May is among them, talking to a man who appears to be setting up a portable DJ booth.

"Is that a DJ?" I ask dubiously.

"Yup. The only one within thirty miles, I think," Liam chuckles.

"A DJ during a softball game, that's a new one," I muse. Liam smiles sheepishly.

"We only play a few innings. The main attraction is the buffet and the dancing," Brett explains.

"Dancing? Boy, this really is some small-town stuff," I say, unable to help myself.

"Is that bad?" Liam looks up from the grill.

"No, it's just kind of crazy the whole town shuts down for this."

"What? You don't have softball games in the city? Or do people not talk to each other enough to organize something like this?" Brett teases. He crosses his incredibly huge arms.

"We definitely don't have events quite like this," I say with an uneasy laugh. Liam shakes his head, the same look of disbelief on his face that I'm sure is on mine.

"Well, Lucy, prepare yourself for some serious action," Brett says, and he exchanges a look with Liam. "Wish me luck!"

"Good luck," I say, waving him off as he jogs toward the other players.

I jump when I hear the shrill sound of a whistle. May stands at the center of the diamond holding a megaphone. She clearly takes her council job *very* seriously.

"Five minutes!" she drills. Almost everyone in the crowd covers their ears, including me.

"Jill and the twins are here, over by the picnic tables," Liam says, pointing to a handful of tables. "You should join them." He smiles.

"Okay, okay, I'll leave you to work your magic," I throw my hands up in mock surrender. He rolls his eyes at me, smirking.

I edge around the field and the players warming up. There are several other families picnicking nearby, they offer kind smiles as I pass by. Just as I hoped, a cast of characters to populate Ruby's town with.

"Lucy!" The twins squeal in perfect unison. They leap off the bench to greet me, Mia wraps her arms around one of my legs.

"Ah, Lucy," Jill turns and beams up at me. "This one hasn't stopped talking about you," she says, making room for me on the bench beside her.

"All good things I hope." I ruffle Mia's head affectionately.

"Lucy, this is my friend Nora. Nora this is Lucy," Jill says, gesturing to the woman sat across from her. Nora looks to be about thirty. She has curly, dirty blonde hair and is rocking a stroller back and forth with one hand.

"Hi there," I say, putting on my best "meeting new people" smile.

"Hi, Lucy," she gives Jill a knowing look. "It's lovely to finally meet you, I've heard so much about you."

"Word travels fast around here, eh?" I laugh, and Nora laughs as well, shrugging. "It's nice to meet you, too. And who is this?" I ask, gesturing to the stroller. I can just make out the small, milky face of a sleeping baby.

"This is Cammy. I'm afraid she's finding the picnic a bit dull," Nora jokes.

"Ah, in that case I hope May and her megaphone don't wake her up," I reply.

"You're telling me," she grumbles sarcastically. "So, what's it like being Liam's neighbor?" She flashes Jill a look.

"It's good," I say, clearing my throat. "But I'm really just using him for his boat. Don't tell anyone." Jill and Nora giggle. The twins settle on the grass behind us, and Robbie reaches out to hold onto my leg. *Really, kid, boundaries.*

"He looks the happiest I've seen him in a while," Nora says, laying her head on her hand. "Don't you think, Jill?" I'm not sure if I'm meant to be catching on to their silent conversation, but the tone in Nora's voice is obvious.

"Oh no, Liam and I are just friends," I start. "I'm only here for a few weeks."

Nora waves her hand dismissively. "Oh, sure. You do you, girl." Jill gives Nora a stern look. "It's just that," she continues, "I don't know if you know Liam and Jill's mother passed last year—"

I nod. "Yes, he told me, I was very sorry to hear that," I say, directing my eyes at Jill.

"Seeing his face the other day, you know, when I came to pick up the twins," Jill interrupts, swallowing before she continues. "I haven't seen him like that in a while."

"I'm glad," I say, hoping that this will put the conversation to bed. "But really, just friends. Besides, Liam and I are *very* different," I add, because really, what else can I say?

"Being different is often a good thing," Nora intones. "Although, do you remember what he was like with Molly?" Nora tips her head to the side, a grin spreading across her face.

"Ugh, Molly was the *worst*," Jill groans.

I can't help but laugh. They speak so bluntly about Liam's life—as if he isn't standing twenty feet away.

"Molly was Liam's last girlfriend." Nora leans toward me like she is telling me a secret. "She lived in a neighboring town but was never really happy here. Had bigger dreams and all that."

"Oh," is all I can manage. I feel my pulse quicken and I'm not sure if it's because we're talking so candidly about Liam's dating history, or the insinuation that there is something happening between us. And then there's the guilt, the knowing that I'm only here temporarily, and that despite anything else that *might* happen, I haven't been entirely honest with him, or with anyone else. Even so, this is *exactly* the kind of gossip I've been dying to hear about.

"Why did they break up?" I ask, unable to downplay my curiosity.

"She couldn't cope with my mom's illness," Jill says quietly.

"Or she couldn't deal with not being Liam's first priority," Nora adds, shaking her head.

"Hmm," Jill muses. "When our mom got sick, Liam was overwhelmed. My dad did what he could, but I think the shock of it all really took a toll on him. It still does." She pauses and looks over toward Liam, her brow creasing subtly. "I was a single mom with two toddlers, I could only give so much, you know?" She sighs. "Liam took on a lot of the responsibility, too much if I'm honest, but when my brother makes a commitment, there's nothing he won't do."

"I'm so sorry," I say. "It sounds like Molly wasn't a very kind person." Although I don't know her, I'm sure she had her reasons for breaking it off with Liam, or why she didn't want to be supportive of his family's struggles. But as I watch Liam laugh with one of the locals, I can't help but feel like any girl would be a fool to let him go.

"Anyway, it's in the past now," Jill gives me a knowing

smile before she pivots in her seat. I follow her gaze. May stands in the center of the field waving her arms. She lifts the megaphone to her lips and wails "*PLAY BALL!*"

Jill whoops and claps her hands, encouraging the twins to root for Liam. It's perfectly charming, and I can't help but smile. I turn back to Nora, who watches on bemused. She raises her eyebrows at me conspiratorially.

"Which one is yours, then?" I ask Nora.

"That one," she points, "with the dad bod." I follow her finger to a man in the outfield. He's on May's team and looks extremely bored. His hair is gelled to one side of his head and he stands with his hands on either side of his hips.

"He looks thrilled to be here," I muse.

"Ah yes, he's missing the golf tournament on T.V. today. And then there's the matter of sleep, or the lack thereof." She nods toward Cammy. "I think he would much rather be snoozing on the sofa, but since he's a half decent player, May forces him to join."

"She would probably deport him from town if he tried to skip out on this," Jill adds in agreement.

"It's true. She has *that* much power," Nora adds, widening her eyes. We all laugh at her serious tone.

"Have you always lived in Hudson Hollow?" I ask her.

"I have, yes," she says.

"And your husband as well?"

"No, actually," she pauses to rub Cammy's tummy, "he's from downstate, a town called Croton-on-Hudson. We met in college."

"How did you get him to move here?"

"That was easy. I was here," she smirks. I chuckle at her cockiness.

"So, I guess you've never wanted to live anywhere else, then?" I ask, wondering if my questions sound too reporter-like. I want to get to know what makes people love Hudson Hollow. I think the heroine in Ruby's book will be a true city girl, like me, so I want her to fall in love with the town and not just the hero. I'm finding that a little difficult when the closest Target is thirty minutes away.

"This is home," Nora says with a shrug. "My family's here and my parents are getting to that age where they don't want to be anywhere but their own house," she adds. "Plus, I've never been a city person, which I'm sure is hard for you to imagine. I've always found it a bit overwhelming. There are so many people on that island, it's going to sink one day."

"I've actually had that thought myself. But it's become my comfort zone now," I explain. I can imagine how jarring Manhattan would be to someone who is used to single-lane roads with two cars on them at any given time. I was shocked when I came to Hudson Hollow, so it must work the same in reverse.

"So, you see what I mean? This town is all I've ever known. I liked growing up here, and I want that for my kids too." She bends down and places a kiss on Cammy's forehead.

When the game is over, everyone huddles around the snack bar, where Liam is overwhelmed trying to get to everyone. Brett rescues him by joining him behind the grill. He ties a bandana around his head like *The Karate Kid* and claps his hands when people approach him. It's quite entertaining.

Jill takes the twins for some food while I hang back with

Nora. Her husband joins us, delivering a plate of food, and I'm suddenly jealous that I don't have someone who does that for me. I need a man to deliver food without me asking. The closest thing I've ever had to that is the DoorDash delivery guy.

Once the line dies down, I mosey over to the food table and get a good glimpse of Liam flipping meat—a surprisingly sexy act.

Stop it, Bowen.

"Hey," he says when he catches me ogling. "Can I get you something to eat?"

"Yeah, although I heard the chef at this place is just okay." I bite my lip. He lets out a quiet laugh.

"Chicken, ribs, or pork sandwich?"

"Hm, not sure, I was expecting the regular burger or hot dog question."

"And which of those would you prefer?"

"A burger. Why? Is that an option?"

"No. I just like knowing things about you," he replies quickly. He doesn't hide his flirty smile. He dips his head and leans over the bar with his arms stretched out. I'm beginning to think that's his signature position. When I don't answer right away, he moves on. "I was going for a southern barbeque theme. Everything has been smoked for about fifteen hours with a dry rub and then I top it off with my special sauce."

"My experience binge-watching *Diners, Drive-Ins, and Dives* should really be paying off right now," I joke and Liam laughs. "You don't do anything the easy way, do you?"

"Not when it comes to food," he says bluntly. "So, what will it be?"

"Pork, I think."

"Good choice. Do you want mac and cheese or greens on the side?"

"Mac and cheese, of course. I don't even know what kind of question that was."

"My kind of girl," Liam beams, dolloping a scoop of mac and cheese on my plate. "Enjoy," he says, handing it to me.

"I'll see you later," I say, grabbing a soda from the cooler.

"Miss Lucy!" I hear a deep voice bellow. I turn to find a very sweaty Max heading my way. I smile and wave, waiting for him to fall in step beside me. "How are you enjoying your time at our lovely lake?" he asks, patting me on the back.

"I love it. It's beautiful here," I say, glancing over my shoulder at the distant sunset.

"Look at this little one!" he says, moving his attention to Cammy. The baby is sitting on Nora's lap, eating small pieces of chicken off her plate. She smiles and mumbles gibberish to him. "She's getting so big, Nora."

"You're telling me. She's a giant," Nora says, rubbing the baby's head.

"That's good. Maybe she'll grow up to be a star ballplayer and finally put my wife out of business," he mumbles and we all chuckle.

"What about your wife?" May calls, walking over in three big strides from the next table over. She stands next to Max with her hands on her hips and eyes him accusingly.

"Only good things," Nora says in a placating voice.

May continues to eye Max. "Likely story," she says, pursing her lips. When she's finished her stare-off with Max, she moves her attention to Cammy, taking her off her mother's lap without even asking—a trait I'm learning is essential to the May character.

"Hey Lucy," Nora says, nudging my arm to get my attention. "Why don't you come to Cammy's party next week?"

"Oh, I wouldn't want to impose," I say, covering my mouth as I finish chewing. I know I'm supposed to be learning all I can about the people in this town, but attending a party at someone's house I met an hour ago seems like a stretch.

"Oh please, you don't really have a choice in this town. We impose ourselves on you," Jill answers from across the table.

"It's in my yard, super casual," Nora adds.

"Oh, then sure, I guess so. That sounds great," I say, feigning excitement. I never understood the point of birthday parties for babies. They don't know what is going on. Seems like a waste of money to me. But if it is a birthday party, there is sure to be cake. I like cake.

"Great. I'll text you my address," she says, pulling out her phone.

After we exchange numbers, Nora turns her attention back to the baby, and I observe the conversation among the group. I watch them swoon over Cammy, joking with each other, as if they are one family, rather than two separate ones. I'm realizing that this town is like one big family, with roots that stretch for generations, like the ones I'm looking at right now. It's no wonder Nora would want to raise her family here. In Hudson Hollow, you get several families for the price of one.

After I eat, I wander onto the beach and kick my boots off. I try to remember the last time I felt sand between my toes. Elle and I took a trip to Long Beach Island last year at this time, but I never made it back to the beach again that summer. That's the thing about publishing, everyone takes the summer off, *except* the assistants.

I sit down on the sand and prop my arms behind me. The sun has dipped below the mountains and the sky is hazy with tones of purple and pink. I love summer skies like this. You don't get to appreciate them too much in the city—the tall buildings get in the way.

My solace is interrupted by the DJ starting his set, kicking off with some heavy dance beats. I hear the protests of people being dragged onto the dance floor by May, who is clapping her hands and singing along to the music. Brett and his bandana are among the small crowd, his arms flailing behind him as he pushes his chest out. He might just give me a run for my money for *worst* dancer. I stifle a laugh. When I said I wanted to become one with the locals, I didn't actually expect to be sitting around the campfire, singing kumbaya or anything.

Well, there is definitely some kumbaya shit happening here.

Nora and Jill join the group, and soon almost everyone is on their feet. I think back to the last family wedding I went to when barely anyone left the tables. Soon, the song transitions to line-dancing country, and I immediately recognize the introductory notes of "Cupid Shuffle."

"Lucy!" Oh, no. I've been spotted. The twins come barreling toward me, their breathing ragged from jumping around with the other kids.

"Come dance!" Mia whines, grabbing my hands with both of hers. I let them drag me to the dance floor, where I see May doing the same to Liam.

I fall in line with the twins, Nora and Jill are behind me, and Max and May in front. My back bumps into the person next to me. I turn around and am chest to chest with Liam. I wait a moment, taking the time to appreciate how marvelous he looks. He smiles my favorite crooked smile. We're so close that I can't help but breathe him in. I let the scent of smoke and aftershave fill my lungs and feel the tingles that his touch against my arms send throughout my body.

The moment doesn't last more than a few seconds before we both step back and gain our composure. I give Liam a tight-lipped smile and he opens his mouth to say something, but we are both almost thrown over by the line of people shuffling from right to left. Liam laughs and makes a motion that says, "Shall we?" And we do.

"To the right, to the right, to the right, to the right...

To the left, to the left, to the left, to the left...

Now kick, now kick, now kick, now kick...

Now walk it by yourself."

We move in sync to the lyrics, except when it comes to "moving it by yourself" which Liam interprets as subtly swaying side to side, shaking his hips like he is doing a hula-hoop—the twins laugh so loud they practically shriek. I shake my hips in a circle when we change direction, a smile never leaving my face the entire time. Jill stares at her brother in disbelief, and I have to assume he's not usually this animated on the dance floor. Our eyes meet and she smiles.

I hold Mia's hands as we shuffle back and forth. I show her how to kick her legs in rhythm to the music. Liam lifts Robbie over his head and does the dance with the kid dangling over his shoulder. In the movie version of this small-town adventure, this moment would take place in slow motion—the light from sparklers glowing in the distance, the bodies and faces around us blurred except for the main characters, my hair bouncing as I shake my body, and the light in my eyes matching the warmth I feel from the people around me.

I don't remember the last time I danced. Maybe sometime last summer when Elle dragged me to a club? It wasn't as fun as this. I remember wanting to leave and get as far away from the crowd of people as possible. But here, this moment, with these people…

I never want it to end.

When my head hits the pillow that night, I start to fall asleep but my eyes quickly fly back open. I'm in too deep. The shallow feeling in my stomach tells me that. Because if I was impartial, if I was just in this for a job, I wouldn't feel a smile spreading across my face when I think about the moment Liam reached for my hand as we danced.

ELEVEN

Fish out of water.

It's one of my favorite elements of romance. It's not often in other genres that you see a main character so completely out of his/her element. In romance, it just adds to the tension sometimes. Or the trope.

I've never felt so much like a fish out of water as I do on this trip. Like in these books, I am completely out of my comfort zone… and it's changing me. The heroines in these books from @HeartwarmingRomance leave their hometown or city lives to renovate an inn or care for a relative… and they end up finding themselves—and love—in a new environment.

What's your favorite fish-out-of-water romance? Let me know in the comments.

Operation Small Town, Day 19

"So, you admit that you're liking it there, then?" Josie says, her voice crackling from the other end of the phone. She wouldn't FaceTime with me today, probably because she's working on the other end of the phone and doesn't want me to see how distracted she is. I roll my eyes at her question.

"I don't know what you're trying to get me to admit," I reply, a bit defensive. "It's a beautiful place, great for a vacation." My mind flashes back to telling Liam that I was in Hudson Hollow for vacation, a lie which he still believes. "I'm not as anti-small town as everyone—well, mainly you—makes me out to be."

"I don't believe you are. But your mother is, and I know how persuasive she can be," I can sense the judgment in Josie's tone.

"You're not that far off, you know," I reply.

It's been a few days since the picnic, and in that time, I've been doing a lot of solo scouting. Yesterday I made it my business to go into every establishment on Main Street, from the gas station to the post office. It didn't take me long. While Hudson Hollow is a quaint town, it doesn't have an idyllic used bookstore with a grumpy owner looking for an out-of-towner to revive her small business. There's no small coffee shop with a pun for a name or a historic site that could inspire a novel. There's Liz's, Lucia's, the library, the post office, and Stewart's/the gas station.

I also spoke with Anne yesterday, who was ecstatic about my notes from the picnic.

"You actually line-danced with these people? I would have paid to see a video of that!"

"Well, that sounds like workplace harassment," I deadpanned.

"Was there a campfire? Did they sing?"

"You don't have to talk about them like they're an exhibit, Anne. But no, thank goodness, there was no actual sitting by the fire and singing folk songs. I think I would have lost it."

"Are you getting soft on small-town life, city girl?" Anne said, and I could feel the condescension in her voice.

"And prove you right? Never."

I could tell from Anne's voice when she asked about the "hero character" that she wanted to know more about Liam, whom she must have heard about from Elle. So far, most of my notes she's seen have been about the town, and the heroine. After the picnic, I started to list out some side characters that could round out the town's ensemble. Of course, I had to add a bubbly, intriguing library assistant who loves to share stories about the town's rich history, just to stick it to Beth. But I haven't been able to paint a clear picture of who the hero will be. I knew going in that Anne basically expected me to infiltrate Hudson Hollow, but I didn't realize just how *personal* of a job it would be. The way Jill talked about her brother's happiness, and *me* somehow playing a part in that, has made my outlook on this project completely different.

"Can't you see the benefits of being in a place like that?" Aunt Josie says. "The slow pace, the nature. I would love it."

"You're the one who jumps from big city to big city," I remind her.

"Hindsight is twenty-twenty, my love," she says, sighing.

"There's a bit too much hustle and bustle in this life for me these days. A lake house and a quiet life sounds magical."

"Then why don't you come home?" I ask, my chest aching, yearning for one of her tight hugs. "We can quit our jobs and move to the sticks. We'll start a sewing circle and have a garden and do outdoorsy shit."

"Doesn't sound so bad, does it?" she muses.

As reluctant as I am to prove Anne and Josie right, maybe I am getting a little soft on this small-town life. "I mean, things are slow here. Like, in no rush to get anywhere-level of slow. And people actually use the crosswalks and wait for the light to turn before crossing the street." Josie cackles. "But I guess there are perks to not having to fight elbow-to-elbow with people to get off the subway car first, or dodging oblivious people wearing air pods in the grocery store, I'm not spending my lunch hour rushing down the block to pay $15 for a soggy salad..." My voice trails off. *I'm not sitting behind a desk all day, watching the rat race on the street below me.*

"Mhmm," Josie hums. I don't have to be able to see her to know the look on her face right now. It says "I told you so" in about seven different languages. "Refreshing, isn't it?"

When I hang up with Josie, I head outside to collect the mail. Part of my "rent," as Anne calls it, is collecting Al and Mella's mail and forwarding anything urgent. The sun is setting over the mountains, and of course, I take my phone out to snap a picture. No photo will ever do it justice, though. And every time I do it, I think of Liam, and his *Outsiders* reference. *We all see the same sunset.*

The sky seems to have so many more colors here than it does in the city. Of course, I realize that doesn't make a lot of sense, since it is the same sky. But I can see so much more of it here. My favorite is when it looks like it does tonight, with layers of colors, one on top of another. Red is closest to the mountains, then orange on top of it, yellow blush on top of that, and purple-pink clouds scattered across the top.

I start to go back into the house when I hear a deep "woof" behind me. I turn and see Blue galloping over like the clumsiest horse I've ever seen. I can't help but giggle. "Hey, buddy!" I squeal, squatting down to pet him. When he nudges me with his big head, it knocks me off balance, and my butt hits the gravel with a thud. "Oh my goodness," I mumble as he licks my face. I laugh until I'm out of breath and I'm finally able to sit up and calm him down. "How are you today? How are you?" I say, my voice pretending like I'm talking to a baby instead of a dog.

"Blue!" I hear Liam call in the distance, but Blue makes no move to listen. I'm scratching his neck behind his ear, and he's moaning in response.

"I think you're wanted elsewhere, my friend," I say, standing up. "Let's go find Liam. Come on." I pat my leg and Blue follows, brushing against my thigh every few steps. I walk around the side of Liam's house and spot him on the dock. He's looking around for Blue, and seems aggravated when he sees him with me.

Liam claps his hands for Blue to come to him. Blue looks up at me and appears to smirk. We walk toward the dock together. Liam takes a step off of the dock once Blue starts to approach him. I see Brett on the dock behind him, zipping a cooler shut and throwing it over his shoulder.

Liam puts his hands on his hips, looking at Blue knowingly. He's in one of his long-sleeved shirts, much like what he wore on the boat that day, and a pair of board shorts. There are three fishing lines leaning off the dock.

"Hey, sorry he bothered you," he says, patting Blue's back.

"Don't be silly, Blue could never bother me," I say, sitting down on the grass. Blue comes back over to me to continue his rubdown. He collapses beside me and flips onto his back, lifting his leg up so I can rub his belly. Liam can't help but smile.

"You're going to lose your free rein privileges, B," Liam tells him. Blue looks up at him lazily, barely able to keep his eyes open.

"Hey, Lucy, nice to see you again," Brett says, coming up beside Liam.

"You too," I say with a shy smile. Brett is the kind of handsome that can be a shock to the system. His voice is deep and strong, and his smile could make anyone blush.

"I'm off to feed the missus," Brett says, clapping his hand across Liam's back.

"You're married?" I ask, not quite able to keep the surprise out of my voice.

"Newly, yeah. Just under a year." Brett flashes his hand at me, where a black ring adorns his finger. I try to lower my eyebrows and hide the expression on my face. Elle will be so disappointed in this development. Brett has been her favorite character in my stories as of late.

"See you soon, bud," Liam says, giving Brett a fist bump. Brett and I exchange small waves as he walks away.

Liam and I exchange glances for a moment, and I suppose one of us should say "How are you?" or something of the like, but neither of us can seem to work up the courage.

He finally breaks away to look back at his fishing poles. "Want to join?" he asks.

"Sorry, join what?" I say, looking between him and the dock.

"Fishing," he says, in a tone that makes it sound like it should be obvious.

"Hah, um yeah, I don't think I'm the fishing type of girl," I reply. I know Liam probably wants to make a comment about how "city girl" that sounded, so I beat him to it. "Have I mentioned I'm from Manhattan?"

"An island surrounded by water in which fish live?" he asks, squinting his eyes and pursing his lips in a jokingly condescending manner.

"Excuse me, sir, I don't like your tone," I say, waving my finger at him.

"Prove me wrong then," he says, holding out his hand.

Why my mind flashes to the 2005 *Pride and Prejudice* hand flex, I have no idea. But I take his hand anyway, which he immediately drops after he pulls me to my feet.

I don't really think of myself as a "girly girl," or one who has no concept of how to hold a football. I'm not judgmental of girls who are, but I don't know if that is how I would describe myself. I'm willing to get my hands dirty, I'm up for a day on the boat, tubing in murky lake water, and whatnot, but a twenty-minute session on the elliptical is my maximum. I'm not delicate, but I'm not a go-getter, nature girl. I'm not about to go rock climbing or anything, but I can usually handle myself. Usually.

But I don't think I've ever looked as awkward as I do when Liam hands me a fishing pole.

"Here, I'll hook the bait on the end," Liam says, handing me the pole and guiding me to hold the line swinging off it.

I hold the thin wire he hands me and slide my fingers down to the end with the hook. But of course, my fingers slip and I prick myself with said hook.

"Ouch!"

"Tell me you did not just poke yourself with the hook," Liam says, not turning around from his supplies.

"I did *not* just poke myself with the hook," I recite back to him, biting my thumb.

Liam turns around with a menacing look on his face. When he glances up at me, I force a smile around my thumb. Liam closes his eyes and shakes his head slowly.

It's moments like these—when I have a blonde-haired, blue-eyed, could-be-on-the-cover-of-a-romance-novel man sitting next to me winking at me—that I feel like I could literally burst out laughing.

Thankfully, I don't. Count one point for Lucy's usually lacking self-control.

Elle would call me cynical for even thinking this, but men like Liam don't exist in real life. Towns like Hudson Hollow don't exist in real life. These past few weeks have felt like an out-of-body experience, and every time I look at Liam, I'm reminded of just how ridiculous this whole thing is.

I'm an editorial assistant, the lowest man on the totem pole of the publishing industry, being paid to work remotely from a lakeside cabin. I've somehow transplanted myself into a Hallmark movie where my neighbor happens to be a real-life blonde-haired, blue-eyed hunk with a tragic past and an adorable family. I cannot wrap my brain around the fact that in a few weeks I'll be back in the city, where guys who look like Liam are the ones on dating apps who are in open relationships or don't understand the difference between *you're* and *your*.

I look down at my phone and see that I missed a call from my mom on my walk over here. "Do you have to take that?" Liam asks, nodding toward my phone.

"Nah, it's my mom. I'll call her back later," I say, putting my phone in my pocket.

"What do your parents think about you being here? They must be jealous that you're not spending your time off work with them," he says, fiddling with the fishing line.

"They're definitely not thrilled about it," I say with a small laugh. "They very much think my focus should be on my work, not gallivanting in a small town."

"They're city people too?"

"Oddly enough, no. I grew up in the suburbs. I guess I thought of it as a small town, until coming here. Now I know what puts the *small* in *small town*." I shake my head, hating the way I just said that. "Not that I think there's anything bad about it—"

"Kind of sounds like you do," Liam replies, obviously a little peeved.

"No, or... I don't know. I'm starting to see that a small town has its perks." I pause, gauging his reaction. "Growing up, I was an only child, and I was lonely a lot. More than I think my parents ever knew. When I moved to the city, I thought my problem would be solved. I was on an island with millions of people. I'd read so many books where the characters were *enraptured* by Manhattan, the sense of community, the hidden treasures, the experiences only New

York could offer. But I didn't find any of that when I got there." I pause, thinking about the early days when I moved to Manhattan, trying and failing to make connections with people, desperately searching for that once-in-a-lifetime feeling that I'd seen so many characters in movies and books experience. "I felt lonelier than I ever had in my life." Liam watches me intently as I speak, and I know he is analyzing every word I say. "But here, I see that sense of community. It's really something special."

Liam absorbs every word that comes out of my mouth like he's calculating something in his mind or trying to store my sentences in the memory bank behind his eyes. When I stop speaking, he looks at me quizzically.

"Why do you have that look on your face?" he asks me, furrowing his brows. It's only then that I realize my brows are scrunched too. I'm not sure how to answer him, because I'm a bit taken aback by myself. Why did I just say all of that? What possessed me to choose this moment to become the over-sharer that Elle is always pushing me to be?

"I don't know. I guess I'm just surprised I said that. I'm not usually very forthcoming with my feelings. That's what my friend Elle says anyway."

When Liam smirks at me, the answer is clear.

It's him. Liam brings out the truth in me.

"Well," he starts, gazing out over the water. "I don't know about feelings, but it seems like what you're saying is that Hudson Hollow is where you need to be right now. I believe that."

"That sounds like something Elle would say too," I say with a smile. "She's always manifesting things into the universe and whatnot."

"I'd love to meet her one day," Liam says with a smile. "And I'm just going to say this," he says, placing his fishing pole against his chair and leaning toward me with his elbows on his knees. I stifle a gasp when his knee bumps mine. "I don't think you have anything to be afraid of. With your parents, New York, anything. When I look at you I see someone who moved to one of the most intimidating cities on her own." I nod at the questioning tone in his voice. "Then she had the courage to come to a strange place all by herself and open herself up to this community. That's bravery. That's what I see, Lucy Bowen."

I don't say anything right away, because how does one respond to that? Liam lets our legs nudge each other without breaking his gaze. I can't help but look away. The weight of his eyes makes my stomach flutter. As soon as I look down, Liam's hand reaches out and gently brushes a piece of my hair behind my ear. My eyelids shoot open and my eyes find his.

"Liam—ahh!" My hand jolts forward with a thrust from my fishing line. Liam jumps up like he's assessing the surrounding area for danger. I grab the pole with both hands and try to resist the pull of the taut line. I stand up and frantically look at Liam. "What do I do? What do I do?" I scream. Blue jumps up and barks, his big paws pitter-pattering in rhythm with my flip-flops on the wooden boards.

"First of all, calm down," Liam says, wrapping his arms around me and covering my hands with his. "I'll hold the pole; you reel it in."

I remind myself to exhale when I feel Liam's strong chest behind me and the flex of his arms on my shoulders.

"Oh my goodness. Oh my goodness," I mutter, keeping my left hand under Liam's and moving the other to the reel. Liam's hand clenches over mine as the tug on the other end of the line becomes stronger, and I feel a warmth as I admire his strong fingers. They're full of dirt from rummaging in the bait box, but they're perfect and strong, and everything that the heroine in a romance novel would admire. I laser my focus on the task at hand and reel the line in the direction Liam showed me. As it gets a few feet away, the water beneath it stirs and a small fish emerges on the other end of my line. I swing the pole over the dock and thrust it into Liam's hands.

"Oh my God! It's flipping around!" I squeal, watching the poor creature helplessly flop over and over on the wooden surface. "Why does anyone do this? This is *horrible*!"

Liam chuckles and grabs the line with his hand, leading the fish into a bucket of water he's set aside and that I, shockingly, haven't managed to knock over with my outburst. "So, I guess that means you don't want to take the hook out then, huh?" he asks playfully.

Blue barks and paws at the bucket as Liam sticks his hands in and somehow emerges with the other end of the fishing line. He puts his hands up with a shrug and shows me the hook. "And that's how it's done."

"That was so stressful. It was like a *massacre*!"

Liam bellows a loud laugh and actually clutches his chest while he does so. Blue is so surprised by the noise that he must think something is wrong with Liam. He bounds over to him and jumps up, matching Liam in height as he places a paw on each of Liam's shoulders. Liam's laugh grows and I can't help but join in as Blue attacks Liam with kisses. The dog nuzzles his face against Liam's and slobbers all over him.

"I'm okay, Blue! I'm okay!" Liam says, placing the dog's paws back on the ground. "He hasn't heard me laugh like that in a while," Liam admits, rubbing the dog's head.

"I'm glad my fishing brought it out of you," I joke, crossing my arms and pretending to look offended.

"Honestly, me too," Liam replies, smiling brilliantly at me.

My last conversation with Jill flashes through my mind, but it's not something I'm willing to address right now. No, right now, I'm going to enjoy the smile on this man's face. The man who, ironically, is holding a fishing line, but isn't in a Tinder profile picture, but who is real, right here in front of me, looking at me in a way I have never seen before.

And it scares the hell out of me.

TWELVE

Operation Small Town, Day 24

"Inhale and lift your left leg up," the instructor says calmly from my phone. I follow her cues and work my way into warrior two. Elle teaches yoga classes as a side hustle, and she's gotten me into it. At the beginning, I was a complete mess. I honestly felt bad for the other people in the class that had to watch me. I was a one-woman game of Twister, with a puzzle of outstretched arms and legs, and every time I laid down, I left a sweat angel on my borrowed mat. Since then, I have definitely improved, and luckily, here in my lakeside retreat, the only people who can see me are a couple on their deck across the way.

I made myself a big breakfast and enjoyed it on the deck, but at ten o'clock I found myself staring at my phone, willing it to ring. When I realized I didn't want to be *that* girl, I pulled up a yoga video on YouTube and got to work.

When I hear a throat clear behind me, I jump so hard

that I completely fall out of warrior two and flat on my face. "Ow," I say, rolling on to my butt.

Of course, it's Liam. Of course, the one person in the world I would be the most mortified about seeing me do yoga is standing six feet away. *Of. Course.*

"Hey," I say, rubbing my head. "You scared me."

Liam runs his hand through his hair and avoids my gaze. He's wearing a pair of board shorts and a blue tank top. I remember mocking men who wore tank tops at some point in my life, but from this view, Liam in a tank top is my new favorite thing.

"Sorry. I knocked on the front door but then I heard a voice outside," he says, gesturing to my phone where the yoga teacher is still talking. I scamper over to where I have it propped up and turn her off.

"Well, I'm sorry you had to witness the hot mess that was me doing yoga," I say jokingly.

"I'm not," he says. I squint at him. "But I had to say something before you started lifting your legs up again and I embarrassed myself," he adds, bowing his head to hide the smile on his face. I giggle.

I'm sorry, did Liam Miller just imply that he is attracted to me? No, that couldn't be right.

All this back and forth I've been doing with Liam, it's been fun, but there's no universe in which this man could actually *like* me. I mean, just look at him. In my experience, guys who look like him don't give me a second look. At least in Manhattan they don't. I have several years of dating app history to prove it.

"So, what's up?" I ask, crossing my legs under me.

"Oh, I wanted to see if you were free today."

"No work today?" I ask.

"That's one of the perks of being the owner. I have a bunch of minions who work for me. They can handle lunch. I'll go in for dinner."

"Oh, well aren't you just *so* big-time?" I tease.

"I try," he admits with a shrug. "So, are you free?"

"I am," I say almost immediately. *Cool, Lucy. Cool.* "What did you have in mind?"

"I thought you might like to see my favorite place in Hudson Hollow," he says, smiling.

"Still trying to sell me on the small-town life?" I say, before my brain has a chance to catch up. Ugh, I hate that I said that. Think before you speak, Lucy. Think. "Sorry, I—"

"Yes, I am trying to sell it to you. But I don't think I'll have to work too hard," Liam replies, crossing his arms across his chest.

The smile that breaks out on my face probably looks goofy, but I can't help it.

"That sounds perfect. What kind of attire does this perfect small-town setting require?"

"Something you can hike in. I'll come back to pick you up in a half hour," Liam says, turning on his heel. Before I can process what he just said, he's jogging off my deck.

"I'm sorry, did you just say hiking? *Hiking*?" I yell, but I'm only met with a deep chuckle in return. "Do I look like I hike?" I yell, knowing Liam is already out of earshot.

An hour later I'm in the best hiking attire I could find—capri leggings, a moisture-wicking tank top, and a pair of sneakers. I tie my hair into a single braid and let it fall over my shoulder. I throw a water bottle, sunscreen, and my sunglasses in a bag and meet Liam out front.

"Ready to jet?" Liam asks, slinging his backpack over his shoulder.

"Just so you know, Elle can track my phone. And if I don't call her when I get back, she is going to go all New York detective on you," I say hurriedly. "Just in case, you know, you're taking me on a hiking expedition to murder me in the woods," I add for clarification.

Liam scoffs. "Well, you're the worst planner ever. You can't tell your captor your rescue plan! Now I'll have to have you call Elle *before* I kill you, leave your phone at the house, and drag you all the way back into the woods to bury you. That just makes way more work for me."

"*Okay...*" I start, taking an obvious step back from him. "I'm slightly concerned at how much you've thought this through."

"*I'm* slightly concerned about how much *you* thought this through."

With the way he accentuates his words, I can't help but burst out laughing. I don't think I've ever physically keeled over before, but Hudson Hollow, and Liam, are providing so many firsts for me. I laugh until a tear forms in the corner of my eye. Liam's laugh is magnetic. Before I can stop myself from thinking it, I'm wondering what it would be like to stop his laughter with my lips.

My expression must be telling because Liam's smile quickly fades. "You good?"

"Oh, fine, perfect," I say, wiping the tear from my eye with a big smile. "Ready to not get murdered."

"Let's do it."

When I approach the passenger side of his Jeep, I notice it's missing a few key elements.

"Uh, Liam? How are we driving up a mountain with no doors on the car?" I ask skeptically.

"I never said we were *driving* up a mountain. We're driving to the entrance of the trail. Then we're hiking," he says with a wink. "Come on, City Girl, let's see how country you can be."

Well, *damn*. If that line doesn't make a girl want to hop in that truck, I'm not sure anything will.

With Blue sequestered to the back seat—he was *not* pleased—we head down the highway.

As we drive with the wind battering our skin and my hair whipping in the wind, I take a moment to marvel at myself. I'm in a strange place, away from home, away from my parents, with a somewhat stranger, in a car with no doors, about to hike up a mountain. Who the hell am I and what have I done with Lucy Bowen?

Hudson Hollow Lucy is independent. She can go where she wants, with who she wants, and doesn't feel guilty about it. (Okay, she's working on that last part.)

Liam catches me smiling and flashes a brilliant one back at me. I try to remember the last time I was this happy.

Nothing comes to mind.

On impulse, I unbuckle my seatbelt, ground my backside into the seat behind me, plant my feet on the floor, and stand up.

"Woohoo!" I scream, stretching my arms out wide. I can barely hear Liam's laughter over the wind. He revs the engine and picks up speed, and I let out a screech.

We only travel a few miles before Liam pulls into a gravel parking lot where a few other cars are parked.

"Witnesses," I jest. He lets out a light chuckle.

"You watch too much T.V.," he says, shaking his head. He clips a leash on Blue who quickly jumps out of the truck behind him. When Liam takes a few steps toward the one and only break in the towering trees where the path begins, I hesitate by the truck, an anxious feeling in my stomach.

"Lucy," Liam's voice snaps me out of my panicked state. He returns to my side in a few quick strides. "What's wrong?"

"Oh nothing. Just planning my escape route in case things turn sideways," I say with a nervous smile.

Liam turns his whole body to face me and leans one hand against the car, so that his arm is caging in one side of my head. It could be claustrophobic, but instead, it's extremely attractive.

"You know you don't have me fooled, right?"

I raise my chin to meet his eyes. "What?" The word comes out with a shaky exhale.

"You make jokes to deflect. It usually works for you, but I'm catching on," he looks down at me. He pushes his sunglasses up the bridge of his nose and purses his lips to the side.

I see his eyes moving side to side behind his glasses, and I want to ask what he is thinking. I wonder if he wants to kiss me but is holding back. He moves an inch—the movement is so subtle that I almost don't catch it, but it's like we're opposite ends of a magnet, pulling and pushing at one another, unable to meet.

A sound escapes Liam's throat, something between one of his signature grunts and a moan.

It's at that moment that I realize how much *I* want to kiss *him*. Yes, he's gorgeous, and yes, I've been attracted to him from the moment we met, but the more I've come to know him, the more my body wants to reach for him. It's as if my heart is literally guiding me to him, like he's an anchor on some imaginary finish line, pulling me closer and closer.

Suddenly, he leans back, and I feel an emptiness around me, and I'm exposed to the elements. Back to reality.

Liam looks away and clears his throat. "Ready, Freddie?"

I smile. "My aunt always says that." Liam smiles back as he holds his hand out to me.

"So, shall we?" he asks. Blue looks at me expectantly, his tongue hanging out the side of his mouth.

"We shall."

That's the truth of how easy it is. One step. Then another. Winnie the Pooh always said that he got to where he was going by walking away from where he's been, right? What if it was really that simple? What if all I had to do to make a change for myself was take one step forward?

So, I do.

We manage to make it half a mile up the wooded path before Liam breaks our silence.

"It's about three miles up to where we're going," he says, letting Blue lead the way for us.

"And will there be snacks at the top of this mountain?" I ask, trying to hide the fact that I'm already out of breath. I really need to go to the gym more.

"I think I know you well enough at this point to know

the only way you won't push me off this mountain is if I feed you at the top," he says with a knowing smile.

"I don't think there's anything inaccurate in that statement," I say confidently. I stick my tongue out at him too.

Liam slows his pace and allows me to catch up once we've made it onto more level footing. We're surrounded by towering trees without a person in sight, so this really would be the perfect place to kill someone. I need to stop watching so many scary movies. Why does my brain keep going there?!

Blue matches Liam's stride and finds a place in between us. He seems to know where he's going. "Do you two come up here a lot?" I ask, as if I'm expecting either one of them to answer.

"Probably once a month, I'd say. Blue needs all the exercise he can get, otherwise he does zoomies around the house. This will tire him out for a few days, at least," Liam replies, patting the dog's head. *And me*, I think, trying to take an inconspicuous deep breath.

"Something tells me that you're not used to going out of your comfort zone a lot," Liam says, and I'm caught off guard by his question.

"I traveled by myself to this town, didn't I?" I remind him.

"That's true, but you also hesitated to hike up a mountain with me," he replies. He brushes his hair off his face and shrugs.

"Hey, I don't think that's fair," I say. I stop walking, the mulch crunching beneath my feet. "You don't know me well enough to say that."

"Then prove me wrong," he says, not slowing down his

pace. I note that that's the second time that he's said that to me. I think he's playing a game with me, and I don't know if I like it.

"Ugh," I grunt, annoyed. I take a few quick steps to catch up with his long stride. "You know, this is exactly the type of cat-and-mouse game that a murderer would play," I mumble.

"Seriously, I'm concerned about where your mind goes," he says, shaking his head.

I catch up to him and our steps fall into sync. "I will have you know that I do go out of my comfort zone."

"Well, from where I'm standing, it seems like you're a little close-minded," he says.

"Close-minded?" I practically shout. He turns to look at me. I put my hand up to my ear like I'm making a phone call. "Hello, pot? This is the kettle. You're *black*."

Liam looks down and chuckles. "I guess that's fair. We both have a little bit of pride in where we come from."

"So, why are you giving me such a hard time about it?" I ask.

"Maybe because I want to know more about you. Something tells me that you don't love the city and your job as much as you say. When you talk about it, you're almost like... reciting a speech."

I stop in my tracks again. "Okay, if you keep stopping every time I say something, this is going to be a very long hike," he says, waving his hands at me.

I stomp my foot and continue walking.

"I think you're making assumptions about me that have no basis," I say, my frustration starting to show. I don't have to put up with this. I like Liam, I really do, but

I don't appreciate it when someone speaks to me like they know me better than I know myself. "I've worked very hard to get where I am."

"I don't doubt that for a second," Liam interjects.

"It seems like you do. Things haven't always been easy for me. School was hard, reading was hard, and now I have a career where I read books for a living," I explain. "I'm proud of that. My parents worked really hard to provide me with opportunities they didn't have."

Liam looks at me for a moment and then smiles.

Dude fucking *smiles* at me.

"What are you smiling about?" I snap, putting my hands on my hips.

"That was a very impassioned speech," he says. "And it's great that you overcame obstacles to get where you are now. All I'm saying is, just because it was supposed to be your dream job, doesn't mean it's actually going to be."

Liam's words make me pause for a moment. I slow my pace, and it takes him a moment to realize I've broken my stride. He stops and looks back at me, expecting me to say something. But I'm so flustered, I'm not really sure what to say.

"What?" Liam asks, sliding his sunglasses onto his head.

"I don't know. I guess… I never thought of it that way," I reply, a confused look on my face.

"Lucy, it's your life. It's great that your parents support you, but the only person you have to answer to is yourself," he says, taking a step closer to me. "If you don't like something about your life, change it."

I shake my head. How did we get into this discussion? "I—Thank you for the psychoanalysis on this nature trail, sir, but as I keep telling you, I *do* love my job. I'm happy where I am. I don't know what makes you think otherwise," I say, picking up my pace again. "Let's talk about something else." Is he right? Of course, he's right. What he is saying is completely logical, but it couldn't possibly apply to me. Could it? No. I've worked too hard. And I really do love my job!

Don't I?

"Made you think, though," Liam says knowingly.

I grimace at him. "Stop looking at me. I clearly can't hide anything on my face when you are around," I say, shoving him out of my path. I take a moment to wipe the sweat from my forehead before continuing up the trail.

"What would you do, if money didn't matter and you could quit your job tomorrow?" he asks, jogging to catch up with me.

"What would *you* do?" I say, turning his question on him.

"Exactly what I'm doing," he says with a shrug. "Don't dodge the question. Don't think about it. Just answer with the first thing that pops in your head."

Up ahead, the trees are starting to clear, and I can see a glimpse of water in the distance. I let out a slow breath. "I love my job. I know I might complain about it, and Manhattan sometimes…" Liam opens his mouth to speak but he decides against it. "I'm happy where I am. Really. Being an editor has always been my dream."

"Dreams can change," he says, matter-of-factly.

I put my hands on my hips, a bit annoyed at his continued line of questioning. "Mine hasn't," I reply, sternly.

"All I'm saying is that if a dream doesn't work out, find a new one. Life is finite. Days are finite. Dreams aren't."

I sigh and walk past him, following Blue up the trail without another word. I don't know what he's getting at, but I know my dream. How long has Liam known me? A few weeks? I've known I wanted to work in books for years. Am I tired of being an assistant? Of course. But that is why I am here. If I write enough about this town, I will be on my way to acquiring books.

I just have to finish the job I came here to do. No distractions.

THIRTEEN

Everything hurts and I'm dying.

Three miles, my *ass*.

I'm about to let Liam experience the full wrath of tired, hungry, sweaty Lucy when we suddenly break through the trees. Liam turns around and smiles as I inhale a small gasp.

We've arrived at a small glade on the side of what, to me, looks like an actual mountain, but is really a cliff on the edge of an impressive hill that I just climbed.

"We call this The Point," Liam announces. "That's the Hudson."

"The Hudson River?"

Liam snorts. "The very one. You can take a boat all the way down to the city."

"Holy crap. This nature shit is crazy!" I love that the same Hudson I see in the city is the Hudson I'm seeing here, two different parts of the same river.

It might be the most amazing view I've ever seen. Some people love beach views, which are great in their own right. But the more time I spend here, and the mere seconds

I spend taking in this view, I think this might just be it. The riverbank below is practically undisturbed, with jagged rocks lining each side. When I look to the left, I see the outline of proper mountains in the distance, they look so unreal, so magical, that they almost appear to be fake. I feel like I could have drawn them on a postcard, that is how perfect their soft peaks are. The Point is definitely making it into my proposal for Ruby's book. The series could even be named after this vantage point—*Something's Point. Love at the Point*. I'll work on it. I was never good with titles.

There is a rickety picnic table to our right, which has certainly seen better days but is charming in that Hudson Hollow way I've come to appreciate.

"Come on," Liam says, pulling off his backpack and setting it down on the table. He pulls out some Tupperware and napkins.

"Liam Miller, did you make us a picnic?" I ask, sheer delight in my voice.

"I told you I was going to feed you," he says in a resolute voice. I watch as his hands move thoughtfully, arranging everything. The whole scene is feeling *very* romantic. I take a deep breath.

"What are you thinking about?" he asks, a lightness in his eyes.

"I'm thinking this was totally your high school hang out spot, wasn't it?" I tease. Liam scoffs as he sets a water bowl down for Blue.

The sandwich that Liam hands me is neatly wrapped in parchment paper. I love that he takes such care with things like this. I take a bite. "Oh my God, what is in this sandwich?" I say, mouth full.

"It's pesto. Why? Do you not like pesto?" He creases his brow, concerned.

"No, no, it's amazing," I exclaim. I hold my hand in front of my face in an attempt to appear polite.

"Thanks," he says sheepishly. "I make the sauce from scratch."

"I wouldn't respect you if you didn't," I muse, pretending to be serious.

"And to answer your earlier question, no. I only came up here by myself in high school."

"The brooding teenager, I get it." I flash him a grin.

"I wasn't *brooding*. I was just trying to get away from my sister."

"It's like your Spider-Man spot."

"My what?"

"Your Spider-Man spot, where you go to get away from it all. Empire State Building. Chrysler Building. Top of a mountain," I say, listing the places on my fingers.

"You really like your pop culture references, don't you?" Liam says, sitting beside me on the bench.

"It's a way of life," I reply, finishing off my sandwich.

Everything is so easy with Liam. Talking, laughing, even hiking. Okay, maybe not hiking. I think back to a few weeks ago when I told Elle that everything in my life seemed like a struggle. Walking to work, taking the subway, trying to show Anne (without being too subtle) that I was eyeing a promotion. That seems like a distant memory now. But I quickly realize that it's not a memory, it's my life. What I'm doing here, with Liam, *isn't* real life. I'm not really a writer. I'm not someone who spends her Saturday nights line dancing with children. What is going to happen when I have to go back to reality?

"Does that brain of yours ever stop?" Liam asks, nudging my side with his elbow. I'm suddenly aware of just how close he is to me. I think back to that moment by the car, when I thought I could muster up the courage to kiss him. I want to scold myself for that now. It was a lapse in judgment, something that shouldn't even be crossing my mind. I'm here to do a job. In two weeks, I'll be back in New York, presenting Anne with all the information I've gathered.

"Yes," I say, "I'm just taking in the view."

I have to be logical. I have to let the mathematical, calculating side of my brain take over here. Because despite what Liam says, working at Heartwarming was my dream, *is* my dream. And I can't give up the chance of making editor, working with my own authors, everything I've worked for. To what? To go backwards into small-town living?

And then I look into Liam's eyes.

They're beaming at me, the color of tropical waters with the smoldering intensity of a typhoon; they're hard to look away from. I see his Adam's apple bob in his throat, and I forget how much time has passed between us. When his eyes flutter toward my lips, I lean back.

"Liam," I whisper.

His focused gaze breaks and he meets my eyes. Concern flashes across his face, followed by confusion, and then finally, rejection.

"It's okay," he says, "I get it."

"No, Liam, don't misunderstand," I start, I physically remove myself from the table so I don't get lured in by his orbit again. "I'm not saying no to *you*, not in a million years. I'm saying no to this... *situation*." I gesture at the space between us.

Liam raises a brow at me and presses his lips into a firm line. He's confused, but he also looks slightly amused at my attempt to explain myself out of this moment.

"What I mean is, I like you a lot—"

"Right. But..." he says, resting his chin on his hand.

"No, no but, there should be no 'but' after that," I stammer. How did this situation turn around so quickly? Is the altitude up here diluting my cognitive abilities or something?

"But there is, isn't there?" Liam says, matter-of-factly.

"Only because I'm leaving in a few weeks. And I—"

I think about what to say next. What if he rebuts my argument by saying he can handle me leaving in a few weeks? I realize that not only would that thwart my one good excuse, but also I don't know how I'd feel about. What if he only sees this as a temporary fling?

"I don't want to start something I can't finish," I say, letting out a long-held breath. "My life, my job, it's in the city. This, me, here, is temporary."

And that's the truth of it. Liam has to know this too. Sure, I'm a new face in town, and maybe I was interesting to talk to for a while, but I'm sure that at his core, he knows this could never work out.

He studies me for a moment and I try to meet his gaze, but if I look into his eyes for too long, I'm afraid I might just admit everything. I shrug and let out a long sigh.

"Lucy," Liam says, standing up. "It's fine." He closes the distance between us in two steps and puts a finger in the dimple on my chin, turning my head to look at him. "Don't overthink this. It's okay."

I really want to believe him, but I see the hurt in his eyes. The hurt that I put there. I remind myself that it would be so much worse if I went through with it.

I repeat that thought about a thousand more times to try to erase the look on his face from my brain. We sit in silence for a few minutes, letting the moment pass.

"So," he says. "Ready for dessert?" Liam, being Liam, brushes it off. "Chocolate chip cookies," he says with a smile.

"Marry me," I joke awkwardly. Liam shakes his head as he chuckles.

We devour our cookies and take a few selfies with the mountains in the background. I also get a few good portraits of Blue, which he was less than thrilled to participate in. As we head back down the trail, I tell Liam more about Elle, the number of times I've come home to her burning sage in the living room, and the time she scolded a man at Bryant Park who was, in her opinion, "not being nice enough to his dog."

"She sounds like a very fun friend to have."

"She's something, that's for sure," I say smiling. "She's very sure of herself."

"And you're not?" Liam questions, raising a brow.

"I think we've established that," I answer, knowingly. Liam lets out a loud cackle and shakes his head.

"You have such an infectious laugh," I say, smiling at him.

I used to daydream about dating a guy like Liam. I spend my days reading books with heroes like him—ones with smiles that brighten a room and stop your heart at the same time, ones that make their heroines feel... like I do right now.

"Well, you're the first one who has heard it in a while," Liam says, kicking a rock in his path.

"Don't say that," I say, closing the gap between us.

"It's true," he says softly. "I know you're not the type of girl who does confessionals, but you've changed things for me Lucy. I know I said it was fine up at The Point but—" he stops, both his speech and his stride, and turns to face me.

"What?"

Liam lets out a breath. "I'm really struggling with the fact that you're leaving in two weeks."

I swallow hard. I have to tell him the truth. I shouldn't have gotten so close to him, it was selfish. As soon as I realized how much he was starting to mean to me, I should have told him everything. How would he react if I told him now? I've never seen Liam angry. I've seen him be silly with the twins, with me, I've seen him be a caretaker to his sister, a boss at the restaurant, and worker and a force for good in this town, but I've never seen what happens when someone crosses him. And I'm not sure I want to.

"Liam, I have to—" I start, just as my phone dings from my bag. "We must be back in the land of service," I say sarcastically. My stomach relaxes and falls from its position in my chest.

"There goes my murder plot," Liam says, snapping his fingers.

I take out my phone and see five missed calls from my mom. There's also a text message:

Call me when you can.

FOURTEEN

My heart plummets into my stomach. Instinctively, my mind jumps to the worst-case scenarios. Was my dad in an accident? Did he have a heart attack? I told her I'd be out all day...

Liam watches me as I rapidly call my mom. I try to match his pace as we walk back to the car. I dial and watch him give Blue another drink of water, listening to the echoing of the dial tone.

"Lucy?" my mother finally answers. "Where have you been?"

"I was hiking and didn't have any service," I explain, trying to suppress my irritation at my mother constantly having to know where I am. "What's going on?"

"Oh, honey. It's Josie—"

I don't hear much after that.

I make out the words "collapsed" and "hospital" and "London," but my mother's voice sounds distant, like when you're underwater and everything is muffled. My fingers feel numb around the phone and I slide down against the

Jeep, my legs folding like paper beneath me, my sneakers skidding across the gravel like sandpaper.

"Lucy?" I hear Liam's voice, but I'm still under the water. I'm looking up and the view is blurry, like I can see him on the edge of the pool, the sun behind him, the ripples on the surface making the outline of his figure sway back and forth. "Lucy, look at me." It's finally his touch that snaps me back to reality. He reaches down and wraps his arms around my wrist, and my gaze falls to his tight grip. When I follow the trail of his arm, I meet his concerned gaze, his jaw in a tight line.

"Lucy?" my mom's voice says in my ear. Liam nods reassuringly.

"Yeah, Mom. Sorry, I'm here," I say, not breaking contact with Liam. I feel the warmth of his arms subside for a moment, only to feel his fingers thread through my free hand seconds later. "I'll be in the car in an hour, I'll get to you as fast as I can."

"Honey, there's no point in that. I can't get a flight to London until tomorrow night, and the doctors say that she is stable now."

"Mom, I need to see her," I say, my voice weakening with every word.

"I know, Luce. But the doctors say she'll make it through this, but the cancer may—"

Cancer.

"—be too far progressed at this point."

My forehead falls to my knees. I'm not a crier—I never have been. Anne's been pushing sob stories at me for years, but none of them ever make me crack. In this moment, all I want to do is cry. I want to feel the release of a sob coming out of my throat, of not being able to catch my breath, of my nose filling with phlegm and tears painting lines down my face. And yet, I've got nothing.

"I can't believe this is happening."

But I *can* believe it. I've always admired my aunt's lifestyle. She's always been chasing this idyllic life, and now it's caught up with her. Wasn't it just a few weeks ago that she was telling me that she might be getting too old for the fast-paced life she leads? When she told me about her plans for Paris in a few weeks, she said over and over again how tired she was. How could I not pick up on it?

"She'll get through this, Lucy. I'll bring her home and she'll be taken care of, I promise." I nod as my mom speaks.

"I want to come with you," I say, noticing the shift in Liam's body next to me. Anne will understand. This is an emergency. I know I'm on a deadline here to produce something for Ruby, but these are extenuating circumstances.

"Lucy, it's not feasible, and besides, you're busy with work." I move away from Liam, hoping he can't hear my mother's end of the call. "We both know Josie wouldn't want you to give up on this opportunity. Let me worry about getting her home, and then you can see her as soon as she's back, okay?"

I shake my head. I know she's right, but I hate that I can't help, that I can't see Josie right now. I feel awful knowing I can't be there for her, and for my mom, in person.

"Okay, keep me updated, as soon as you get there." We say our goodbyes and I take a slow, deep breath.

"Hey," Liam says, giving my hand a gentle squeeze. "What's going on?"

I look up and I'm met with the most comforting face I've

ever seen. Liam parts his perfect lips to say something, but holds back, deciding to rest a hand on my shoulder instead.

"It's my aunt," I say, my voice shaky. "She's sick." I rub my hand across my forehead, running my fingers through my hair. I look at Liam in disbelief, because... where has this day gone? How did I end up in a dirt parking lot with Liam's hand in mine, and Aunt Josie in a hospital thousands of miles away?

"Do you need to go home?" he asks, his voice low.

I shake my head. "No, she lives in London. My mom is going to go and bring her back. I have to—" I'm about to say, "*stay here to work*," but I catch myself. "I'll be there when my mom brings her home."

Blue lays down at my feet, his big mouth wide, and his giraffe-length tongue hanging out of his mouth as he pants. I lean forward to pet him, wrapping my arms around him and relishing the comfort that hugging a dog can provide. Liam's hand falls down my back, and he rubs circles into my spine. All I want to do is turn into him and let him comfort me, but I resist.

"Come on, I'll take you back," he says, stepping back. And just like that our physical contact is broken.

We don't speak much on the way back. Every so often Liam flashes me a sideways glance or places a hand on my knee. I mostly look out the window, remembering just a few hours ago when I felt free enough to stand and scream in the wind—thinking about how proud Josie would be that I did that.

When we get back to the house, I get out of the car and start to prepare my "*Thanks for a nice day*," speech to Liam.

But he follows my lead, letting Blue out of the truck as well, and I'm wondering what his plan is.

"Blue insists that we keep you company tonight," Liam says matter-of-factly. "He won't take no for an answer."

I manage a smile. "Is that so?"

"Yep, we discussed it in the truck," he says with a nod. He gives me a sympathetic smile.

"Liam, I—"

"Lucy, please," he puts his hand up to stop me. "At least let me make you dinner. I'm really shit in uncomfortable situations. I never know what to do or what to say. But I *can* make some banging food. So let me do that for you. Please?"

The urgency in his voice lightens the mood a little. I press my lips together. "I was just going to say that I really want to take a shower first, so maybe you and Blue could come back in half an hour." That's not what I was going to say, of course, but the look on Liam's face took away any objections I had about wanting to be alone tonight.

"Oh, right," Liam responds, nodding a bit too much. "A shower sounds like a good plan. I'll do that too." Is he flustered? He shakes his head to get the hair out of his eyes but avoids looking directly at me. I feel like he was trying to be all assertive with his "Blue insists" plan, and I totally killed his mojo. I try to keep my giggle to myself.

"I'll see you in a little bit," I say, giving him an awkward wave. I pat Blue on the head and step inside, anxious to get the sticky sweat of the day off my body. I feel bad that Liam feels like he needs to stay with me tonight, instead of going to the restaurant. But it's not like I asked him to. He offered.

And maybe with him here, I'll think less about how much I wish I could teleport myself across the ocean to Josie's side.

The shower is regenerative. I always feel better when I'm clean—and feeling refreshed takes on a whole new meaning after hiking six miles today. The muscles in my legs are twitching from the hike, a clear sign I'm out of shape—shocking given all the walking I do in Manhattan.

I throw on a pair of yoga pants and a soft T-shirt. I don't feel like I need to impress Liam, it's not like this is a date. He's just making me dinner after a rough day, and rough days call for yoga pants.

Once I'm dressed, I clear my notebooks and put away all my work stuff, trying to suppress the guilt that surfaces as I look over some of my sketches. But I can't deal with any more complicated emotions tonight.

I check my phone and find a text from my mom.

> Just talked to the doctor at the hospital. Josie is awake and talking. She wants to leave already. They said we can call her in the morning.

I smile at the thought of my rambunctious aunt fighting with a bunch of British doctors. She's probably threatening to take her IV out and leave against medical advice. I honestly wouldn't put it past her.

Oh Josie.

I don't know much about the fight that is in front of her, but I'll feel better once she's on this side of the ocean and I can fight it with her.

A firm knock on the door catches my attention, followed by Blue's deep bark. As I approach, I can hear Liam's muffled voice as he speaks to Blue. "It was me, buddy. I knocked. It's okay."

I chuckle when I open the door, Blue's ears are perked up and his tail wags manically. I need to get a dog.

"Hey," I say, and Blue comes rushing in, the nails on his paws click-clacking on the wood floor. He makes himself right at home, sniffing the perimeter of the foyer and dashing straight into the kitchen.

"He's looking for Mella. She feeds him. Usually cold cuts," Liam explains, stepping into the house. He's carrying two reusable grocery bags that are stuffed to the brim. His hair is wet and scraggly. He is in some variation of a Liz's T-shirt and sweat shorts. I inhale the scent that follows him into the house—he still smells like the woods but mixed with fresh, minty soap. It makes my stomach flip, the scent of him.

"I didn't know what you had, so I just brought what was in my fridge," he says, gesturing to the bags.

"Well, I have some eggs, wine, and some of the cake you brought me. Not sure there's a meal in there though," I reply with a laugh. I follow him into the kitchen. "Is it weird being here without Al and Mella?"

"Not really," Liam answers, emptying his groceries onto the counter. "They've been spending less time here in recent years. I actually think they'll move to Florida full-time, which is where they are now. Blue will certainly miss them though, and all the treats." He looks down at the dog and shrugs.

I nod with a smile. "Do you need help with anything?" I ask, knowing that I really wouldn't be much help.

"How are your knife skills?" he asks, raising a brow.

"Depends on how much blood you like in your food," I answer. Liam makes a face.

"Never mind then," he says. He goes over to the fridge and pulls out a bottle of white wine. "I think we deserve a little bit of wine, don't you?"

"Today is definitely the day for it," I agree, accepting the bottle from him. I grab two glasses from the cabinet and pour one for each of us. I sit down on one of the barstools and Blue wraps his body around the legs of the chair, settling in.

I watch as Liam dices tomatoes, onions, and garlic, tossing them into a pan with oil. The fragrance of those ingredients sautéing together is rivaled only by the scent of the chef himself. Liam looks up every so often and smiles at me watching him.

The result is a bowl of pasta with zucchini and a light tomato sauce. He plates them fancily, swirling the pasta with a spoon so it sits perfectly in the middle of the plate. He sprinkles cheese over the top and joins me at the bar.

"You're welcome to ditch the restaurant and become my personal chef anytime," I say, taking a bite. The pasta is heavenly. It's light and fresh, with exactly the right amount of bite. I love it when pasta is just al dente enough that a few pieces stick together. I moan in pleasure as I eat.

"And you're welcome to make that sound anytime you eat my food," Liam replies, a smug smile on his face.

How far we've come from our conversations that consisted of my awkward babbling and his cranky grunts. I used to think I could never get a read on Liam, then I thought the only read I could get was that of a proud small-town boy, too terrified to see that not every out-of-towner was there to steal his home or look down on him. Now, though... now we're at this happy medium. We've formed our own kind of friendship.

"What are you thinking about?" Liam asks, turning his stool to face me. Our knees knock together under the counter.

I let myself smile a bit. "About how just a few short weeks ago, you weren't my biggest fan," I say smugly.

"I don't think that's true," he says, placing his fork down.

"Um, yes, it is. You were *skeptical*, to say the least."

"Only a little bit," he says seriously. *Maybe he would be more so if he knew how much I was lying to him*, the voice in the back of my head says. "I'm sorry if I ever made you feel that way. And I'm sorry for today. I know I pushed you a little bit."

"You mean *cardiovascularly*?" I joke.

"Ha! No, I mean I pushed your buttons a little. It wasn't my place, and I'm sorry." He folds his hands on the counter and turns to face me.

I sigh. "You did, but I understand. You're a bit like my aunt in that way actually," I explain, lifting the side of my mouth.

"Am I?"

I nod. "She's always pushing me to see the best in things, especially life outside of the city. I didn't mention this earlier, but I actually have dyslexia." Liam's brows furrow. "School was always kind of hard for me. But now I read for a living, which is rather ironic." Liam smiles softly.

"And pretty impressive," Liam interjects. I smile shyly.

"My parents pushed me really hard, and Josie never agreed with how... *disciplined* they were when it came to school. They always thought, and they made *me* believe, that if I got this great job and lived in the city and proved that I could work just as hard or harder than everyone else, then I would be happy and successful."

"Your aunt didn't agree?"

"Hmm," I muse, thinking about Josie's animated rants about my lifestyle. "She just wanted me to consider my options, I guess. I've always had a bit of a one-track mind."

"I can't imagine," Liam prods. I grimace at him.

"She's pretty much the same way," I add. Josie spends so much time telling me to enjoy life and embrace this opportunity in Hudson Hollow, but she's the one gallivanting all over Europe, and look where that's gotten her. I rest my head on my hand, thinking about my exotic aunt, and how much I wish I could hug her right now.

"She's going to be okay," Liam says, putting his hand on my leg. He squeezes my knee. I smile and nod. She will. I'll see her soon. But in the meantime, I have this gorgeous man sitting in front of me, admiring me like a painting. He keeps staring, his face serene and curious.

"What?" I finally ask, as his eyes continue to move across my face. He reaches out and traces a line with his finger from my temple to my chin. I gasp quietly at his touch and let my eyes flutter closed. A satisfied sigh escapes my lips. Even if it's just this once, I let myself fall into his touch. I let myself be held by him. And I love it.

And then his lips are pressing into mine.

I don't jump in surprise. I don't gasp. I don't shudder. Because I'm not shocked. It's as if he read my mind. This moment was inevitable between us. An understanding.

"I can't tell you how long I've been thinking about this moment. About learning what you taste like," he murmurs against my lips. He presses his lips to mine again, gently at first, and then more hungrily, like he truly is tasting something delicious for the first time. I gasp against his mouth, relishing the feeling of his fingers threading through my hair, pulling me into him with delicate urgency.

Kissing Liam is like taking a deep breath after being stuck underwater. It's like the first gasp of air after you've been tossed around by an ocean wave, the oxygen filling your lungs in a way that you never thought you'd feel again.

I let my hands trail up his back and I wrap my arms around his neck. In one smooth motion he lifts me up and places me in his lap, so I'm pressed between his chest and the back of the counter.

I can't believe this is happening. It feels so natural, Liam kissing me, holding me. I'm trying desperately to silence the part of my brain that is sounding every alarm bell.

He shifts my weight and suddenly I'm straddling him, feeling his hardness beneath his shorts. The feeling sends a wave of wanting through me. I haven't done this in so long. I forgot how good it can feel. I forgot what it was like to want someone this badly.

I kiss him harder as his hands reach under my shirt, his fingers exploring my torso, his thumbs tracing the bottom of my bra. I dig into his hair, deepening our kiss, and pressing my tongue into his mouth. Liam groans and responds quickly, sitting up so my back is arched into the counter. I reach for the bottom of my shirt and start to lift it up, but Liam grabs my wrists and stops me.

"I'm sorry," he says, inhaling sharply as he leans his

forehead against mine. "I quite literally couldn't help myself. I've been wanting to do that all day."

"Then why did you stop?" I whisper, desperate to get that feeling back, the satisfaction of his arms around me, the comfort of being held by him, so tightly.

Liam sits back and studies my face. He pushes some stray strands of hair out of my face and tucks them behind my ear. Why is that move so heart-meltingly amazing? Why?

"Because you're hurting right now," he says, his voice aching.

I let myself fall back against the counter, running my fingers through my hair. I can feel the heat in my face—am I embarrassed? I don't really have anything to feel ashamed of, we were both pretty into that kiss. But I still feel self-conscious about how far I was willing to go just now. Just today I said I needed to focus on my work here, and not get distracted.

That was a whole lot of distraction right there.

"You're right," I say, struggling to believe my own words. Because I don't. He's not taking advantage. I am hurting, but every second I spend with him makes me feel exponentially better.

FIFTEEN

If you had the chance to live inside of a romance novel, would you take it?

I'm sure most of you would, considering you're loyal romance readers. As you all know, I'm off doing a super special project for @HeartwarmingRomance and I wish I could tell you all about it. And it has me thinking… what if one of my favorite small-town romances could actually come to life?

What #romancebook would you want to live in? Let me know in the comments!

Operation Small Town, Day 25

"Lucy, I'm so sorry, babe," Elle says softly on the other end of FaceTime. She lays her chin in her hand and tilts her head at me. If I was in a better mood, I'd crack a joke about the stereotypical pity head-nod she's giving me, but I let the moment pass. "But it sounds like she's going to be okay."

I spoke to Josie on the phone briefly this morning. Her voice was weak but she was complaining about the "sorry excuse for breakfast" they fed her, which gave me a bit of hope that she must be feeling better. My mom is headed to London tonight.

"I know. I can't wait for her to get here," I say, plopping down on the couch. I raise my fingers to my mouth, gnawing on the edge of my thumb. "Counting down the days."

"Soon!" Elle says. "So, would it be insensitive of me to change the subject now?" Elle asks. I love how blunt she is. It's why we get along so well. There's no bullshit between us.

"Not as insensitive as me making out with my cute neighbor on the same day I found out Josie was in the hospital," I say quickly.

See? We both get right to the point.

"You *what*?!" Elle screeches. "And you waited until *now* to tell me?"

"Elle, Josie is in the hospital!"

"I think I speak for Josie when I say this is bigger news," she says confidently. She's right. Josie would get a kick out of this.

I recap the events of last night with her, leaving out some of the more *intimate* details—the ones I keep playing over in my mind on loop. She listens diligently, waiting for her moment to speak.

"You know what," Elle starts, dragging out the words like she is hatching a plan.

"What?" I grunt, not moving my head to look at her.

"Anne's plan is kind of coming true." I jump up, flipping myself onto my stomach and practically smacking myself in the face trying to brush the hair from my eyes.

"No, it is not," I say, firmly.

"You're falling for your very own small-town hero, you're believing in love again, you're even embracing a bit of nature, it's everything Anne talked about!" She practically cheers the last words, the smile on her face growing with every passing second.

"Stop being excited about this," I say angrily. "That is not what is happening. These are people's lives I'm messing with."

I let out an exasperated sigh. I'm angry at myself for letting this happen. I'm angry at Anne for putting me in this situation. I'm angry at Liam for being so wonderful. And I might be the angriest at Elle for being so damn happy about it.

"Lucy," she says, trying to snap me out of my silence.

"I just feel so *icky* about the whole thing, Elle," I say, looking down. "I didn't expect to feel this way, but the more time I spend with the people here, the more I'm realizing that if they ever actually found out why I'm here—"

"Your concerns are completely valid," she says in her perfect editor voice. "And since you're so worried about it, then you did the right thing not going any farther last night. You don't want to hurt him, I understand."

I knead my thumbs into my temples and try to let her words sink in. In a few weeks, I'll leave Hudson Hollow and never see these people again. I try to ignore the sharpness in my chest that follows that thought.

"So, are you going to tell him the truth?" Elle asks in a soft voice.

"That I'm not actually here on vacation? I don't think I can."

"Maybe he won't even care," Elle offers.

"He'll care, Elle. When I first met him, he basically said that any out-of-towners that come to Hudson Hollow just try to exploit the town."

"Awkward. That's a bit on the nose," she says.

"Ugh! See? I can't tell him. And what happened last night…" My voice trails off. "It was a mistake. I'm in too deep." I can't admit to Elle how wonderful it felt to be held by Liam. Oh my God, when was the last time I was held by a man? "Me coming here, Liam being interested in me… It's all too much. I'm here to do a job. I need to finish that job and come home. I have my career to think about. I've worked so hard for this. One kiss isn't going to change that."

"Ah, Cynical Lucy is back, I see," Elle responds.

"Not cynical. Realistic," I reply curtly.

"I'm sorry that you're going through this," Elle says, her lips forming into a pout. "But I think you have to admit, this town has been a bit of a spiritual awakening for you."

"Speaking of spiritual awakenings," I start, hoping to change the conversation. "I really do think I'm getting some good material for Ruby's new series. I've even written out some scenes myself. I know they probably won't be used, but I've really enjoyed writing them."

"I *knew* the universe had sent you there for a reason. Hudson Hollow is literally infusing its energy into you. It's making you the best version of yourself. Even if you are cynical, at least you're a cynical *writer*, Lucy. I almost don't want you to come home."

"If the word goddess comes out of your mouth I am going to hang up. I'm not kidding," I say, pointing at her.

Elle squeals with excitement. "I am so happy for you, Lucy. So many good things are coming your way, I can feel it."

"Is my aura visible through FaceTime?" I ask jokingly.

"Don't mock me, but yes, it most definitely is." She sticks her tongue out at me and flips her perfectly curled hair back over her head.

"Now shut up and help me pick an outfit for this stupid toddler party I've been invited to."

When I step into Nora's backyard, the sheer scale of the celebration stops me in my tacks. Dozens of pink and white balloons cascade along the fencing, while and a grand tent dominates the patio. Oh, and there's a bouncy castle.

"Lucy!" I try to wipe the shocked look off my face when I see Nora coming toward me. She's wearing a pink maxi dress with wedge heels that she can barely walk in. I suddenly feel underdressed in my jean shorts and floral tank top. But then again, this isn't a freaking wedding. And someone should definitely tell Nora that.

"So glad you made it!" Nora says, throwing her arms around me. I'm caught off guard and momentarily just stand there with my hands limp at my sides. When my body finally gets the memo that, apparently, we're doing the hugging acquaintances thing, I awkwardly pat her back.

"Happy to be here," I say, relieved when she finally pulls

away. "This is for Cammy," I add, handing her the gift I managed to pick up yesterday.

"Thank you! You didn't have to do that," she says with a modest smile.

"Where is the little birthday girl?" I ask, scanning the crowd for her.

"She's napping," Nora smiles, shrugging.

"Oh," I say with a small chuckle, thinking about Emma's first birthday party on *Friends*. Elle would get the reference if she was here.

"Well, go get yourself something to eat. Liam's made quite a spread," Nora says, waving to greet another guest. My head perks up at the mention of Liam's name. I turn my attention to the buffet table where I spot him. I'm beginning to think he doesn't own anything besides jeans and T-shirts because the only other thing I've seen him in is his bathing suit. Not that either option looks bad on him, or that anything ever could.

"Hey you," I say, walking up beside him. I resist the urge to place my hand on him, my mind flicking back to the way I felt with my legs wrapped around his waist. I'm not really sure how to approach things with him today. I'm going for casual; we definitely didn't have a life-changing make-out session twenty-four hours ago vibe. I think it will go well.

"Hey," he says, smiling. "This setup is crazy right?' he asks, gesturing to our surroundings with tongs.

"Insane." I raise my eyebrows. When I look around, I notice Liam's other half is missing. "Where's Blue?"

"He's at home. I didn't want him scaring any of the little kiddies," he says, unpacking Tupperware from his many boxes.

"He is the complete opposite of scary," I whine, disappointed that my furry friend won't be here to keep me company.

"Yes, well, the soccer moms over there have a different opinion," he says, nodding to the group of women on the patio.

"Rude," I say bitterly. Our arms brush as Liam reaches for another bag, the contact makes me jump. I half expect him to bring up our unfinished conversation from the other day, but I'm relieved when he presents me a glass instead.

"It might not be your thing, but this sangria is a fan favorite," he says, passing me the fruit-filled red liquid. "Try a sip."

"Thanks."

He tips his beer toward my glass. "Cheers," he says, taking a long, slow sip. I follow his lead.

We stand awkwardly, staring at each other for a few moments in silence. The tension between us is palpable, electric. It's almost unbearable.

"I have to head back out to the truck. Be right back," Liam murmurs, placing his beer on the table.

I watch him walk away and giggle when I see him steal a kid's hat. He whips it around his back and puts it on another kid's head before laughing and running out of sight.

"Well, you could definitely do worse," someone mumbles behind me. I turn and find May standing a few feet behind me with her arms crossed. She purses her wrinkled lips and nods her head toward Liam.

"Oh no, there's nothing—" I start to say, but Jill turns around from her conversation with someone to poke her head next to May's, following her gaze to Liam.

"Worse than what?" she asks.

"Than your brother," May answers in a serious tone.

"May," I scold in a muffled voice. I pinch her arm.

"It's common knowledge already, sweetie. Roll with the small-town punches," May responds in a matter-of-fact tone.

"It's true," a deep voice agrees. I turn around and see Brett over my shoulder. Where did he come from? *What's with this town?!*

"Brett, what—?" I start, getting whiplash from discovering all of the people circled around me.

"See?" May adds, smirking at me before walking away. I let out a loud sigh as I watch her switch from the calm demeanor she just had with me to loudly embrace someone on the deck.

"You kind of walked right into that one," Brett says, winking at me.

"Yeah, I know," I mumble, taking another sip of my sangria. "Hey, Brett, is your wife here?" I ask, looking around him.

"Nah, she's working. She's a nurse at the hospital in Catskill," Brett explains with a shrug. "Have you had some food, Lucy?" he asks, gently nudging my shoulder.

"Why don't you go grab us some snacks like the gentleman you are?" Jill intercedes, scrunching her nose at Brett.

"Girl thinks just because she babysat me, she can tell me what to do," Brett says, shaking his head.

Jill rolls her eyes playfully. "Liam just went to grab more

sliders for the grill, so I think you should get over there." She winks.

"I am going to get something to eat, but because I *want* to, not because you *told* me to," Brett teases, smirking at Jill.

"Whatever you have to tell yourself," she deadpans. I can't help but smile at their banter.

Jill takes a long sip of her beer before turning to face me. "Liam told me you guys have been spending a lot of time together," Jill says, just as Liam rounds the corner with a large box in his hands. He smiles at me and I try to casually smile back, hoping not to draw Jill's attention to it.

"We're really just friends," I say, trying to believe it myself. I did tell Liam at The Point that me being here is only temporary, but after last night, I feel like I need to repeat it.

Jill eyes me knowingly. "Look, I don't want to sound too 'big sister' here, but I just hope you'll be careful with Liam. I know you're here on vacation—which is great—but you'll be leaving soon, and Liam will still be here—"

"I understand," I say, interrupting her. I turn to face her, so she can see the seriousness in my eyes. "I know Liam has been through a lot recently."

Jill doesn't respond right away. She looks past me, at Liam, who has Robbie in his arms and is spinning him around.

"He has been through a lot," Jill says, keeping her gaze on him. "You know, I'm older than him, but most of the time, it's *him* taking care of *me*."

"I guess sometimes it works out that way," I say, stifling

a laugh when Liam puts Robbie down and he falls to the ground immediately from dizziness.

"I wish I could do more for him," Jill says, her eyes not meeting mine. "But he's probably told you that I've had my own struggles the last few years."

"Yes, and I am really sorry for everything you've been through," I say, touching her arm.

"It's not like things were great between us. He just couldn't have chosen a worse time. I can't even say I was heartbroken. I was just angry. I wasn't sad for myself, honestly, I was sad for them," she says, sighing. "They deserve so much more than that, than him."

Liam is now busy spinning another kid around. Just watching them is making me dizzy. "Liam really made the transition as seamless as it could be for them," Jill adds. She smiles at the scene of her brother surrounded by toddlers all begging to be spun around. "All while he was taking care of my mom, trying to keep my dad from drowning in grief, and running a business. It was very overwhelming for him."

"I can only imagine," I mumble, taking the last sip from my drink.

"But ever since you arrived, I've seen him smile more than I have in a long time," she says, eyeing me knowingly. A pang of emotion seizes my chest. I'm not sure how to describe it—guilt, like I've been caught doing something wrong? Or the guilt that I've made an impact on this man who I'm lying to? Maybe both. Definitely both.

"My mom had these flowers on our windowsill when we were growing up," Jill starts. I shift to face her again, seeing that her gaze is somewhere in the distance. I try to hide the confusion on my face, because I'm not sure where she is going with this.

"I don't know what they were called, but they had really long, straight stems and gentle, purple petals on the flower. She wasn't a gardener by any stretch of the imagination. She tried to plant herbs every year, but they never lasted for more than a few weeks." A soft laugh escapes her lips. I can tell she's picturing the scene in her mind, her mom bent over in the garden, maybe on a hot day like today. Her eyes don't look sad at all. Her lips perk up at the corners, and I smile along with her.

"But these awkward-looking, lanky things held on for *years*," she continues. "They were so resilient. No matter how much she tried to kill them, unintentionally, of course, they hung on. I mean, she kept them in the corner of the living room where literally *no light* could get to them. But they reached for it anyway. It kind of creeped me out sometimes, how I would look at them and they were in one position, and then a few hours later they were leaning to reach for the sliver of sun on the wall behind them.

"Liam reminds me of those flowers sometimes. He internalizes a lot, but he feels this responsibility, to me, to my dad, to this town, that he shouldn't. He lets anything and everything get thrown on his plate and he still tries to make the best of it. When I tell you how distraught he was last year, when our mom—And I mean we all were, but he... he was with her a lot near the end." She pauses for a moment, her smile growing wider as she watches Liam. "And yet here he is. Reaching for the sun."

I feel a ball in my throat as we both gaze at Liam. My

words come out in a crackled croak, and I try to hide my face from Jill.

"No, he *is* the sun."

SIXTEEN

I've never understood why people drink so much. In movies, books, television shows—even in my own life—I've watched alcohol turn people silly, angry, and sometimes too laid-back. And then it makes them throw up. Yet here I am, unable to resist the lure of a cold sangria amid this oppressive heat. Plus, I actually need to relax right now. The conversation with Jill has left my stomach in knots, and now my appetite has vanished. I manage to pick at some cheese and dip while I nurse my drink.

When Cammy wakes up, the crowd surrounds her like a magnet, and I sneak off to take a moment to breathe. I'm keenly aware of where Liam is—behind the buffet tables making sure everyone has what they need. I even sit down on the swing set and pull out my phone, so it doesn't look too obvious that I'm in the corner having a panic attack.

This thing with Liam, this secret, it's starting to become too much for me. I need to come clean. I couldn't bear to see the look on his face if he found out I've lied to him this whole time, and worse, that I didn't have the courage to tell him the truth, when he's been nothing but honest, and kind, and vulnerable with me. The worst part is that I'm not any different from those big-city leeches in the Hallmark films—I'm exactly what Liam feared I would be, and for that I don't know if I can forgive myself.

"Hey, Bowen," Liam says, stopping a few feet short of me. I take a deep breath.

"Liam—"

"You and me, bouncy house race," he challenges, cutting me off. He nods toward the massive inflatable, swaying from the small bodies jumping inside. His serious face gives way to my favorite full-face smile, and I can't help but match his smile.

Oh, Lucy, you're in serious trouble with this one.

I look over at the inflatable death trap. It is about the size of a small house. There are two holes at the beginning of the course that I've seen kids jump through. Then, they climb up a "rock wall" and go through some other obstacles before climbing up a rope to the top of a slide. I've yet to see an adult attempt it, but that certainly isn't going to stop me.

"What'll it be, Lucy?" He extends his hand, and for a moment I just look at him, *really* look at him.

"Alright," I say. "You're on." I stand up and take his hand. He leads us over to the ginormous contraption, where a group of kids is lined up around it. Mia spots us and runs over, launching herself at Liam.

"Uncle Liam, I beat Robbie!" she squeals.

"I don't doubt it for a minute you little monkey," Liam says, tickling the girl's belly. "Think Lucy and I could have a turn to race?" Liam asks her, who responds emphatically.

We kick off our shoes and take our places at the imaginary

starting line. Mia stands at one end of the obstacle course to tell us when to start, and Robbie stands at the other to call the winner. When Mia says "Go!" I catapult myself through the hole and smash my face into the rock wall. I see Liam on the opposing side already halfway to the top. I scramble to the top, hurling myself over the wall. Up, down, and around I go through protruding walls that lead to the rope ascent. Liam gets stuck in the wall obstacles because his limbs are so long. I reach the rope before him and slip three times before I make it to the top. I somersault over to the slide and awkwardly roll down it. When he makes it to the bottom, we're both laughing uncontrollably. The force of his weight bouncing to the bottom of the slide sends me flying off the course. Luckily, I land on my feet, tears forming in my eyes from laughing so hard. Liam jumps off the course and wraps his arms around me, the biggest smile I've ever seen on his face. He places his hands on my hips to steady us, and when our gazes meet the laughing ceases.

"Sorry, I feel like I'm going to fall over," I say, leaning on him to steady myself. I just need the world to stop spinning so much, then I'll let go of him.

I let out a slow exhale and close my eyes.

"Hey, Lucy, are you okay?" Liam asks, taking a firm hold of my shoulders in either hand.

"I'm just really hot," I mumble, not opening my eyes. With my eyes closed, I can pretend everything isn't spinning. It's a much more comfortable place to be. My grip on Liam's shirt tightens as I wipe my forehead with my other hand.

"Let me get you some water." As soon as the words leave Liam's mouth, I feel a lurch in my stomach.

I push Liam away and throw my hand to my mouth. The

lurch comes again. I manage to make a run for the house. I barely make it to the toilet by the time the sangria, fruit, and the little bit of charcuterie I've ingested makes its way out of my stomach. When it's over, I collapse next to the toilet feeling exhausted. I'm absolutely mortified by what just happened, and to make matters worse, I hear a knock at the door.

"Luce? It's me," Liam says in a concerned voice. I groan in response. "Everything okay?" I murmur something unintelligible. "Do you need me to come in?" he asks.

"Liam Miller, if you come in here, I will cut off your hands and staple them to your shoulders!" I growl, flushing the toilet and trying to make my way to the sink, worried that he won't listen.

"Wow, that's very *graphic*," I hear him say on the other side of the door.

When I see myself in the mirror, I groan again. My makeup is running down my face and my hair looks like the worst case of bedhead I've ever had. I splash my face with cold water and throw my hair up into a messy bun. *I just have to make it home*, I say over and over in my head. I take a deep breath and lean against the sink. *Just make it back to the house.*

When I open the door, Liam is standing outside, propped against the wall with his arms crossed. I see May peeking her head around the corner from the kitchen. Liam gives me a pitiful smile. I grimace, the embarrassment washing over me again.

"Well, either I'm the world's biggest lightweight," I say, not meeting his gaze. "Or I am super dehydrated."

"Maybe a bit of both," Liam replies, gently. I narrow my

eyes at him. He cups his hand around my cheek and I lay the entire weight of my head into it. "Let's get you home."

★

Liam drives us the short ride back, leaving me to concentrate on steadying my breath. *In. Out. In. Out.* I keep my eyes firmly shut, especially as Liam navigates the bends of Puke Parkway. His hand rests on my leg, moving in a gentle, soothing rhythm. I channel all my attention to the warmth of his touch, willing it to drown out the relentless churn of my stomach.

Liam helps me into the house, and I go straight to the bedroom. I collapse on the bed and kick my shoes off. I groan at the feeling of the soft mattress beneath me. It must be getting close to eight o'clock, because the sun is just starting to set. I really wish it would get on with it already so I can wallow in the darkness by myself.

The world is still spinning a little bit, but as long as I'm curled up in a ball and don't move my head, everything seems to steady. I just want to sleep. I snuggle my face into the pillow and notice that Liam has left the room. I wonder if he's gone forever. I wonder if he went to get me some food. *He makes good food.*

"You make good food," I mumble into the pillow. My stomach gurgles in response.

"Well, thank you," I hear Liam say. I pry one eye open just in time to see him enter the room with a glass. "Water is the best I could do, since you didn't have any ginger ale or anything."

I slowly sit up and take the glass from him. I lay my head back down and watch him as he sits on the edge of the bed. He folds my legs over his lap and runs his hands over my calves.

I turn my head and blink a few times to try to see him more clearly through my dazed vision. It doesn't work too well.

"You always say just the right thing," I tell him in a rough voice. Liam furrows his brows at me. "You even furrow your brows like a romance love interest. You're perfect for it," I mumble, trying to poke the spot between his eyebrows with my finger, but I miss it and hit his forehead instead. He raises his brows even more and crosses his eyes in an attempt to see my finger. "I could see myself falling for you, if this was real," I add, floating my eyes closed.

My head feels heavy, too heavy to keep it raised. I want to keep my eyes open so that I can see Liam. I love seeing him. He's nice to look at. "You're nice to look at," I whisper, willing my eyes to open, but they don't budge. It feels like they're glued closed, and no amount of strength will separate them. I try to focus on the feeling of Liam's hands on my legs, the kneading of his fingers into my muscles, the rubbing of his skin against mine. I think I hear him say something, but I'm too far gone.

The last thing I remember is a feeling of warmth against my cheek and the lingering moisture that stays on my skin before I fade entirely into sleep.

SEVENTEEN

Operation Small Town, Day 26

Fuck, my head hurts.

I woke up around four, still in my jean shorts and tank top, groggy and disoriented. After fumbling my way to the bathroom in complete darkness, I stripped down, pulled on the first shirt I could find, and collapsed back into bed.

The sun wakes me up next, glaring through the window. I give it the finger. I roll over and search the nightstand for my phone. I eventually find it tangled in the sheets with me. It's past nine. I groan and curse the sun. My body is in no condition to be awake right now. I roll over and see a note on the nightstand.

> Breakfast will be on the front porch when you wake up. Call me later.
>
> —Your Perfect Love Interest

What.
The.
Hell?

I spring upright, immediately regretting it. I whine as blood rushes from my head and pressure compounds at my temples. I roll back, willing the pain to dissipate. When I can finally see straight, I grab the note off the nightstand and read it again.

I cover my mouth with my hand.

I didn't.

I didn't.

Please, God, tell me I didn't.

Maybe I did.

Shit. Shit. SHIT.

I didn't tell him *everything*, did I? I remember playing on the bouncy castle with Liam. I remember puking—a lot. I remember the drive home, and talking to Liam, but I can't remember exactly what I said. But if I had said something incriminating, he wouldn't have made me breakfast. He would be mad. Those are not the actions of someone who is mad. I take a deep breath. I collapse back on to the pillows and open my phone.

Lucy: Any chance you woke up with amnesia this morning and completely forgot who I was and anything that happened yesterday?

Liam: Not a chance. You?

Lucy: It's a little foggy.

Liam: Happy to fill in the blanks for you. You went on a

bender at a one-year-old's birthday party and had to be dragged out under duress. There was talk of calling the police. Real bad influence on the kids.

I send him the middle finger emoji.

Liam: Kidding!

Liam: I guess you didn't eat or drink enough yesterday because you were too busy losing to me on the bouncy castle. Rookie.

Lucy: I feel like I'm going to die.

Liam: You're not going to die. Did the pancakes help?

Lucy: I haven't made it out of bed yet.

Liam: SMH. Have something to eat before the raccoons get it. You'll feel better. I'm at the restaurant all day if you want to drop by.

Lucy: I will be hiding from you for several days, hoping you forget me and the embarrassment that I am.

Liam: Not possible.

My stomach is in knots from my performance yesterday, but even more so because I miss Josie, and I can't bear being apart from her when she is hurting.

After I clean myself up in the bathroom, and try not to

scream at the horror that is my face, I make my way outside and see a takeout bag from Liz's outside on the porch. I heat up the large stack of pancakes and try to FaceTime Elle, but she doesn't answer. A few minutes later, she calls me back using audio, not video.

"Hey! I'm at the store, what's up?" she says.

"Well, we've reached the point in the story where I make a small-town fool of myself," I say, my throat raspy.

"Uh-oh," she says, concerned. "What did you do?"

I relay the whole miserable story to her, scowling when she snickers at my many memorable antics.

"You drank sangria? And nothing else? Maybe not the best idea on the hottest day of the year," she says once I've finished the whole sad story.

I drum my lips and sit down with my pancakes. My stomach grumbles. No wonder I'm hungry. My anxious stomach and the extreme heat took away any appetite.

"Yeah, I think it may have had something to do with the fact that I'm falling for a guy who I'm lying to," I say bluntly.

"You're falling for him? That's quite a confession," Elle says, a wary tone in her voice.

"I don't know what to do," I murmur, the thought making my stomach tense.

"Lucy, you need to stop asking everyone else what to do and ask yourself what is best for you! Only you know how you feel," Elle says, the sympathy back in her voice. I stare down at the food on my plate, my appetite quickly fading. "That was an invitation for you to tell me how you feel, by the way," Elle adds.

"Oh," I say surprised. I struggle to find my next words. "Can I get back to you on that?"

"No," Elle says with a laugh. "Just don't think about it. If I asked you right now, how do you feel about Liam, what would you say?"

I could see myself falling in love with you.
Oh shit.

"Oh shit," I say out loud, shocking Elle.

"What?" she says, concerned.

"I think I told Liam I was falling in love with him last night," I mumble, trying to piece together the flashes of my memory. I rub my temples as if that will magically clear up the night for me.

"Come again?" Elle says, the panic in her voice mirroring mine.

"I was so out of it and I was falling asleep and... Oh man, I am *so* not equipped to handle this," I say defeated. I slump back in my chair, my mind going in a million different directions.

"Tell me exactly what you remember," she instructs, and I comply. I say that Liam drove me home and we talked before I fell asleep. I don't remember everything, but I think I compared him to a love interest.

"Well, this is a lot to process," Elle mumbles.

"Oh!" I exclaim. "I also got the big sister talk from Liam's sister yesterday," I explain, cringing at the memory.

"What did she say to you?"

"Basically, that Liam's heart has been broken before and he's the most amazing person who puts off his own dreams to take care of his family, and basically I'm just a monster who came here and is threatening to destroy him," I ramble.

"I'm going to assume you're paraphrasing there," Elle says sarcastically.

"That was basically the gist," I reply flatly.

Elle lets out a big sigh. "Well, here's the good news. You're coming home in a week. So, whatever is going to happen, will happen."

"Are you freaking *kidding* me? How the hell is that good news?" I practically scream at her.

"I'm not sure. I'm working on the fly here," she says casually.

I lay my head on top of my folded arms on the counter. "I can't do this, Elle. It's too much. Everything that's happened... There's no way this ends without me hurting Liam. And I don't want that."

"What do you want to do? Do you want to tell Liam that you were basically sent there to plot a romance series and just so happened to fall for him in the process?"

"Not when you put it like that," I mumble.

"He might understand. He might think it's cool that you're using him for the book," Elle says, trying to be empathetic.

"But I'm not *using* him," I say quickly. "I think I'm using the setting more than I'm using the people. Either way, I would throw this whole book away just to keep him," I admit, my heart physically aching at the thought of leaving Liam in a few days. "I really believed that I would never feel something like we read about in our books, that all of it was just a fairy tale, but with Liam—"

"Then I think you have your answer," Elle says, pithily. I look at the Liz's bag on the counter and think about all the times I've smiled over the past few weeks.

I was in a rut before I came here. I needed a change. I needed to remember why I loved romance, and this lake, this town, this man, has done that. As much as I hate to admit it—and never will publicly—Anne and Josie were right. This city girl needed to experience small-town life. And now that I have, I think it may have changed me forever.

"I think I just need some processing time." Elle likes to compare my "processing time" to Sherlock going into his mind palace. I say it whenever I need to take a break from reality, sit by myself with a manuscript, or go for a walk. It's the time when I let the logical side of my brain take over and push my creative, emotional thoughts to the side. I think that is the only thing that is going to get me out of this situation.

"I feel like the past few days have just been too emotional for me, with Josie and then this Liam… situation. I just need to take a beat."

"That sounds like a good idea, call me later," Elle says, with an oddly upbeat voice. She hangs up before I have the chance to respond.

I wander outside and lean against the railing on the deck. I take a photo of the sun shining on the lake. I've been waking up to this view for weeks, but it hasn't lost its appeal yet. I wonder if it ever will. As I finish my pancakes at the kitchen counter, I write out a post to go with the photo on my Instagram.

> What. If.
> So many of my favorite romance novels explore the complex relationship between these two words.
> What if?
> What if there is a novel-worthy romance out there for me? For all of us? Isn't that what we all believe when we open a book?

I'm waffling, I know. A few weeks ago, I might have answered a HARD no to these questions. But now… what if?

I hit "Share" and feel the urge to keep writing. Now that my body is nourished and hydrated, I have a lot to decompress from in the last few days.

I turn to my computer and alternate between speech-to-text and typing. I start by taking notes, with setting descriptions, but soon I find my mind wandering into character profiles. Every small-town romance has a customary cast of characters. Once I start, I find it hard to stop.

Heroine
Hero—librarian, library assistant? Researching for grad school on Native American history?
Small-Town Head Bitch in Charge
Family—hero's sister/brother? Kids?
Small Business Owner
Side character who befriends the heroine, shows her the town?

I type HEROINE on top of the page and HERO on the bottom. I add a table and label each row with a heading: PHYSICAL DESCRIPTION, LIKES/DISLIKES, BACKSTORY, CHARACTER ARC.

I'm a bit hesitant to start with the heroine because I feel like Anne would definitely call me out if she turned out too much like me. I turn my attention to the hero section and get to work. I write pages of character profiles, setting descriptions, and plot charts.

Outlining is a lot harder than I imagined.

The problem is, I need to make the characters different from the actual people I met here.

> *Small-Town Head Bitch in Charge: shoulder-length gray hair, small brown eyes that can be daggers in the right setting.*
> *Small Business Owner: coffee shop, café; happy-go-lucky guy, married to a strong-willed woman (HBIC?), father-figure for heroine.*
> *Hero: tall, lean muscles, hair falls just below the ear; tragic past*
> *Parent deceased?*
> *Character Arc – learning to accept help/laugh again from heroine?*

After typing and deleting on repeat for what seems like forever, I sit back and take my hands off of the keyboard, defeated.

As much as I try, I can't escape the similarities. Because it's them. It's May and Max, and Liam and Jill, that make this story. It's May with her megaphone. It's Max with his big belly laughs and overgrown mustache. It's Liam and his grief, his loss, and big heart. It's Jill with her kindness, her determination. It's what makes them... *them*. That's what this story is.

Without them, there is no story.

Who was I kidding? I can't pretend that the characters I came up with are any different from the people in Hudson Hollow. I can't sketch out a setting and give it a different name when this place is the heart of the book. The whole plot of the story I dreamed up for Ruby, it's *them*. It's all the people I've met, it's this town. And I've betrayed them.

Anne sent me here to map the setting of a small-town romance, and Elle's right, I've started living one.

I'm frozen at the counter with my hands on either side of my face, the heels of my palms pressed into my temples, the contents of my brain swirling so fast I feel like I should be frantic. But instead, I can't move.

I scroll through pages of the document—pages of work that I sat here toiling over for the past two hours. Work that, up to this point, I would have been proud of. Now I just feel… *ashamed*.

I hate that I've proved Liam's initial suspicions right, and that I've been lying to myself the whole time. I was never going to be able to keep this place separate from the town I created for Ruby's book. I did it. I succeeded in my mission. I did exactly what Anne sent me here to do. I created the *perfect* setting and cast for a small-town romance.

How am I going to hand this proposal to Anne with pride? How could I have been such an idiot?

I look back at my laptop on the counter. This is it. This is the arsenal of information I would need to get a promotion. Anne will eat this up. She's not an evil person, but I doubt that she would understand the crisis of conscience that I am having about my time here, about Liam. The "think-like-a-reporter" mentality can only go so far. These are people's lives.

The doorbell snaps me out of my turmoil.

I make my way to the door and stop in the foyer. I freeze mid-step, my socks sliding on the floor in dramatic fashion.

What if it's Liam? What do I do? What do I say to him?

Nothing. I have to keep my mouth shut. I have to protect his feelings. As far as he knows, I'm recovering from a shitty day yesterday. I can't make any rash decisions right now.

I continue toward the door and don't bother looking through the window to see who it is. I whip it open and squeal at the person on the stoop.

"Surprise!" Elle shouts, raising her hands in the air. I stare at her, dumbfounded.

"But... I was just on the phone with you," I sputter, still standing in the doorway like an alien has just rung my bell instead of my best friend.

"I was on the train!" she exclaims. "Best surprise ever?" She throws her arms around me in excitement, and I allow myself to melt into her embrace. I don't think I realized how much I missed her until this moment. But boy, am I happy to see her, here, in the flesh.

"I missed you," I say breathlessly when she finally releases me from her grip. "Did you take a few days off?"

"Yeah, I just got the sense that... I don't know, maybe you needed me? With Josie and everything, and then I saw your last few insta posts and—"

"And our conversation this morning pretty much cemented the fact that I'm losing it, is that it?" I finish for her.

"I don't know if I would use those exact words, but yes," she says, taking more than a step into the house. "Oh man, look at that!" she says with a gasp, her gaze fixed on the back windows. "Look at that view! Look at the water! It's actually blue, not brown!"

"That it is," I say, somewhat amused.

"Our standards are pretty low, huh?" Elle jokes. I follow

her to the kitchen counter. "Wow, look at this," she says, finding the mess of papers I left in my wake. She picks up my notebook and glances at my laptop, where my HERO/HEROINE table is front and center. My chart is so perfectly color-coded, it could be in a bullet journal. Her fingers roam over some notes I made earlier in gel-pen. It's all about the hero. About Liam.

"Is this the motherlode? Are you fully infiltrated?" she says, sarcastically.

"Practically a ninja," I groan, running a hand through my knotted hair.

"Wow, Lucy," she mumbles, still flipping through the notebook. "This is... more than I expected." Elle's tone is serious as she reads through my notes. She looks up at me and immediately frowns. "What's wrong?"

I fold my hands behind my head and bite my lip. All of a sudden, I feel so tired I could cry. "Elle, I—" My voice croaks and I can't finish my sentence. I fall into a chair at the kitchen table and place my head in my hands.

Elle puts down the notebook and sits at the barstool next to me. "What is it?" she asks in a gentle tone.

"There's so much wrong about all of this. It's *them*. It's him," I say, rubbing my eyes with my knuckles. "I was here to plan out the series, but I got so caught up in the creativity, I basically outlined an entire book. And—it came out as all the wonderful people I've met. I've been spying on them. Using each and every one of them. Using *him*."

Elle slowly turns her head to evaluate the scene in front of her. I doubt she was expecting this when she chose to surprise me today. I sigh and lay my head against her shoulder, defeated.

Elle sighs heavily. "Lucy, I think you got a lot more than you bargained for, coming here."

"No shit," I reply, my voice hoarse. I sit up, rubbing my face like it might actually remove some of the sadness from my head. "I came here with a goal, and I achieved it. It just doesn't feel good... at all."

"Maybe you should just tell him. It will be better than wringing yourself in knots like this and wondering *what if*," Elle answers quickly. "You don't necessarily have to use all of this, but you're right. You haven't been honest. And before you can get upset about the ramifications of this," she says, picking up my notebook again, "you have to see if there is something worth fighting for."

I let out a loud exhale and lean my head against my hand. I admire my friend, whose Bohemian-chic overalls and wild curly hair look like they belong on a runway or on the streets of Manhattan, not in my dingy rental kitchen. My heart tugs at how happy I am to see her, though. For all the jokes and digs I make about the city, without Manhattan, I wouldn't have Elle. I grew up watching *Friends*, thinking that one day if I moved to Manhattan, I'd have the same set of supportive, unbelievably loyal friends who would do anything for me. It took me a while to find them, but I did, in Elle.

I pause, wondering if I can believe what Elle is saying. *Something worth fighting for*, I repeat in my head. Do Liam and I have something worth fighting for? Of course, I wish that we did. But in reality, how long have I known him for, a month? I've been working toward becoming an editor for *years*. But the real battle I'm having here is with my conscience. Can I live with the fact that once I return to the city—to my real life—I'll never see these people again, and worse still, I will have used them for a story?

I don't know if I can answer that question yet.

"I don't know if I can do that, Elle," I manage to squeak out. The throb in my throat is threatening to explode. Elle must be able to see that I'm on the verge of tears, which startles her. She wraps her arms around me and squeezes.

"Lucy, take a breath, babe. Everything is going to be okay."

I wish I could know that for sure.

EIGHTEEN

Lucy: Hey, thank you for the pancakes. It was just what I needed. Hope I didn't ruin your day yesterday.

Lucy: PS: Elle surprised me for the weekend and we're having a cozy night in, so I won't be by the restaurant.

Liam: Glad you're feeling better. You could never ruin my day. Have fun with your friend. Talk tomorrow.

"Sounds kind of abrupt, don't you think?" I ask Elle, showing her my phone.

"Only to someone overthinking the situation who may or may not have hinted at the fact that she has hard and heavy feelings for this man last night," Elle says matter-of-factly.

I spend the rest of the night thinking about it, about Liam. Hours later, once we're both settled on the couch with the television on, Elle turns to me.

"What if you actually got together with Liam? What

would that look like?" Elle asks. It's comforting to be sitting next to her again. As fun as it's been to be on my own, being able to dance in my underwear or go to the bathroom without closing the door, I've missed my best friend.

"I don't think I can let myself picture that right now. Not when there is a good chance I won't see him again after next week," I say, running my fingers through my hair. I pull a blanket over me and snuggle myself further into the couch. The last twenty-four hours have been draining. The last *week* has been draining—ever since my trip up the mountain with Liam, things have been tough. Thankfully my mother texted me soon after Elle got here to say she had landed and was on her way to see Josie, and she would call when she could.

"You've thought about it, though. *Everyone* thinks about it," Elle prompts.

"Of course I have, but it feels like a dream." I sigh. "I have to go back to my life in the city because that's what's *real*."

"But Liam is real. Your feelings for him are real. What's happened to you here, that's also real. You're doing yourself a disservice if you can't admit that," Elle says, placing her hand on top of mine.

"The truth is," I start, but I can't bring myself to finish the sentence. *Why is it so hard for me to say it?* Why can't I just admit what I want?

"The truth is what? What do you want, Lucy?"

"Sometimes I really think you can read my mind," I say, warily.

"I just know you," she says with a comforting smile. "You think about everyone else and then alter your actions to fit what you think their reaction is going to be. You can't go on like this."

"You sound like Liam," I mumble. Elle looks at me curiously. "He asked me what I would do if money or my parents didn't matter, what was the first thing that came to mind."

"And what did you say?"

"I said being an editor was my dream, and that dream was in the city."

"And did you mean it?" she asks, widening her green eyes at me.

"Yes," I reply, almost automatically.

"I feel like you're saying that because you feel like you have to," Elle says, turning her body to face me. "Don't you feel like this trip has changed you?"

"I love it here," I admit. "I'm... at peace here. In New York, I'm in a constant state of *'avoid that pile of garbage on the street, dodge that cab crossing 6th Avenue, try not to get too upset when I see dogs that have no grass to run around and play on,'*" I ramble. "But that doesn't change the fact that publishing is my dream."

Elle doesn't have to say anything for me to know that she thinks it's all bullshit. The expression on her face says it plainly. "I mean—it really is my dream. I've waited so long for it." I throw my arms in the air, thrumming with frustration. "Why does no one believe that I know what I want?" Elle is taken aback by the tone in my voice. "I'm sorry, but first Liam and now you. I love my job. I will be so happy when I get the promotion. It's what I've *always* wanted."

"Just because it's what you've always wanted doesn't

mean you can't change your mind," she says, her eyes wandering to the lake.

I follow her gaze. "*This* won't change my mind. I'm here to do a job, and next week, I'll be back in the city. That's it." But even as I say it, I know my voice lacks conviction.

The next morning, Elle climbs into bed with me, her face bright and refreshed from a good night's sleep. Mine, after hours of relentless tossing and turning, tells a very different story.

"Yes?" I croak, groggily.

"I've developed a plan," she announces.

"Does it involve breakfast?" I mumble, rubbing my eyes.

"Yes, but after that, it is going to be *Get Lucy on Track Day*," she proclaims.

"Get Lucy *what*?"

"Alright, I admit the name is a bit rough, but it's the thought that counts," she says, grinning.

I throw my hand over my eyes to block out the sun.

"And what does this entail?" I groan.

"Admitting that this trip has been more than just an emotional roller coaster for you," she says confidently.

I mumble something unintelligible back at her.

"I've spent the morning snooping on your laptop," she says without an ounce of shame.

"You'd make a terrible thief," I grumble.

"Lucy, your notes for Ruby's book are incredible. The scenes you wrote out? It's basically like you're writing the book yourself. Reading them made me realize that editing is not your calling. *Writing* is." I scrunch my face at her. "I think this trip has shown you that you're missing out on something important in your life."

I toss the duvet and plant two firm feet on the ground.

"Where are you going?" Elle whines.

"I'm not talking about revitalizing my life until I've eaten something."

"Be honest," Elle says sternly. "If we asked Josie about this, what would she say?" She's right behind me, following me into the kitchen.

"Oh, that is a low blow, *Eloise*!" I save that nickname for when I'm mad at her, because I know she hates it. I'm not actually mad at her for bringing up Josie, but I know that she knows that Josie would agree with her. And she's using it to her advantage.

As if on cue, my phone rings.

"Oh my goodness!" I squeal, Josie's face filling up my screen. "Ah, aren't you a sight for sore eyes!"

Her hair is pinned back off her face, which appears pale and gaunt. And her eyes, usually so full of life and color, are tired. Seeing her like this hurts my heart, but I've promised myself I'd maintain a brave face. My mom also comes into view, their two heads bobbing side by side, and the sight of the two them together, in her bright apartment, gives me a feeling of joy and calm.

"I'm sure my appearance at the moment is cause for sore eyes," Josie teases, her voice deeper and raspier than usual.

"Oh stop," I say, shaking my head.

"Is that Elle I can see?" my mom asks, turning the camera to face herself. "What's she doing there?"

"Hey Mrs. B!" Elle offers an animated wave. "I came for a surprise weekend."

"Hi Elle!" Mom beams. "That was so nice of you."
I pivot the screen back to toward my face.

"It's so good to see you guys," I say, my voice shaking. "What's the plan from here?"

"We're going to spend a few days getting packed and then we'll be on a flight home on Friday," she explains. "And no—" she holds up her finger in my aunt's direction. "We will not be discussing this again, you're coming home with me, end of discussion," she says sternly.

I raise my brows at Josie. "You're complaining about coming to see me?" I accuse.

"No," Josie says grumpily. "I'm complaining about the ten thousand doctor appointments *your* mother has made."

"How's it going there, Luce?" Mom asks, choosing to ignore Josie.

"Yeah, tell us more about that quaint little town," Josie adds.

"Well," I start. I take a moment to cough while I try to read Elle's face. She raises her eyebrow knowingly. "I'm making a lot of progress on my assignment," I say, cringing at the sound of my own voice. It sounds *so* rehearsed.

"That's good," mom answers.

"Anne has been really happy with my notes. I've even started sketching out some scenes," I explain, gaining a little enthusiasm in my voice.

"Have you forgotten all about the city yet, Luce?" Josie asks.

I shoot Josie a sharp look. "I'm not sure I'll ever forget about it, Josie, seeing as I live there. But now that you're coming home, we're one step closer to having our garden together."

"*Your* garden?" my mother questions.

"Josie keeps trying to sell me on small town life. I told her I would only give in if she agreed to live with me," I explain. My mother's face is dubious. "It was hypothetical, Mom, relax." She shakes her head.

"Anyway, what are you two up to today?" she asks.

"Just relaxing, really. Elle has to be back on the train in the morning."

"Ah, well, enjoy yourself, and keep up the good work."

When I put the phone down, I can't help but feel a small bit of pride over the work I've done here. Maybe what I've accomplished *could* have some place in my new reality? The only question that remains is whether that new reality includes Liam, too.

Elle and I spend the afternoon exploring Catskill, losing ourselves in the town's only indie bookstore. With our reader hats firmly in place, we gush over the romance section. We hunt down Heartwarming titles, and—like true insiders—subtly rearrange a few to claim prime spots at the front. It's a quiet tradition among publishing folks. We all do it.

When we get back to the house and change, we find a few floats in the garage and bring them down to the lake. We spend the next few hours floating around the lake, our toes being bitten by little fish as we attempt to not float too far away from the dock.

I find serenity in the silence of the lake water and let my eyelids flutter closed. I try picturing what my life with Liam would look like. I imagine living in his house, with an office that overlooks the lake. There's an antique wood desk that Elle would probably spot at a flea market, and I'd write for hours while admiring my favorite view. Maybe I could be a freelance editor for Heartwarming if my books do well. I mentally shake my head at myself. It's one thing to dream about things like this, but it's another for them to come true.

I just don't have that kind of track record with the universe.

"Have you decided what you are going to do?" Elle asks, her voice soft and thoughtful.

"I don't know," I say, opening my eyes and turning to face her. "I really don't know how, or where, to even start." I've played the scenario out in my head. Maybe I will stop by Liam's house when he gets home from the restaurant later today and tell him I have to talk to him. Maybe he won't hear me out, or maybe he'll be more understanding than I deserve. It's all maybe, and I don't like to deal with unpredictability.

"Start with the truth, that's all you can do. Everything else will fall into place from there," Elle says, infusing as much confidence in her voice as possible. She gives me a sheepish—although I think it's meant to be encouraging—smile. "Remember, Lucy, we don't get to choose love. We don't get a say in the when, or the where, or even who. We don't get to decide. Love finds us. And the only decision we get to make is what we do with it when it does."

NINETEEN

"Love is showing up. That's all it is. Take out the grand notions of happily ever after and flowers and candy and knights in shining armor and just accept that being there for someone is all it takes. Get out of your own way and just show up. Because otherwise, what are we all doing here?"

This author guts me with this line every time I read it. Because if that's all love is, then why is it so complicated? When all people really have to do is tell each other how they feel? Why is that so difficult for some of us?

(not a rhetorical question... asking for a friend)

Operation Small Town, Day 28

I post a photo of one of my favorite Heartwarming novels from the Catskill bookshop. It's an enemies-to-lovers story with a clever twist on *Pride and Prejudice*, where the hero and heroine are both too stubborn to admit their true feelings.

When I get back from dropping Elle off at the train station, I decide to take some time to process. Or more honestly, I straight-up procrastinate. When I get back to the house, I delve right into work, adding to the outlines in my notebook and drafting an email to Anne with an overly-labeled plot diagram of the book.

I'm writing a character profile on the local bookstore owner based on the one we met yesterday, when my phone vibrates on the counter next to me.

> Liam: Hey, random question. Are you at your house right now?

> Lucy: Yeah, why?

> Liam: I left Blue at home thinking it would be a slow day, but it still hasn't died down. I'm sorry to ask this, but would you be able to take him out for a quick walk?

> Lucy: Of course, don't apologize. I might just keep him for the whole afternoon.

> Liam: Thank you so much. I'll try to get away as soon as I can.

I'm glad for the distraction, especially one as cute and furry as Blue. I slip on a pair of sneakers, head across the street, and find Liam's key underneath a flowerpot in his front landscaping. Terrible security system. Good thing he has a scary-looking dog.

Blue mauls me before I'm fully in the door. He jumps up, putting his paws on my shoulders, his head level with mine, and licks my face.

"Well, hello to you too," I say in a baby voice. I bet dogs hate it when humans talk to them like they're babies. They probably find it so embarrassing.

"Where's your leash? Let's put your leash on," I goad him, and he shows me the hook next to the door where his leash hangs. He sits down on the mat next to it, waiting.

"Geez, I didn't peg Liam for the crazy dog trainer type," I say, scratching Blue's face beneath his ears. As I'm mumbling some nonsensical nothings to him, I notice a small camera on the table behind Blue. There is a small red light below the lens. I bring my face up to it and stick my tongue out. I laugh and look at Blue, as if he is going to join in on the fun with me.

"Weirdo," I mutter at the camera, trying to imagine Liam setting up a baby monitor for a dog who could eat a robber for breakfast. I shake my head at Blue, who is waiting anxiously at the door.

Blue and I head down the gravel street toward the neighborhood's main thoroughfare. Blue picks up his step, trotting alongside me, sniffing at random patches of grass, and peeing on something every five feet. We walk farther than Liam probably anticipated us to, but I get in such a rhythm with the dog's footsteps, and find it so soothing, I don't want to turn back. But eventually, Blue starts turning around and eyeing me, his large tongue sticking out the side of his mouth, basically begging me to take him home.

I squint up at the sky and notice that clouds have started to form in the distance. It's the oddest skyline—behind me, the clouds are low, puffy, and white, but the way the sun is reflecting off them, makes an orange hue in the distance. Ahead of me, the clouds seem higher, and much darker. They're staggered throughout the sky, but they are all thin streaks, like blue and gray watermarks across a canvas.

When I take my phone out of my pocket to check the weather forecast, I feel the first drop.

Blue looks back at me, with a look on his face saying, "Did you feel that too?"

"Uh-oh, Blue," I mutter, gauging our distance from the house. We're still a few streets away, and I am not about to sprint down this road with an eighty pound German Shepherd in tow. "We're about to get *real* wet, buddy."

I pick up my pace as the drops increase in number and speed, but Blue dawdles on, refusing to go any faster than a leisurely walk. I can't believe how hard the rain is coming down when we finally turn onto our street. I break out into a jog just as I hear wheels on the gravel behind me. I turn around and see Liam's truck barreling down the road. I stop and stick my thumb out, laughing. He rolls his window down.

"What the hell are you doing?" he calls over the rain.

"What do you mean? Walking your dog!" I whine, gesturing to Blue, who has his nose pointed up at the sky. I half expect him to stick his tongue out to try to catch the raindrops.

"In the rain?" Liam shakes his head, but a smile tugs at his mouth.

"Obviously it wasn't raining when I started, Liam," I say,

continuing down the street. Liam rolls his eyes and parks up in front of the house. Blue jolts the leash in that direction, desperate to see him. Liam emerges from his car with an umbrella and tries to dodge the drenched dog who has come to greet him, to no avail.

"Seriously? An umbrella?" I tease, reaching for it before he can open it.

"Well, yeah. I don't want my hair to end up looking like yours," Liam says, squinting as he is pelted with droplets. I grab the umbrella and toss it back in his car, letting the rain drench him. I cackle as I lead Blue to the front door, Liam trailing close behind, his deep laugh a comfort to my ears.

Our laughs echo against the gravel in sync with the pounding raindrops as we race to the cover of the awning on the front stoop of his house. Once we reach the top step, we lean against the wall to catch our breath.

"I'm sorry, this doesn't happen in real life. Rain doesn't just appear out of nowhere. There are literally like four clouds in the sky," I say, pushing my sopping wet hair out of my face. Liam shakes his hair so it sprays in every direction. It's so wet that his blonde locks stretch almost all the way down to the base of his neck, where I find my eyes focusing as well. A single drop of water makes its way over the large muscle of his throat and trickles below his shirt.

And then we're not laughing anymore.

Our eyes are locked on one another, and even though the humidity is stifling, goosebumps spread across my flesh as I feel Liam's warmth next to me. Our arms are so close together, I feel a force of static between them that sends lightning into my gut. Something has changed between us. And he can feel it too.

Liam shifts so that the shoulder closest to me is leaning against the wall, and the rest of his body is facing me. We're even closer now, our chests rising and falling in the same rhythm, water dripping down our faces, our fingers just inches from each other at the side of our bodies.

My gaze remains on Liam's neck, because I know if I let myself look into those eyes, I'll lose any last resolve I have left. I watch Liam raise his hand beside me and tuck a wet string of my hair behind my ear. I can feel his eyes scanning every inch of me, but I don't move. I can't move.

"Lucy." My head slowly rises at the sound of his voice. What a shift in the dynamic between us from just a few moments ago. It's a moment like this when the old Lucy would make an awkward joke to get out of this situation, but the new Lucy never wants to move from this spot.

Liam lifts his body off the wall and places one hand next to my head, caging me in. I finally meet his gaze and immediately feel like I'm going to melt from the weight of it. His eyelids lower as his gaze falls to my lips. My breath hitches as he traces a line up my arm with his fingers.

"I know there are more than a few reasons why I'm not supposed to do this right now," he whispers in a low sensual voice. His eyes never move from my lips. His light touch makes its way to my face and traces the outline of my lips. "But I can't seem to remember any of them."

His feather-like touch transforms into a whole hand cupping the side of my face, his fingers threading through my hair. His mouth crushes against mine in the most gentle and passionate way possible. His wet hair rubs against my forehead and I can taste water on his lips. I breathe in every inch of him I possibly can. I place my hands gently on his abdomen and feel the hard, round peaks beneath, which spikes my pulse. Liam moves his lips with mine in a beautiful rhythm, one that lets me forget about what I should be doing, if he's enjoying himself, if I'm enjoying myself, all the reasons why I shouldn't be letting this happen... and just be.

Liam pulls away too quickly, and I'm left breathless with my eyes closed, trying to cement every second of the last few minutes into my memory—the feel of lips against mine, the gentle trace of his fingers on my skin, the warmth of his body up against me. I want to remember everything.

Liam lets go of me for a moment to unlock his front door, pulling my hand to get me inside. Blue runs in, and I can hear his footsteps head for his water bowl. Liam closes the door behind me and quickly presses me up against it. I gasp when he presses his body against mine, wet fabric slapping together between us. He brings his face closer to mine but stops at the point when our noses touch.

"I have to tell you something," he whispers, his voice breathy.

I groan internally. "Wait, I have to tell you something first," I say, barely able to catch my breath. The way my body is yearning for him is almost uncontrollable. I quite literally might burst if he doesn't start touching me again. How can I think like this when I am keeping a secret from him? How can he completely consume my thoughts, the presence of him expelling any reason from my brain?

"No, me first," he says, lowering one hand to press it against my hip. "The other day," he starts, sneaking his fingers under my top. He glides his wet fingers up my abdomen, and I shiver at his touch. "When you said I was skeptical of you when you first got here—"

"Liam, I didn't mean—"

"I wasn't skeptical. I just couldn't believe *you* were here," he finishes, and I tilt my head back, confused by his statement. He cups his hand around my ribs, using the other to fold a piece of hair behind my ear. "I couldn't believe I was seeing you again."

What? "Sorry?" I say a little too loudly.

"I'd seen you before. In Manhattan. I was with Jill and the kids to see the Christmas tree. You fell—"

The rest of his words sound far away. I squint at him as his hands reach for my hips.

"Manhattan—?"

"Lucy," Liam says, snapping my attention back into focus. "I saw you. I saw you fall. And I couldn't get to you. And then you were gone." He pauses, a look of disbelief spreading across his face. "I don't know why that moment stuck with me—seeing you across the way. Then when you showed up here, it was surreal. At first I thought I'd lost my mind."

My eyes are surely wide enough that he understands the level of disbelief I am feeling right now. "I was in disbelief that it was you, the same girl from New York. And that I was getting a second chance to actually meet you. Because I'd thought of you every day since."

He was there. On the other side of Sixth Avenue. He was the one who saw me. The one who looked like he was coming to help me. My knight in shining armor.

"Please say something. And please don't tell me you think I'm some sort of creep," he says, chuckling bashfully.

I can't resist this anymore. I can't pretend like the last few weeks haven't changed something for me. Because this man... this man has changed everything. I was starting to believe that the stories I read about—the ones that talked about meeting your "person," the person who makes all the ones who came before seem like distant memories—I thought they were bullshit. But I'm standing here looking at a man who has been longing for me—*me*—for a year, and I can't believe it. I finally found the moment I've been reading about all my life. I finally found my Big Romance Moment.

And in this moment, nothing else matters. Not Anne, or Ruby, or the book, or my job. I don't care about any of it. I'll throw the book away and delete all my notes. I'll delete any evidence of anything that could hurt this golden soul in front of me. Because I've finally found what I've been looking for my whole life.

I lean forward in what can only be described as an animalistic fashion, crushing my mouth against his. He smiles against my lips, and I can't help but smile as well. Together, we slide to the floor, and Liam presses me backwards. He cradles my head as he lays me down, breaking our kiss to trace my jaw with his lips, licking the last of the raindrops off my neck. I let out a mix between a giggle and a moan, completely intoxicated by his touch.

He kisses my chest while he unbuttons my shorts, my hips already rocking with anticipation. Did I shave my legs last night? What's the situation down there? Do I care? His fingers skate beneath my panties and his palm cups my center. Scratch that, I don't care. Nope. Not one bit.

"Oh my God," I whine, as he starts to rotate his thumb

around the most sensitive part of me. I can't believe this is happening. My body can't believe this is happening. My hips move in tandem with his hand, and I throw my head back. Liam reaches behind my neck to support me and presses his lips to mine again, tracing the inside of my mouth with his tongue. As the intensity of his kiss deepens, so does the speed of his hand, and I moan even more. There's a tingle in my toes that slowly creeps up the backs of my legs, and a squeeze in my abdomen. I tense beneath him, every muscle in my core spasming under his grip. I feel Liam press himself against my hip to show me what I'm doing to him, and in the midst of my pleasure, I think I mumble something about wanting him inside me, but I'm not sure that any of it comes out coherently.

When I open my eyes, Liam is grinning. I smile back, because how can I not? Liam presses his forehead against mine.

"I've been dying to do that," he whispers, his lips moving against mine. I let out a weak laugh. Just as I'm about to respond, I see a flash of white out of the corner of my eye. I turn my head to peek out of the small window that lines Liam's front door. Liam must see the confusion on my face, because he follows my gaze, to where a white sedan pulls up behind Anne's car. Liam looks at me, and I communicate my uneasiness to him with my eyes. *Who could that be?*

We both sit up. Liam looks out the window and I see his shoulders relax. I pop my head up in time to see an elderly man opening the passenger door of his car. A woman of equal age steps out.

"It's Al and Mella," Liam says, looking at me with a puzzled expression. I match his gaze with an even more confused face. What are they doing here? I'm supposed to be here until Saturday.

Liam stands up, pulling me up with him, and opens the front door. Blue scurries out beside Liam. I readjust myself, run my hands through my hair, and follow him.

"Liam!" Mella calls as she shuffles toward the house. Liam meets them at the entrance to the porch of my—their—house and I stand behind him warily, unsure what my next move should be.

When did this day become so derailed? I try to avoid Liam, then I kiss him, and then some other stuff happens, which was totally *not* part of the plan, and now these two show up? My brain is on overload. And boy are my shoes wet.

"Al, Mella, what are you doing here?" Liam says, embracing Mella as she opens the front door of the house.

"What do you mean?" she asks, finally spotting me behind Liam.

"Hi, I'm Lucy," I say with a pathetic wave, coming up behind her. It's odd to be entering my rental without the feeling of it being mine, since its actual owners are opening the door and letting themselves in.

"Ah, Lucy!" Mella exclaims, holding her arms out for an embrace. "It's so nice you met our lovely neighbor Liam. But I have to ask, what are you still doing here, sweetie?" she adds as I give her an awkward hug.

"What do you mean?"

"Why don't we take this inside, Luce? Because it's, you know, pouring," Liam says, ushering Al under the small awning.

"I'm so sorry," I say once we're inside. "Did we get our dates wrong?"

"Should I grab some towels?" Liam offers. Mella nods.

"There are some in the cabinet just through the kitchen," I say as Mella shrugs and shows me a kind smile.

"We thought you were leaving this weekend. Anne said before the fourth," Mella explains.

Ugh, Anne. "Well, as usual Anne is a terrible communicator. She has me scheduled here until the fifth," I say, just as Liam re-enters the room with a pile of towels in his arm.

"Who is Anne?" he asks, handing me a hand towel. I reach my hand out instinctively, but as I take it from his grip, my eyes focus on him in shock.

He doesn't know who Anne is. He doesn't know my connection to Al and Mella. He thinks I'm just renting their house.

I can't open my mouth fast enough. Mella beats me to it. And then it's all over.

"My daughter-in-law. You must have met her, Liam. Penny's wife? She's also Lucy's boss," she says with a smile.

"Why would your boss have you scheduled here?" Liam asks, the furrow in his brow getting deeper by the second. He rises from his crouched position on the floor, where Blue is now rolling on the towel Liam set down for him.

It's as if I can physically feel the blood pumping in my veins. The clench in my stomach feels like a combination of when I got caught after pushing Sydney Dana off the swings in second grade and the lurch I felt a few days ago before I puked at Cammy's party. And yet, I'm paralyzed. My face is sunken in, my eyes wide, and I can't undo it. I can't speak up for myself, I can't explain myself out of the situation.

All I can do is stand by and watch the world I've carefully crafted over the last four weeks crumble in front of me, like a slow-motion scene in a movie.

"For Lucy's work project?" Mella asks, looking between me and Liam. Apparently, she doesn't sense the tension or awkwardness in the room because she keeps going. "I don't quite get it, if I'm honest." She winks at me. "But Anne said something about a new book? Based on Hudson Hollow?"

"I—" I stutter.

"Lucy?" Liam starts.

We're both cut off by Blue's explosion of energy that sends him racing into the kitchen. Liam breaks my gaze and goes after him, calling his name. "Blue, no!" he commands from the other room. I turn my attention to Al and Mella, who are looking at me like I'm a statue. Which, to their credit, I must look like right now. My hair is still dripping wet, lines of water streak down my legs, and my feet are squishing in my sneakers.

"Are you alright, dear?" Mella asks, gently placing her hand on my arm.

"Um, Lucy, what is this?" Liam calls from the kitchen. I snap my head in his direction, as he turns the corner with my notebook in his hand.

My research. My *notes*. My computer. I left it all on the bar top when I went across the street to get Blue. And now it is in Liam's hand.

TWENTY

"Al, Mella, excuse me," Liam says in a hard voice, before turning his attention to me. "But Lucy, *what the hell is all this*?"

"Liam I—"

"Al," Mella interrupts, "didn't you say you were hungry?"

"Starving, actually," Al murmurs.

"Me too. We're going to run down to the restaurant for a quick bite to eat," Mella says, practically pushing her husband out of the door.

"No, you guys don't have to leave," I say, breaking off from Liam's intense stare to meet them outside the door. "I'm sorry, it's just been a bit of a crazy day, I guess."

Mella turns to me and places her hands over mine. "Darling, it's okay. We'll be back in a little bit. It'll give you two a minute to chat," she says with a sympathetic smile. Before I can rebut, they're out the door, and I'm left staring at the door handle, wondering how everything has imploded so spectacularly.

"Well?" Liam presses.

When I turn around, he's reading my notes, the character profile of the bookstore owner. And on the corresponding page is the profile for the hero—the fictitious version of him.

In a moment like this, I'd love to be able to avoid him, to hide from him, to *lie* to him. But that isn't me. I stare right into his eyes.

"Can we sit?" I croak, walking past him and collapsing at the kitchen table. He follows but leans against the counter instead of sitting. For a few beats, no one speaks, and then I start the speech I've prepared in my head over the past few days.

"I didn't come here to run away from a relationship. I haven't even been in a relationship since college." Liam shakes his head. "The truth is that Anne, my boss, sent me here for one of our authors. To outline a new series."

Liam pauses for a moment, and I can see the thoughts working behind his eyes. "To write a series about Hudson Hollow? To... *study* us?" I can tell that he's trying to stay calm but there's anger rising in his voice.

"No, no, that makes it sound so clinical!" I reply, internally panicking. "She sent me here to see what living in a small town would be like, to get ideas, to inspire a new series. My notes were never supposed to—"

Liam turns and grips the counter with his hands. His head hangs between his shoulders. He flings the notebook across the table at me with a loud *thud*.

"Tragic hero. Abandonment issues. *Damaged*." He practically spits the last word. "Is this your opinion of me?"

"Of course not!" I squeal, jumping up and meeting him in the kitchen in three big strides. "These are tropes. It's just a formula. The characters need backstories, things to overcome before they can fall in love with each other." I pause for a moment, wondering how my rambling must sound to him. I meet his gaze to see if I'm getting through to him at all. All I see is anguish. Betrayal.

"Please just let me explain everything," I plead, urging him to sit down. Liam looks at me in a way I haven't seen since I first arrived in Hudson Hollow. He looks at me with unease, like he's not sure if he can trust me. And I don't blame him. I've been dishonest with him from the start.

He takes a deep breath and sits down, and for the moment I breathe a tiny sigh of relief.

"You were right about my job, about me not being completely happy," I start. "Everyone thinks living in the city is glamorous, and maybe it is for some people, but—" I hate that I sound like I'm complaining. This isn't coming out right.

Why did this speech sound better in my head?

"Sometimes my life has felt like one disappointment after another. Not just with work, but with dating, too. And even though I work on romance for a living, I've basically stopped believing in it," I admit, my gaze falling to the floor. Sure, I've told Elle how hard things have been in New York, and I've thought about how frustrated I am with my life there, but saying it like that, out loud, is surprisingly invigorating. It feels like an affirmation.

"The truth is, since I've been here, and since I've been spending time with you, I've felt so happy," I say, my breath becoming more relaxed as I speak, as if I could feel the joy in my voice. "Before, when Anne gave me this opportunity, I couldn't pass it up because it would lead to a promotion.

And I'd been waiting for such a long time to feel recognized at work, to feel *seen*."

Liam leans forward, resting his forearms on his thighs. He doesn't look at me.

"So, you weren't here on vacation? You were here to get yourself a promotion?" he asks, folding his hands under his chin and looking up at me.

God, why does he have to look so handsome when he does that? Why does the pain in his eyes make me want to kiss them, and feel his arms embrace me? How I wish I could reach out and stroke the stubble on his hard jawline, and iron out the tension that fills his face.

"I came here because of the promotion, yes, but when I got here, it became less about trying to prove myself to my boss and more about finding out who I really am." I physically cringe at that statement. "I hate how cheesy that sounds, but it's true. I have a lot I've been needing to process, and I haven't been entirely honest with myself about what will make me happy." I take a deep breath. "But being here… I think I've figured it out."

Liam doesn't speak, he's just looking at me, his face guarded, unreadable. It's only then that I realize I'm crying.

"I never wanted to hurt you," I say. "I'm so sorry that I lied to you." I shrug helplessly. "Yell at me, scream at me, I deserve it. But you have to know that I've been in knots about how to tell you for *weeks*. I wanted you to know the truth, because how I feel about you—" I say, my voice trailing off when I see his eyes redden. "Everything between us was real."

Liam rubs both of his hands over his face and stands up abruptly. "I need some air. I can't do this right now," he says, running his hand through his hair and taking a deep breath.

"Oh, I—um, okay. Do you want to talk later?" I say, pathetically.

"Lucy, I'm not even sure how to look at you right now," he replies harshly. I inhale a sharp gasp at the tenor of his voice. Yelling and screaming would be easier than this.

"Please tell me what I can do to make this better. Tell me what to do and I'll do it," I say, my voice weak.

"Well," he says, his eyes sharp as flint, "maybe you should plug it into your formula." His voice drops to a mutter as he turns and heads for the door.

"Blue, come," he commands, clipped and cold. The dog rises from the floor, casting me a brief, searching look before obediently following him out.

It's impossible to put this feeling into words—the sensation of my heart sinking like a stone, heavy and leaden, dragging me down as I collapse into the kitchen chair.

I grab my notebook off the table and hurl it across the room. As is severing that connection, that lifeless bundle of paper, could somehow erase what I've done. But it doesn't. I can't undo this. I can't rewrite it.

I came here chasing love, just not for myself. From the start, it was a business deal, a transaction, a means to an end. I always knew this trip had an expiration date, and I accepted it.

So why does it feel like I've become the villain in my own love story?

Al and Mella walk in to find me in the midst of a frantic cleaning spree. It hasn't been more than a half hour since Liam left, but already I've packed my clothes, stripped the sheets, and emptied the fridge. Soon, there will be little trace of my presence.

"Lucy, is it alright if we come in, sweetie?" Mella calls from the front door, just as I round the corner out of the master bedroom with my last suitcase.

"Hi," I say, dropping the bag by the front door. "Of course. This is your house. I am so sorry for the mix-up." I rub the back of my hand against my forehead, exhausted by the events of the last hour. My whole body hurts, like I have the flu, only worse somehow. I feel like I could close my eyes and fall over, which is not a great feeling considering I have a very long drive home. I'm going to need some coffee.

"You have nothing to be sorry for. I always said that Anne was a scatterbrain," Al mutters, carrying his fanny pack to the kitchen.

"Can we persuade you to stay the night, and drive home tomorrow? You look a little—" Mella starts, but her voice fades and she gives me a pitying look.

"Like hell," Al finishes for her.

"Al!" Mella yells, way too loudly.

"I don't mean it offensively. But you certainly look like someone who has had a tough day," he says, holding his hands up apologetically. I let out a mock laugh as Mella shakes her head at him.

"I guess that's one way to describe it," I quip, turning my head to look out the windows, gazing at Liam's house.

"Don't pack the car yet," Mella says, taking a step toward me. I look at her, questioning. "I don't mean to overstep," she adds, her hands out like she is cautioning me against something. "I don't know what happened between you two, but I've known that boy for his whole life. You shouldn't give up on him that quickly," she says, a hint of sadness in her voice.

"I'm not giving up on him," I say softly, taking her hand in mine.

"At least let him know you're leaving. It can't hurt."

I blow air out through my lips, my stomach clenching with anxiety at the thought of walking across the street and talking to Liam. I look back at Al and Mella—Al shrugs his shoulders at me, but Mella looks at me encouragingly. I don't know what makes me do it, but I reach out and embrace Mella, much to her surprise. Hudson Hollow *has* changed me; I hug people I barely know now. Whew, who would have thought?

I don't make it more than two steps down the porch when I realize that Liam's Jeep is no longer in the driveway. My shoulders deflate so heavily, I'm sure I might crumble to the ground. He's gone.

None of this was supposed to happen. There wasn't *actually* supposed to be a perfect small-town man that could lure me away from all my problems in the big city. He wasn't supposed to look like a rugged, young Brad Pitt, and be the nicest, most caring person I've ever met. I feel like a balloon, the air inside me slowly deflating. A million thoughts race across my mind, all the what-ifs and maybes. But what's done is done now, and I have nowhere to go but back to my old life.

I sit on the shoulder of the Highway of Hurling for a long time before I have the strength to keep driving. The rain is coming down even harder now, drumming against the roof and the windshield, the perfect cherry on top of this nightmare day. At this point, in this joke of a romance novel that has become my life, it *should* be raining. It seems unbelievable that I'm actually sitting here, a month or so after Anne sent me on this crazy expedition, in her car, 100 miles away from home, crying over a man I met a month ago.

This was my chance, and now I've let my very own happily ever after slip out of my grasp. Now I'm headed right back to where I started.

The hole in my stomach grows deeper as I drive down the main street of Hudson Hollow. I bring the car to a near halt outside of Liz's. I try to force myself to keep going, but it's like there's a magnetic pull dragging me toward the building. I scan the parking lot, realizing that the Jeep I'm looking for isn't there. *He* isn't here.

And then I see Jill.

She's helping the kids out from the backseat of her car. As soon as she lifts Robbie, he bolts toward the restaurant. Mia follows close behind, and my heart squeezes as I watch her carefully navigate the steps, cradling a baby doll in her arms that's almost the same size as her.

I think about the character sketch I wrote yesterday on the hero's cousin who lives next door. The character came out sounding just like Jill. From the first day I met her, I knew she was someone just trying to keep everyone afloat. But by no means was she the type to wallow in self-pity. Even when we spoke at Nora's party, she said her husband leaving was more inconvenient than heartbreaking. I envied her bravery. She was confident in a way I feel like I will never be.

I pull into Liz's parking lot and park beside Jill's car. When she notices me, she smiles, warm and friendly.

"Hey, Luce," she says, slinging her pocketbook over her shoulder.

"I have to tell you something," I blurt out. Not my most glamorous intro.

She brushes a blonde curl out of her eyes and looks at me with concern.

"Is everything okay?" She looks inside, checking for the twins, who we can both see seated in a booth by the window. They're pressing their faces against the glass at us. Robbie's tongue is out.

"No, er, yes everyone is *physically* fine, but..." *Ugh*, why am I like this? I take a deep breath, trying to maintain eye contact as I explain the whole situation. "I haven't been completely honest about why I'm here."

I try to explain everything as succinctly as possible. I tell her about Anne, about the research, about Liam finding my notes. My voice becomes hoarse when I get to that part. Jill doesn't interrupt me but she looks confused, twirling her keys around her finger.

"Wait, I don't get it. You're writing a book?" she asks when I finally stop talking.

"Not me, no. I came here to get ideas for someone else's book," I explain, hanging my head in shame as I speak.

"But why lie about it?" she asks, as if it's the most obvious question in the world.

I wish my answer could be as clear-cut.

"It was part of the research, I guess it made sense

to me at the time," I say, and it feels like it's not a good enough response. She blinks. "I felt weird about it from the beginning and I should have trusted my gut." I occupy my attention with a small pebble, kicking it back and forth with my right foot.

"I've never regretted anything as much as I regret lying to Liam, to you, to everyone," I say, meeting her eyes. "I betrayed his trust, and I can't forgive myself for that."

Jill frowns. She looks like she's struggling to find the right thing to say. "Jill, I—" I start, but stop when Mia comes running toward us.

"Lucy! Come eat with us!" she squeals, wrapping her arms around my legs, her doll still in the crook of her elbow. I look up at Jill, who purses her lips to one side, as if to urge me to explain myself to Mia.

I get down to Mia's level and take her hands in mine.

"I can't today, I'm sorry." Mia sticks out her bottom lip at me. "I actually have to head home, so I may not see you for a little bit."

"But you live here," she says, swaying in my arms.

"I don't, I have to go to—" I stop myself, choking down the lump in my throat, "my home in New York City."

"When will you be back?" Mia asks petulantly. I glance at Jill and she lets out a gentle sigh.

"I'm not sure, but hey," I say, touching my finger to her nose. "I had the *mostest* fun with you while I was here. Take good care of your mom, and make sure Robbie listens to her, yeah?" Mia nods her head excitedly.

"Go ahead inside, baby. I'll be right there," Jill says. I give Mia one last hug and watch her waddle back inside. After a moment I take a deep breath and say. "Jill, I just wanted to tell you how sorry I am, I never wanted to hurt anyone."

"Lucy," she says, taking a step toward me. "I don't know exactly what happened with you and Liam, but you brought him back to life these past few weeks. I'm not saying I'm not angry, or confused, because I am," she says with a knowing look. She puts a hand on my shoulder. "But you reminded him that he still has room in his heart for someone, and I think he knows that."

I swallow the lump that her words caused in my throat. She's being too nice. Nicer than I deserve.

"I just want him to be happy, and not so hard on himself," I whisper. "He needs you. He won't admit it, but he does."

Jill nods, and after a moment she reaches over and embraces me. Her arms wrap around my back and squeeze, and I feel the tears building, threatening to spill over. "Be well, Lucy. We'll miss you."

"Me too."

TWENTY-ONE

It's July 4th and I am not watching the fireworks on Liam's boat in Hudson Hollow.

I'm not sitting on his lap in his captain's chair, wearing the sweatshirt he brought me in case I got cold, my arms wrapped around his neck. I'm on my couch, in Manhattan, throwing popcorn at the Macy's fireworks on my T.V.

"Girl, it's not Macy's fault. Stop throwing things at them," Elle scolds, plopping herself down on the couch next to me. She pulls the blanket that is draped across my legs onto hers, setting a bowl of popcorn on her lap.

She wants to say something else, I can tell. I feel her watching me. It's the same, "*Will she snap?*" look she's been giving me since I got home. I haven't been up for much talking since my tearful phone call on the ride home. I know it's been hard for her and that she's been giving me my space. But I think her patience is holding on by a thread now.

"So, are we going to talk about it?" she says in a wary tone.

When I turn my head toward her, she pops a piece of popcorn in her mouth and smacks her plump lips with a pop. I've missed her so much, I want to reach across the couch and hug her for no reason, just because I can. Because she's not a three-hour drive away, she's right here, with me, on the same piece of furniture. We're back where we belong, watching T.V., me avoiding her invasive, therapist-like questions. All is well.

Isn't it?

"I think I'm all talked out, honestly," I reply with a sigh.

"But you've barely said a word!" she whines, raising her voice.

I almost smile at her outburst, but my body catches itself. The moment my lips start to curl up, my reflexes kick in, and remind me why I am sitting where I am right now.

"I did. I told Liam everything. I was the most honest I've ever been with anyone in my life. You're always saying it's hard for people to be vulnerable," I say, gesturing to her with my hand. "Well, it *was*," I add, matter-of-factly. "I did it, and then he told me he needed space, and you know what, I don't blame him."

"You know he was hurting when he said that."

"Elle, I know you want to believe the best in people, and you really want this to work out, but this is not an *actual* romance novel. When a guy tells you he's done with you in real life, he means it."

"What are you going to do? Go back to Tinder and forget that the perfect guy already exists?" She crosses her arms and glares at me with piercing brown eyes, arching her perfect brow at me.

"I don't see what else I can do," I say, resigned. Elle leans in, taking the popcorn from my lap and placing it on the coffee table. I try to avoid her gaze for as long as possible, but she eventually draws me in.

She looks at me like I'm wounded, and the one thing she wants most in the world right now is to make it better. And usually, that's what she does. That's what we do for each other——we pick up the pieces, but this time, I think we're both at a loss.

"Lucy," she starts. "I'm so proud of you." *Always start with the positive.* Any editor knows that when you give feedback, you have to start with the good news first. "I know you'll roll your eyes at me. But Hudson Hollow changed you, and I think you know that too." I grimace at her, and she knows she's right. "You went somewhere new, on your own, met new people, and proved to yourself that you're a pretty great writer." I flutter my eyes down and fiddle with the strings on the blanket as she talks. "Think about it, you practically wrote a book, *and* you fell in love." I look at her slowly, my cheeks so hot that it feels like steam is emanating from my skin.

"Don't give me that look. I'm not telling you anything you don't already know," she adds in a confident tone. "I'm especially proud of the way you put yourself out there, how you told Liam everything," I wince when I hear his name. "And I think you will find your way back to him, and him to you. I'm manifesting it." I eye her knowingly, swallowing to try to contain my emotions. She nudges my shoulder.

"I love you, Elle. And I hope you're right."

The following day, Elle comes with me to visit my parents' house, and for the first time since I returned from upstate,

I smile; and I mean *really* smile. Seeing Josie is restorative, even if she's looking frail, and sleeping away most of the day. And when we return to our apartment on Sunday, my mind feels calmer. Seeing my family helped take my mind off worrying about Monday, and sharing with Anne everything I wrote in that little notebook, and all the guilt that comes along with it.

When Monday does arrive, my stomach is in knots. Nadine is always the first one in the office, being the newest member of the team, she's eager to please. We've tried to tell her that Nicole and Terri never show their faces before 9:30 am, and Anne usually moseys in a half hour or so later, but she refuses to risk it.

"Hey! How was your trip?" Nadine asks, standing up from her side of the wall as soon as I get to my desk.

"It was good, thanks," I say, hoping she'll leave it at that.

"It's been all Anne can talk about," she says with a knowing smile.

"Ha! No pressure then," I mumble, plopping into my chair and turning my computer on in frustration.

I want to inundate Anne with so much information that even her most specific questions are answered before she even has a chance to ask them. I organized and typed up a simpler version of my outline along with an in-depth setting description, and profiles for each character. It was *a lot* of work. If this project becomes a bestseller, I should really get a piece of the pie.

Elle was right, Hudson Hollow changed me. Even if I can't be as confident as her, I can damn well fake it. I can know my worth, and I can go for what I want. I only need to repeat that about seven thousand more times in my head.

Nicole and Terri don't bother me much when they come in, but Callie is more intrusive, asking if I met any cute guys. I shut her down with a brief answer and a look that says I'm not in the mood to talk.

"Hey!" Anne exclaims when she comes strutting past my desk. "Look how tan you are!" She drops her bag on my desk and stands there with her arms outstretched. I stand up awkwardly and hug her. Callie visually cringes next to me. I've worked here for almost three years and this has never happened.

"I can't wait to hear all about it!" she says, making her way to her own desk. I eye Elle over our divider. She's holding in a laugh.

"I have a conference room booked for us at 11 am, and a call scheduled with Ruby at 11:30," I say, handing her a pile of mail. "You asked me to remind you to email Erin back about lunch and to formally reject that submission from Kelly first thing this morning."

"My God, I've missed you," Anne says with a groan.

Mission accomplished.

"Okay, so tell me everything!" Anne says, sliding the glass door shut behind us. She sits down and props her head on her hands, giddy to hear everything I'm about to say.

"It was great," I start, swallowing hard. "It was such a... *unique* opportunity. I'm very grateful, Anne."

"I'm thrilled to hear that." I force a smile. I already feel the sweat trickling down my neck from my nerves. I desperately hope it doesn't show.

"Hudson Hollow is the perfect small town to set a

series in," I continue, handing her my write-up. "I think you sending me there was great inspiration for our—well, *Ruby's*—heroine. I'm thinking she could be a writer for a production company, sent to work on a new project in a small town. It will give us the fish-out-of-water aspect that you were kind of envisioning with me."

"That sounds great. And our love interest?" she asks, not looking up from the packet.

"A historian," I say, sliding the character profiles over to her.

"Did you get any inspiration from that neighbor guy Elle told me about?" My heart shudders at the question. She finally looks up and moves to the edge of her seat. "What happened with him, by the way?"

If she only knew the half of it.

"He was great. But this character is quite different. He's a complete alpha hero who turns out to be a cinnamon roll. Liam, er, the neighbor guy, well," I sigh, "he was a cinnamon roll through and through." I try to push the thought of him from my mind.

I look down at the time on my phone, and a reminder for our call with Ruby flashes on the screen. Anne follows my gaze, and our eyes meet a moment later.

"Ready for this?" she asks, pride in her voice.

"As I'll ever be," I murmur. Part of me can't believe I'm about to do this. I am about to tell a bestselling author, a professional, what she should write. All the hard work, the writing, the hours spent speaking into my computer, and all my work over the past three years, it's all led to this moment.

"Lucy," Anne starts, jolting me from my thoughts. I turn my attention to her, the anxious voice still mumbling in the back of my mind. "No matter what Ruby says here, I want you to know, I took the liberty of ordering you some new business cards," she says with a sly smile.

Something between a laugh and a "ha!" comes out of my mouth. "Does that mean what I think it means? Because I don't actually have business cards now..."

"You don't have business cards?" she asks, raising a brow.

"You told me assistants don't need business cards," I gently remind her.

"That does sound like me," she says sarcastically. "Well, you'll have them now."

"Anne, thank you. I really appreciate it," I say, less enthusiastically than either of us expected.

I should be elated in this moment. And part of me is—truly. Even if Elle and Josie or even Liam don't believe it, I do love this job. And I'm proud of myself for making it to this point. I did it. I got the promotion.

"What is it?" Anne asks, giving me a curious look. I'm not sure I want to tell her exactly what's going through my mind. I think she can tell that something is off, but I'm not sure she will understand. How do you explain to someone that you're unhappy when your dreams come true, because it's not actually your dream anymore?

"It's just a lot to take in," I say, trying to recompose myself. "And we still have to talk to Ruby. I'm a little overwhelmed," I admit.

"I can handle Ruby," Anne says. She reaches over and gives my shoulder a light squeeze. "You've earned this, no matter what happens today."

I finally let myself smile, but it's reserved.

My hand shakes as I dial Ruby's number on the conference phone in the middle of the table.

"Hello Ruby, how's it going?" Anne starts, putting on her friendly editor voice.

"It's going," Ruby replies. Every time I speak to Ruby—which isn't that often—she always strikes me as burnt out. She didn't get into writing until later in life, and now I think she is pushing eighty. Maybe she's tired of the business? I honestly don't know what her reasoning is for being so grumpy all the time. But everyone has their own issues, I suppose. You never know what someone is going through.

"So, what did your lackey come up with?"

Um, feeling a little less understanding now.

"*Lucy*, I can assure you, has gone above and beyond the call of duty here."

I take a deep breath, feeling assured that Anne has my back. Ruby isn't Anne's favorite person, and while she may be a bestselling author and essential to our company, Anne won't let her bully me. I'm confident in that.

"It's all you," Anne says with an encouraging nod. I press my lips in a line and try to smile back at her.

I relay the basic story elements to Ruby: the main character is a film writer who goes to a small town to research for a new movie. While there, she falls for a historian, but feels conflicted about her feelings for him. She struggles to balance her morals, her desire to impress her boss, and an impending deadline. I elaborate on a few of the side characters, and briefly go over the plot structure as I see it unfolding. Anne and Ruby remain silent, almost ambivalent, and by the end, my mouth is incredibly dry.

While I may not feel proud of how I obtained this work, I am proud of the story I came up with. I worked my ass off in Hudson Hollow, and from the look on Anne's face, I'd say she agrees.

"What do you think, Ruby?" Anne asks after a few moments.

"I—" she starts, and then sighs. Well, that's not a good sign. I crease my eyebrows at Anne.

"Ruby?" Anne prompts.

"I just don't see what is so special about it," Ruby finally says.

Okay, *rude*.

"I'm sorry?" I say. Anne reaches a hand over and gently places it on my arm.

"Why don't we talk through some of your concerns?" Anne says, the consummate professional.

"It's the whole thing, really," Ruby whines. "It just doesn't feel like me."

Maybe because you didn't come up with the ideas.

"I don't understand. You write *everything*. How could this not feel *you*?" Anne asks.

"I know, I know. I guess cowboys always felt the most authentic to me. Even with the suspense, I could model that after my favorite crime shows, but I just don't see the appeal of a city versus small town conflict."

"I understand that this would be new territory," Anne starts.

"Maybe you might feel differently if you traveled to a small town like I did," I offer, trying to salvage things. "I'm sure that could be arranged the next time you are in New York for promo." I look at Anne for validation.

"Sure, we could do that," she says with a nod.

"The town is my *least* favorite part."

Woah, bitch. Take that back.

"The people are bland, too cookie-cutter. There's nothing that makes them or the setting unique," Ruby drones.

"I don't think that's fair—" I say, but Anne squeezes my arm again.

"Ruby—" Anne starts, but Ruby cuts her off.

"I'll think about it, Anne. But I'm pretty sure this is a no." I let out a quiet gasp. "I'm disappointed of course, but maybe it is time to move on."

"Ruby—"

"We'll speak soon," Ruby interjects.

The dial tone echoes in the room.

"Well," Anne says, still staring at the speaker in the middle of the table. "Fuck."

Did that really just happen? Did I really go through all of that turmoil and stress for nothing? How—how could Ruby react like that? How could she say that my characters are cookie-cutter? They are based on some of the most amazing and caring people I've ever met in my life. How could I have failed this spectacularly?

"Anne, I'm so sorry," I say, my voice cracking.

"Please, Lucy, don't be silly. That woman has been giving me a hard time for years. She'll moan about this for a while, and then one day she'll come to me saying she has a new great idea, and this will all be water under the bridge. I just thought maybe we'd do it the easy way this time around," Anne explains, shaking her head.

Anne pats me on the shoulder as she stands. "This is not a reflection of all the great work you did, though. Please know that," she says. But how can I not take it as one? "We'll figure something out. Maybe another author can use your ideas." Anne squeezes my shoulder and slips out of the room.

I crumple in my seat, bringing my hand to my head, and let out a loud exhale.

I failed. I hurt Liam, I hurt Jill, I hurt everyone... for nothing.

I got what I wanted—what I *thought* I wanted. I'm an assistant editor. But this win, if that's what it can be called, feels hollow now. Because what I want now is so different from what I wanted six weeks ago. I want so badly for this story to have a life, for all the little pieces of my soul that went into this outline to thrive on a shelf somewhere.

I can feel Anne's gaze from the other side of the glass, and I retreat into an invisible shell around my body. I want to go home and curl up in my bed and pour over my notes, because that's the only way I will feel close to Liam. That's what I want most of all. I want to be sitting on his deck, his fingers entwined with mine, smelling smoke from his firepit and listening to the giggles of Robbie and Mia on the grass below us. I want to be back in Hudson Hollow.

Today was supposed to be one of the best days of my life—I finally have the promotion I've waited years for. But now it's lost its meaning. Now, all I can think about is Liam, and Hudson Hollow, the past six weeks of my life that brough so much joy and self-discovery. Maybe the only way I can do that is to write this book myself.

If Ruby doesn't want this story, fine. Because I do.

TWENTY-TWO

Liam,

Starting a text like a letter feels odd, but since you haven't responded to my calls or messages for weeks, a bit of formality seems warranted. I know you don't want to speak to me right now, and I understand why, but I just have to get this off my chest.

I know what you've been through this past year, and I am so sorry for being dishonest with you. I know I don't deserve your forgiveness, but I care about you so much, and I would give anything to go back in time and tell you the truth from the very beginning

No matter what happens, I hope you're happy, Liam Miller. I hope you watch a sunset every once in a while and think of me. I think about you every day, and I miss you.

Lucy x

★

July flies by.

My schedule beings to settle into something resembling normalcy, helped by the slower pace of summer in the publishing world, which all but dozes off this time of year. Instead of burning the midnight oil until a hungry stomach forces me to stop, I can leave the office at a decent hour. Elle and I even make the most of summer hours, embracing the season's rare leniency with a sense of well-earned freedom.

Anne was right, and Ruby doesn't make the decision to terminate her contract, which Anne says our contracts department would never allow her to do. She claims she'll spend a month brainstorming a new series, and we'll reevaluate at the end of the summer.

Meanwhile, I spend any moment I'm not working, eating, or sleeping, writing.

And I don't tell Anne about it.

I barely touch my Instagram, because although I'm writing a romance novel, I can't seem to face the fact that I'm no longer living in one. A few followers even message me, asking if I'd ever tell them the secret project I was working on. I don't answer because I don't really *have* an answer.

Writing is not an easy process. And any Tom, Dick, or Harry who says they can "probably write a book" can go to hell. They can't. And anyone who has written one deserves a medal. Deleting all the extraneous uses of the word "just" from a document should be deserving enough of a reward.

What makes the process even more difficult is the fact that even though these characters aren't based on *my* people— the *real* people of Hudson Hollow—and even though it's not exactly *my* story, it certainly feels like it. I've changed the characters' motivations and personalities significantly, especially the hero and heroine, but the experiences they have together, they all lead back to Liam for me.

Instead of a mountain top, I make the hero's "Spider-Man spot" an inlet behind his house. It's a piece of land that juts out into the lake, with a long, winding path that leads to a small clearing with a pebbly beach. I wrote about it one night after Elle had fallen asleep and I was sitting in bed, in the dark with my laptop on my lap. I didn't realize I was crying until I wrote the last line of the chapter and a tear dropped on my keyboard.

Love scenes are the hardest. I can build tension between the couple, but when I try to get them together, I draw a blank. My fingers are incapable of moving across the keys. It's not that I don't know how to write about two people falling in love or depict them being intimate with one another. It's that every time I try to write about the hero *tracing his knuckle along her collarbone* or *placing his large hand around her ribcage and pressing her against a wall*, all I see is Liam.

I see him leaning over me, his elbow on the top of his Jeep, looking down at me, his blonde hair blocking his eyes. I remember myself longing to touch my lips to his, just to see what he tasted like, to close the distance between us that felt like magnets at different poles.

I remember him reaching over and rubbing his thumb in circles on my knee while he drove me home from Nora's party. I remember memorizing the rhythm of his fingers, matching my breaths with his circles to keep the nausea at bay.

I remember kissing him.

I remember his mouth covering mine so gently, that it barely even touched me. If I close my eyes, I can feel his tongue tracing the outline of my lips before he moved it in tandem with mine. I can feel the pressure of his hands against my hips, pressing me into the side of the house.

I can feel him.

I try not to write those scenes before bed anymore, because if I do, I don't sleep. I toss and turn to the memory of him. I writhe in the guilt, the shame of manipulating his feelings, and the ache of missing him.

But still, I write.

Because if I don't, what will it all have been for?

By the second week of August, I'm at fifty thousand words when my word tracker app expected me to be at thirty thousand. By then, Elle is also so sick of me refusing her invitations to go out on the weekends that she is ready to throw me out of the window just to get me out of the apartment.

But all the personal drama I impress upon myself with my writing dream and pining over Liam is nothing compared to the battle Josie has gone through. Stage Four pancreatic cancer can go fly a kite.

I rent a car and drive home every weekend. That is, in addition to the days that my mom and Josie spend at doctor's offices in the city, or nights they stay at our apartment, when Elle and I get to sleep on the pull-out couch together like Joey and Chandler. By the end of July, we had a pretty good picture of how impossible her battle is. By August, she convinced us all that the only one who can decide to fight is her. And she is tired.

She tells me one weekend at the beginning of August, when we're sitting on the deck at my parents' house. My laptop is wedged on my thighs in a lounge chair, and Josie is sprawled out next to me in an over-the-top yellow cover-up with a wicker visor and sunglasses that are two sizes too big for her slowly sinking face. The sun is high in the sky, beating down on us like the world's most powerful heat lamp. "Do you want some lemonade, Jo?" It's so hot out here, it won't take long for either of us to get dehydrated.

"Lucille," she groans, not turning her head to look at me. "Please stop hovering over me like I could just evaporate into dust at any moment."

"Okay, rude, Sassy Pants," I say, flicking her arm. She gasps at me.

"You can't flick me. I'm dying!" she says, wagging a pointed finger at me.

I throw my hands up in the air. "You're dying but I'm not allowed to offer you lemonade? Double standards," I grunt. Finally, she sits up, reaching a hand for me to pull her up from a prone position. "What's the matter? Do you want to go in?" I ask, concerned by how clammy her skin is.

She flicks me.

"Jo!" I whine.

"What I want, my love," she starts, taking a breath after every few words, "is for you to stop treating me like I'm a glass vase on the edge of a counter." She reaches her hands out and places them on either side of my face. Her fingers feel more wrinkled, but still soft in signature Josie fashion.

"Well, that is a very silly analogy," I reply. "I would just move the vase off the edge of the counter. I only wish I could do that with you."

She sighs. I take hold of each of her wrists, and squeeze them, wishing I could hold on to her, hold her still, keep her here, in one place, just a moment longer. It's the same wish I've had my entire life—when holidays were cut too short, birthdays spent over video calls, moments of happiness with a bitter taste of the knowledge they would end in goodbye. But this goodbye will hurt the most of all. And we both know it.

"Lucy, you know I can't keep this up," she says, her hands sliding to my neck. I inhale sharply, but my breath stops short like the air can't physically get past the sob in my throat. "I don't want to fight anymore. I don't have it in me."

"I don't think you tried hard enough," I whisper, feeling a crack in my voice.

"You're right. Because I knew I wasn't going to win." She brushes some strands of hair out of my face, cupping her fingers under my chin. "I would rather spend my last few months just like this, in these special moments with you, than in a hospital. You know I have to do things my way." *I know*, I say in my head. And in true Josie fashion, she's choosing to act like dying is her idea. *I'm going to die, but not because cancer told me to*. Classic.

"Well, then you should have made this decision sooner. We could have been living our best small town lives sewing shit and growing shit and—" I stop talking when Josie wipes a tear off my cheek.

"We have been living our best lives, honey," she says with a laugh. "Every moment out in the sun. If I squint, I can pretend I'm on the coast of Nice instead of the depths of suburbia." I let out a laugh, my nose stuffing with the water building in my eyes. "And you are going to continue to do so. You're going to finish this book. Not for your boss or for me or to prove to your parents or society that you can. You're going to do it for you." She takes a breath, wrapping her arms around me. "I'm so proud of you, my Lucy Loo."

Three weeks later, Josie is gone.

She does it dramatically and on her terms. She lays out in the sun, a smutty book in her hand, and closes her eyes. Part of me wishes she had better planning skills, because she would be the perfect person to have a living memorial for. She would have gotten a kick out of it. Instead, we go all out for her. After the funeral, we drink Bloody Marys and play the music too loudly. Any passerby might have thought we were having a pool party, but we were simply partying on the coast of France, just like Josie would have wished it. I cry more that day than I ever have in my life, knowing that Josie would be shaking her head at me the entire time. *What's the cry about?* She would say. *I'm in Heaven. The digs here are great.*

I have a hard time getting back to work. Elle comes to my parents' house to physically bring me back to the city. Because if I go back, then that means life has to return to normal. And my life can't be normal without one of my favorite people in it. I can't watch millions of people walk by me on the streets of New York, acting as if the entire world hasn't just shifted on its axis when Josie's soul left this plane. How could anything be normal anymore?

And yet I go. I go through the motions of everyday life, trying to convince myself that tomorrow will be better. And every night, I go to the roof of our building and watch the sunset, earlier and earlier with each passing day. I watch the sky change from blue to yellow, to orange, sometimes to purple and pink, and I think of a boy, hundreds of miles away, who might just be watching the same thing. And I think of my aunt, wondering if she can see the sunset where she is.

Josie lived her life to the fullest, and she loved how cliché that sounded. She loved to be the topic of conversation, especially disapproving conversation, in which people would scandalize her for chasing her dreams, working too much, spending too much money, smoking too much, and drinking even more. She said everyone was jealous of her. And she was right. We were.

With every day that passes without her, I become more jealous of my aunt's ability to decide for herself—what she wanted, what she did, where she lived. I'm jealous of her ability not to give a flying fuck what anyone said about it.

I'm jealous because I can't do the same.

TWENTY-THREE

It's not until the end of August that I finally return to my book.

Life without Josie is quiet. There's too much space for my thoughts to drift—to Liam, to a future without my wonderfully eccentric aunt, to the possibility that someone might *actually* believe my book has value, forcing me to confront my career. Writing feels impossible with a mind this still. The quiet amplifies every doubt, every worry, every stray thought clamoring for attention.

In the scene where I left off, the heroine wrestles with the decision to return home after weeks spent pouring herself into the screenplay for her film. She's finally admitted that she loves the hero, but the reality of the distance between them looms large. And she isn't prepared to risk her career, no matter how deep her feelings run, however much she might love small-town life.

It's at this point that I realize that I'm not exactly sure how this book is going to end. In my outline and synopsis, I kind of left that as a "TBD" or a "TK" as we put on everything in publishing (and no one really knows why). I know the couple is going to get together in the end, but I'm not exactly settled on how that is going to happen.

In romance books, there are really only two options for an ending: happily ever after or happy for now. The first implies that the couple's story is complete, and they will be together—married, with children, or a proposal, up to interpretation—forever. "Happy for now" means that the couple has overcome the great obstacle that threatened to tear them apart in the book. "Happy for now" leaves the opportunity for a sequel.

I've always thought of "happily ever after" as a big commitment, especially if the story includes some kind of instant love. I love romance, so much so that I've made a career out of it, but not every aspect of it is my favorite. I've never bought into the plots that have the couple fall in love within a matter of days. At the end of the book, they profess that they can't live without each other, or they'd die for one another, when they haven't even eaten a meal together.

Happily ever after also says a lot about the couple's future. Someday we'll be happy. We'll be happy forever. Fifty years from now, we'll find true happiness. And I just have one question to pose to Disney, Cinderella, and romance writers everywhere: what about *now*? Why can't our happiness focus on the here and now? Maybe we should say "screw the future" because, as corny as it sounds, it's not promised. Maybe we should make "happily ever now" the new "happily ever after."

I scroll to the first page of my document and type in all capitals:

HAPPILY EVER NOW

The next morning, I send the first 200 pages to Anne, with the subject line in the email reading, "Surprise."

Elle says it's the most spontaneous thing I've ever done.

When Anne walks into work that morning, I immediately drag her into a conference room.

"Please tell me you're pregnant with the chef guy's baby. That would be the best plot twist ever," she says as I lead her by the arm through the glass door. I slide it closed behind me.

"What? No. And no it wouldn't." I look down at myself. "Do I look pregnant?"

"Of course not, but a little excitement around here wouldn't hurt," she says, rolling her eyes.

I shake my head. "Anne, I have to tell you something, and I don't know how you're going to react, or even if it's something I'm allowed to do. But here it is," I say, my mind working faster than my words. "I wrote the book."

"What book?" she replies immediately.

"The Hudson Hollow book. I've been working on it all summer. And I know it might be a legal problem because technically I was taking notes and working for the imprint, but I just felt like it was my story to tell. I've always wanted to write; I've tried in the past. And after Ruby said no to it, I just, it just came flowing out of me." I try to gauge Anne's reaction on her face, but she's neutral. This feels like the biggest news I've ever shared in my life, and she hasn't even batted an eye.

"The first 200 pages are in your inbox, and I would love it if you would read it, but I understand if it's a conflict of interest."

Anne doesn't say anything for a solid minute.

Seriously, sixty seconds never passed so slowly.

The whole time, she stares at me, squinting one eye like she's trying to evaluate my credibility. She purses her lips to one side, holding her chin between her fingers.

Ninety seconds.

"Anne—"

"Lucy," she finally starts. "Please stop being in such knots about this. I think it's great. It's a little unorthodox, sure, but unorthodox is kind of my style. Before we talk about conflicts of interest, let me at least take a look and see if it's any good."

Blunt, but okay.

I nod, exhaling for the first time in what feels like all morning.

Anne takes all week to read it.

Yes, I understand that it's not a one-chapter sample, but we're editors, folks, we're inherently fast readers. If we read something we like, we can have it done in a day. Two maximum.

But no. Anne waits until Thursday, a whole four days after I sent her the partial to tell me to schedule a meeting for us the following day. Making it Friday before she plans on even discussing it with me. Five. Days. Later.

I am in agony for those five days. Well, to be fair, Elle is probably in more agony because she has to put up with me. I pace. I snap. I groan. I barely sleep which just makes me crankier. I seriously reconsider my dream of being a writer, because I may not be able to handle the anticipation of critique all that well.

I may have been drinking too much coffee this week as well. My intake might have increased to compensate for the lack of sleep. Whoops.

By the time I make it to the small conference room with Anne on Friday morning, I'm ready to burst. Knowing myself and my inability to keep my mouth shut when it should be, I start talking before my butt even hits the chair. "It's just a first draft," I start, wringing my hands like a wet towel. "I can change and move things around—"

Anne raises a finger at me.

I close my mouth and clench my teeth. She takes her seat and calmly places her notebook down in front of her. Maybe she only looks so calm because I am so visibly not. I take a deep breath to try to still my internal vibration that is out of control. I place my hands on my lap and try to appear much cooler than I am.

"I really like it so far," she says, placing her hands on the table to mimic my position.

"*Really?*" I say in disbelief. Anne nods and opens her notebook.

"It's lovely. The characters are well-developed, it's steamy but not too much to be in keeping with the small-town audience that we usually have. I like the backstories and the setting is just perfect. You clearly took your time writing down everything you saw while you were there. It shows." I smile proudly. There is truly nothing better than working hard and being recognized for it. "But—"

Whoop, there it is.

I give Anne a weak smile and nod, urging her to go on. In my wildest dreams I didn't imagine walking into this meeting to no criticism, so a "but" at the end of the compliment is more than palatable.

"I don't really see where it's going at this point," she finishes with an awkward look on her face.

"Do you mean it's not predictable?" I ask, trying to clarify her words.

"Well, we don't want it to be predictable, do we?" I shake my head. "What I'm saying is that you've built this world and these characters and I feel like the writing is fading off toward the end. Like you're not sure where you want to go."

"Well, it's a romance so there are only a few options," I joke.

"Do you know what happens next? I don't exactly recall from your outlines," she says, flipping through her notes as if the answer will somehow be in there.

"The ending has always been a bit fuzzy for me," I admit, looking down at my hands. Why wasn't I more prepared for this question? Why didn't I have an outline for the end prepared?

"Why do you think that is?" Anne asks, sitting back and tilting her head.

I let out a loud breath and do what has come to be a natural behavior in the recent weeks, I think of Liam.

While I may have changed a bit of the story to distance it from Liam and I, the truth is, every word that my main character says about her hero are my words. They're my feelings. My feelings about Liam. And the reason I can't pinpoint an ending for their story is because I didn't get one for mine.

"Here's the thing," I start, sitting forward and making eye contact with Anne. "You know how I told you about that guy I met? How I thought we had something?"

"Of course," Anne says, nodding quickly.

"Well, it was a bit more serious than I told you. At least,

I thought it was. But when he found out that I was there to collect information for the imprint, he felt like he couldn't trust me anymore. Which is very understandable," I say, swallowing the sob in my throat and looking down to hide my glassy eyes.

"Oh, sweetie, I'm sorry," she says, placing a hand over mine.

"I think—I think the reason I'm struggling with the ending of this book is because it's based so much on my story and my story didn't have an ending. Not a good one anyway." I let out a long breath when I finish talking, all the emotions from that day with Liam flooding my mind and making my body quake with sadness. I sniffle softly and pull myself together. I won't be the girl who cries in front of her boss. I won't.

"Lucy, are you alright?" Anne asks, leaning toward me.

Am I? I really don't think so.

What would make me okay? Isn't that what Elle is always asking me? What do I want? I thought I wanted this promotion, Anne telling me I could acquire books, that I could finally move forward at the company. Then I thought it was Anne telling me that she would read the book. And she's done that. And yet, something is still missing.

The end of my story. The place where I feel at home. The clear path I've been looking for my entire life.

That's what's missing.

And the thing is, I found it. Somewhere I never thought possible.

What do I want? What would make me be okay?

Liam.

Sitting on his deck, Blue curled around my feet, Liam

coming up behind me to wrap a blanket around me while we drink coffee on a misty morning. Helping him load the twins onto the boat for a day on the lake, Blue begrudgingly standing on the boat in his life jacket. Hiking up to The Point for a dinnertime picnic after a long day of writing.

All this time, I thought dreams like that were just that... dreams. I thought ideas like that belonged in books, and only in books.

I want a life like one in a romance novel. I want a man in a dark Henley leaning up against my doorway with his forearms flexed. I want passion and excitement. I want devotion and heart-aching love.

Maybe when I first started in this business, maybe even just a few months ago, I saw romance as a dream. I've loved romance novels since I was in high school. They were my escape from the mediocre life I found myself trapped in.

Maybe romance used to be an escape for me. But after years of believing true love was nothing but a fantasy, I'm starting to think... no, I know, it's what I deserve.

"I'm really not," I finally stutter, breaking out of my catatonic state, and blinking my way back to clarity. "Anne, I don't think I can do this."

How has it taken me this long to realize so much about myself? I'm always thinking about what everyone else around me is thinking. I picture how situations will work out for everyone else, besides myself. I thought I wanted to be in publishing, but maybe that was just some way to appease my parents' dream for me to live a corporate life. I thought I wanted to live in the city because that's where publishing was. I thought living in the city would be like my favorite episodes of *Friends*, when really, it's nothing like that at all. I was justifying my choices by having to explain them to people, and I could never answer the question: *What do I want?*

And now the answer has never been clearer.

Anne is taken aback. "Do what? Finish the book?" I look down at the papers in her hand, the neurons in my brain making their way back to full capacity, then forging into overload.

"No, I mean, yes. I can. But not yet. I can't finish it yet because I don't know how it ends." Anne looks at me quizzically. I stand up abruptly and start to walk out of the room, but I turn back and lean against the desk across from her. "I really hope you're serious about publishing this book. Because if you are, I'll write you another one and another one and another one. Because I don't think I can be your assistant anymore. Or even your assistant editor. This isn't how my story ends. And I have to go find out how it does."

"And where are you going to do that?"

"Hudson Hollow."

The smile on Anne's face is unlike any expression I've ever seen her make. "I was hoping you would say that." With that, she jolts out of her chair and rushes out of the room before I can comprehend what she said.

I furrow my brows and awkwardly follow her into the hall. The people in the rows of cubicles are staring at us like they're angry librarians and we coughed in a silent library.

"Um, Anne?" I say, peeking my head out of the conference room. She's already back at our desks. I grab my stuff from the conference room and speed-walk back to our row. Anne is waving her hands at the rest of our team. "Anne, what are you doing?"

She pulls out her phone and starts typing ferociously. "Going to Hudson Hollow," she says matter-of-factly.

"*What?*" Elle and I say at the same time. Nicole, Terri, Callie, and Nadine take their earphones out to see what the commotion is about.

"What are you talking about?" I ask, my heart starting to race a bit.

"Exactly what I said," Anne says, finally looking up at me. "We're going to get you an ending to your story."

"What's going on?" Nicole chimes in, all of us now standing around our desks and attracting the attention of the entire department.

"Anne, that's crazy—" I start. "I—I didn't really think it was a group kind of thing," I say, staring at my boss in disbelief. Did I not explain myself well? It almost kind of sounded like I quit back there, and this was definitely not the response I was expecting. This is supposed to be my big montage moment, where I decide what I want and go get it. Anne is kind of stealing my thunder here.

"Where are we going?" Nadine asks, rounding the corner with Elle and Terri to be closer to the conversation.

"Hudson Hollow," Anne answers.

Elle smiles brilliantly. "You're going back? You're going to tell him you love him?" She runs down the line of cubicles, drawing the attention of the rest of the floor.

"Tell who, what?" Callie asks, swinging her chair back from her desk.

"Liam, the chef guy. She loves him and we're all going

to Hudson Hollow to find an ending to her book," Anne explains, dialing her phone.

"I'm sorry, *we all*?" I say, looking between my co-workers. I turn my attention back to Anne and she raises her phone to her ear and puts up a finger to silence me. "Hey babe, I have a work emergency, I have to run up to the Catskills... I'll explain everything later..."

"This is not a work emergency!" I whine in a whisper. "This is the exact *opposite* of a work emergency!"

"We're all going!" Elle announces, and I look at her like she's gone mad. How did this get so out of hand?

I look around at the rest of the team. "I have to say, I think that might look a little bit like we're ganging up on him," I say with a look of hesitancy on my face.

"We won't all *talk* to him!" Elle says in an obvious tone. "Come on, ladies! Let's get going!" The women jump up and we all begin to gather our belongings.

"This is so exciting!" Callie squeals, throwing miscellaneous items into her purse. Nicole and Terri look unsure but Anne is already halfway to the door.

"Nicole, Terri, let's go! Time to be a little spontaneous! Don't you want to see how this turns out?" she calls from the end of our aisle of cubicles.

"I do," Nadine says, slinging her bag over her shoulder.

"Nadine, find out what time the next bus is. Let's get a move on!" Anne says, clapping her hands. I look over at the desk of our publisher, who is turned around with a curious look on his face. Anne follows my gaze and gives me a wide-eyed look. She really didn't think this through. "Team-building exercise!" she yells across the floor. "As you were!"

Wow, Heartwarming Love Stories has really gone to the zoo today.

TWENTY-FOUR

Once we're on the bus, it all clicks into focus—this is happening. The feeling in my stomach churns with a chaotic mix of anticipation, excitement and dread, like I'm perched at the apex of a roller coaster, bracing for the inevitable drop. The journey here felt like the agonizing climb, each turn of the wheels cranking me up, inch by inch. Now there's no going back. The only thing left to do is to hold tight, steady my breath, and resist the urge to let the adrenaline spill over.

Elle spends the entire ride trying to calm me down. Every time she places a hand on my shaking leg, it ceases for a moment, but minutes later it's revving again, and I'm unable to control it. We're not the only ones on the bus, so when she blasts music from her phone and tries to start a dance party, it's ill-received by the rest of the riders. I manage to grab her and pull her back into her seat just before she flips them all off.

"Tough crowd," she groans and the team laughs at her.

"There's really a delay in the excitement here, Anne," Nicole says, leaning over her seat to talk to Anne.

"Well, I didn't make the town so far away," Anne whines.

"I know. I just feel like in the movies when there's a grand romantic gesture or a chase, they don't show you the boring bus ride the heroine takes to get there," Nicole says, shooting me a knowing look.

"Thank you for making me even more nervous," I say, hitting my head against the seat.

"There's nothing to be nervous about," Elle says, hitting my thigh. "This is going to be great. Happy ever afters all around!"

"If you say one more obnoxious, upbeat thing, I'm going to punch you," I say, raising my fist.

"Noted," she replies with a nod.

I text my mom to say that Elle and I have decided to take a spontaneous trip upstate for the long weekend and I'll call her tomorrow. I can't believe I'm really doing this. My mother texts back her equivalent of "WTF," which is mainly just a bunch of question marks. I explain that it was very last minute and that we are staying in the same place I lived for a month, and not to worry. She tries to call me, but I text her saying I don't have good service. I need to compartmentalize right now. One thing at a time.

I can feel Josie with me every step of the way. I can feel her courage in my heart. I can hear her cheering for me in my brain. She is getting a kick out of this. I know it.

I can't stop my mind from racing the entire ride there. What if I get there and he refuses to see me? I won't give him the option. This is the stuff of romance novels, dammit, and I'm going to get my high-stakes ending, even if I have to fight for it. I'll say what I have to say and if he really doesn't feel the same way, then at least I'll know that I tried. I would have tried to make a commitment and be vulnerable for the first time in my life. And if he does feel the same way? I'm not sure what to do with that ending actually...

We live three hours away from each other. I realize it's not 3,000 miles, but it's not right around the corner. We have established lives in separate places, and I don't know if he's going to want to commit to something like that. I stop myself. I'm doing it again. I'm thinking of all the reasons why this won't work instead of focusing on the one important reason that it should—it will: I love Liam. These last few months without him, I've been frozen. It was like I was only going through the motions and watching my life happen from a movie theater seat. The only thing I was invested in was the book, and mostly because it felt like spending time with Liam again. I could delve right back into our story at all the good parts and feel the way I did when I was with him. I feel a smile form on my face at the thought. A montage of my favorite moments with him passes through my mind and the feeling in my chest reminds me why I'm doing this. I want that feeling back. Elle is right, I deserve it.

I scan my phone for a photo from my time in Hudson Hollow and find one I took of Liam while his back was turned at The Point. I don't want to post a photo of his face to my public Instagram, so I decide this one works best. His broad shoulders are perfectly framed, and the mountains in the distance look like they could have been painted, they are so perfect. Looking at that view makes my heart clench in a way I've never felt before. Is it excitement? Like this thing I'm doing right now—putting myself out there, making a change, being honest with myself about what I want—might actually be a good thing?

> A lot of you may have noticed I've been MIA lately, and some have even messaged me wondering why. My trip earlier this summer was work related, but eventually became more than that. Thanks to this man right here.
>
> He doesn't follow this account, so I can say anything I want about him. Most importantly, that I love him. He doesn't know this yet, but I hope he will soon. (continued in comments)
>
> Before my trip, I was having a hard time (well, more than a hard time) finding the joy of HEAs in my real life. There's only so many times you can be ghosted before you start to lose hope. When I went to a small town for a project (that is still under wraps!), I thought it was ridiculous. I thought it would be a complete waste of my time. But instead, I found everything I've been looking for my entire life.
>
> I'm not sure how this story will end. But whatever way it goes, I promise not to doubt HEAs again. They're out there. I know it.

Anne orders an Uber when there's twenty minutes to go on our trip, because unlike Manhattan, there's not exactly one waiting on every corner in Catskill. The knots in my stomach had loosened somewhat in the last hour of the ride, but when I start to see the familiar signs, they clench right back up. Not least of all because I still haven't figured out one word of what I'm going to say to Liam.

"Are you ready?" Elle asks as we squeeze into the minivan with one too few seats for us.

"Not at all," I mumble. The driver looks at us like we're nuts. As I look around—Nadine, Callie, Elle, and I are squished together in the third row, Terri and Nicole are in the captain's chairs and Anne is chattering the driver's ear off without looking up from her phone—I realize that we are a little nuts. I also realize that this group of women has become so important to me over the last few years. When I moved to the city, I didn't have a solid group of friends to ground me and help me find my way. Since working at Heartwarming, I've found a family. I didn't recognize that until this moment, as I make the most impulsive and scary decision of my life, that these people are here for *me*. They may be here out of sheer curiosity—Terri in particular—but they are here to support me. And that's a pretty good feeling.

When I see a sign that says "Welcome to Historic Hudson Hollow," I think my heart might just pound right out of my chest. I swallow hard as we enter the town and tell Anne to stop in front of Liz's with a shaky voice. I can't believe I'm here. I can't believe I'm doing this.

"Is it too late to go home?" I ask Elle, wrapping a death grip around her forearm.

"Yes," she says confidently. I roll my eyes at her. We all climb out of the cab like clowns exiting a P.T. Cruiser on the opposite side of the street from Liz's. It's scorching hot out, and I have to cover my eyes to shield myself from the sun.

I approach the doors of the restaurant slowly, as if there is some dreadful form of doom waiting for me on the other side. Elle must sense it, because she's Elle, and she wraps her arm around my elbow. I look over as she gives me a reassuring smile. Anne takes a few steps around me to get to the door. She smiles a gummy smile which squeezes her glasses up her nose as she opens it.

My stomach clenches as I step into the restaurant. The familiar scent of flat-top grilled burgers and maple syrup hits me and I feel a wave of something wash over me. Relief? Comfort?

Home.

I feel home.

Maybe this was a mistake. Maybe I'm setting myself up for failure here. Because if Liam still doesn't want to see me, and just being in Hudson Hollow for two minutes makes me feel this good... what will I do if I never set foot here again?

"Lucy!" I turn around at the sound of a deep voice bellowing my name. I see Max and May heading toward me from a booth in the back. My eyes start to travel behind the bar, but I don't see Liam anywhere.

"Hey, Max!" I smile as he puts the box he was carrying down and makes his way over to us. The rest of my traveling Motley Crew are still making their way into the restaurant.

"It's so nice to see you. What are you doing here?" Max asks, giving me an awkward hug.

I exhale, feeling like I'm admitting to a crime. "I'm looking for Liam," I say with a hesitant smile. I see in Max's eyes that he's curious about the backstory behind my statement, but I really don't want to go through it all right now. After a moment, he smiles confidently, giving me a knowing look of approval.

"I knew there was something going on between you two," May interjects as she embraces me. She looks around at the crowd of Heartwarming employees behind me looking very out of place.

"Sure you did, May," Max says sarcastically.

"I can't wait to tell Mella; she'll be so happy that you found your way back to us," May says, beaming.

The air is heavy with expectation between us. I'm waiting for them to say something or for Liam to walk out of the kitchen, but neither happens.

"LIAM!" Elle screams into the restaurant, causing us all to jump.

"Elle!" I scold in a whisper.

"What? No one spoke for like thirty seconds," she says, widening her eyes as if her actions were warranted. "We're all kind of on edge with anticipation here."

May and Max look at each other grimly, and then back at me, but their eyes are full of pity.

"He's not here," May says solemnly and something in my chest drops.

"He's meeting suppliers out west this weekend. He won't be back until Monday," Max adds.

I inhale sharply, a mixture of relief and disbelief swirling in my stomach. I feel Elle's hand on my arm, but her words don't register in my mind. This was the single most ambitious and exciting thing I've done in my life, and it was all for nothing.

"Lucy, I'm so sorry, sweetheart," Anne says from behind me. I feel a soft hand on my back.

I shake my head quickly. "It's fine—" I start.

"Of course it is," Elle interjects. "This changes nothing. You still want to see him. You still need to talk to him. This is not the end."

"Of course not," Anne adds. "It may just be the end of today's adventure," Anne says with a reassuring smile.

My face suddenly feels very hot, like the reality of the situation has finally hit home with my nervous system. I came all this way, and Liam is not here.

That makes my stomach lurch.

"We should go," I mutter.

"You guys should have something to eat," May starts, placing a hand on my forearm.

"That's sweet, May, but I don't think I could eat anything right now." I feel Elle's eyes on me like lasers as I talk. "You guys get something for the road if you want," I say to the team. I quickly embrace May. "It was so good to see you guys again," I stumble over my words as I move from one Lucia to another. "I'll go outside and call an Uber."

I turn and walk out the door of Liam's restaurant, feeling like a hole is growing in my heart with each step I take. When I see the mountains in the distance, as picturesque as the day I first saw them, I yearn for the feeling of reassurance I thought I would feel when I saw Liam again. I thought I would feel like this choice, this crazy spontaneous choice that I made for myself, that it was right. That I was finally doing something for myself and it was going to pay off.

But instead, I feel regret. I feel ashamed. My entire team of colleagues just saw me crash and burn. But that is not the worst part. The most significant piece of emptiness I feel comes from the unknown. If I made this jump once, will I ever be able to do it again? At this point in a romance novel, the hero should be in the place where the heroine goes to confront him. This is the happy ever after, *right now*. And yet, for me, it's not. What comes next in my story?

The bus ride back to Manhattan might be the most silent the Heartwarming team has ever been in the time that I've known them. Elle tries and tries and fails to get me to speak about the clusterfuck of a situation I just found myself in. She holds my hand for most of the ride, squeezing it occasionally when she sees me gazing out the window without blinking for too long.

When we arrive back in the city, it's just about the end of the workday, so we all head back to the office together to gather our belongings for the weekend. Elle was supposed to go to her mom's in Jersey for the weekend and she invites me to go with her, but I decline. I know by the time we get back to our desks, she'll have found an excuse to stay at the apartment with me instead.

We walk from Port Authority to our office on Sixth Avenue, the warm breeze of late August blowing my hair along the way. I'm in a daze as we exit the elevator into our lobby. I've been staring at the floor for most of the walk anyway. As we turn to enter the glass doors of our department, Elle stops suddenly, her sandals scuffing on the floor. She places a palm on my arm and my head snaps up, looking for any signs of danger.

"What's wrong?" I say, but before the last syllable is out of my mouth, I see a wisp of blonde hair in my peripheral vision.

Holy shit.

He is standing at the reception desk, a line of sweat showing through the back of his uniform black T-shirt. His hair is longer, the end of the waves reaching the bottom of his neck. The secretary sees me before he does. But not five seconds pass before he turns around.

"Lucy," my name is an exhale on his lips. I don't say anything for a moment, and I'm sure the look on my face is not the least bit attractive, so Elle slaps my side so hard I wince into focus.

"Oh," is all I manage.

"Do better than that," Elle commands, awkwardly.

The whole of the Heartwarming imprint is still behind me and the secretary and the few workers still left at their cubicles are now watching this spectacle unfold. Great. This is great.

"Lucy, I'm sorry to just show up like this—"

"Stop." My voice even surprises myself. Elle looks at me concerned, and then smirks. She ushers the rest of the team to the side, giving Liam and me some space. Liam's face is stoic, his brows arched in concern.

"I'm sorry," I stutter. I flex my hands at my sides. I try to alternate glances between Liam and the floor until I find my courage, and the two dozen eyes watching me are not helping.

"I'm sorry, that came out harsh. I just mean—" I take a deep breath and finally meet Liam's eyes. On my exhale, I let his gaze wash over me like a comforting wave. Liam is here. He came to Heartwarming to see me.

I push my disbelief to the side and inhale another breath.

"I need you to ask me where I just was. Don't say anything else. Just ask me."

Liam looks at me and tilts his head. "Where were you?"

"Hudson Hollow," I reply without missing a beat. His confusion deepens and then he smiles.

"You see," I start. "I had to go there… to tell you I love you."

I swallow hard. It's not because there's a bunch of people watching us or because I'm embarrassed, but because I've finally said the words I couldn't all those weeks ago. That afternoon when Liam was so angry, and I was so desperate to explain myself, I wanted to say those words, and I couldn't. And I've spent the last two months wondering if he even noticed my hesitation or felt the same.

"I like… really love you," I blurt out. Liam lets out a soft chuckle, and a bit of the pressure releases from my chest. I shake my head, mad at myself for sounding like such an idiot when this should be my eloquent, heroine grovel moment. But Liam is smiling. He's not angry. He's not walking away. He's coming toward me.

"And not just because you feed me delicious food all the time and don't judge me when I embarrass myself at a baby's birthday party," I say with a laugh. "But because you're the kindest, most empathetic, caring, and fun man I've ever met. I love how you love your town. I love how you love the people in it. I love that you're a dorky dog dad that sets up baby monitors for his German Shepherd." Liam bellows "Ha!" that reverberates through the office.

"Most of all, I love how you make me feel. I love being around you, and I'm sorry. I'm so, *so*, sorry for lying to you. I'm sorry for hurting you. But the last two months without you have been miserable. So, if you give me a chance, I promise never to knowingly lie or hurt you again. Because I love you, Liam Miller. A lot."

We are quiet for a moment, but I don't break my gaze with Liam. Speaking my truth, telling him how I feel, has given me a confidence that I didn't have moments ago. The adrenaline I felt when I was back in Hudson Hollow is back, and I need Liam to speak. I need to know what he is thinking.

"So, you're the romance expert," he starts, his hand reaching for mine. I shudder at the sound of his voice. I can't believe I get to hear it again. I wasn't sure that I ever would.

Liam's smile grows wider as he closes the distance between us. I can't do anything but hold my breath and wait for his next words. "Would you judge me too harshly if I said you had me at hello?"

I bark a laugh of relief and jump into his arms. He wraps them around me and squeezes, all the pain and loneliness of the past two months lifting out of my body like dust from a fan. He sets me down and takes my face between his hands. He presses his lips against mine for just a moment before we both jolt at the sounds of applause that roar around us. I look around and see Anne, Terri, Nadine, Nicole, and Callie cheering and embracing one another. Elle is jumping up and down and screaming like she's just seen a celebrity.

I shift my gaze back to Liam, my vision glassy with tears. He swipes a thumb across my cheek and lifts a corner of his mouth. "I love you, Lucy Bowen," he says, before pressing his lips to mine again.

TWENTY-FIVE

The moments between kissing Liam in the Heartwarming lobby and arriving back at my apartment are a blur.

Elle decides to go to Jersey for the weekend after all, but not before hugging me like she's leaving for a month when we parted. There is so much to be said between us, and I'm sure she'll drag it all out of me when she returns on Monday.

I'm not sure how to leave things with Anne, so I just tell her I'll see her on Monday, because that is definitely a Monday problem.

So that left Liam and me... alone.

"Where's Blue?" I ask as Liam stands uncomfortably in the foyer of my apartment. I take his hand and lead him to the couch.

"With Brett," Liam replies, weaving his fingers in mine. "I was really supposed to be meeting with suppliers this weekend. But my car kind of just drove itself here." His voice trails off as we sit on the couch together.

"I feel like we have a lot to talk about," he says.

I scoot to the edge of the couch and prop myself up on my knees. He raises his hand to place a piece of hair behind my ear. I lean into his hand, the corner of my mouth turning up at the feel of his fingers running through my hair. I look up at him and give him a soft smile.

"We do, but is it okay if I go first?" I say, sitting back on my heels. He nods.

I take a deep breath before I start. "I don't know what this is going to look like, you and me," I say, gesturing between us. "I don't know what the next few months or years of my life are going to look like. But I want to go through them with you."

Liam smiles my favorite shy smile and folds his legs under him to sit next to me on the couch. I let myself reach out and run my hand through his hair, taking a moment to marvel at the fact that I'm really looking into his eyes again. Part of me still can't believe that today happened. Maybe I'll wake up tomorrow morning, my laptop still on my stomach after falling asleep writing, and realize this was all a dream, the perfect ending to my story. But this is real. I did this. I found my ending.

"I started writing the book," I start, looking down to avoid his gaze. I wish I could sidestep this conversation, but this all-consuming idea of a book has been a third wheel in our relationship since day one, and we both need some closure from it. "It's not about you. It's not even about Hudson Hollow." Liam eyes me, an unsure expression on his face. "It's still a small-town romance, the heroine is a lot more cynical than me, if you can believe that," I say with a nervous laugh. "And she finds herself, at least, I think she will, with the hero's help." I lift a corner of my mouth up. "Okay, maybe you did inspire some parts of it. But I want you to know, I didn't mean any of the things I wrote about you. You're not damaged, you're so strong, and so put-together all the time," I add with a laugh.

"I understand, Lucy. It took me a while, but I think I finally get it," he says, his voice gravelly. He reaches over and takes my hand in his. "In truth, I don't know how you qualified for this research mission in the first place, I don't think you have one bone in your body that is slimy enough to do what you set out to." I look down for a moment and squeeze Liam's hand, hoping that our connection can communicate what my words are failing to in this moment. I think he knows how sorry I am. I think he's forgiven me. Now I just need to forgive myself.

"You asked me once why I chose to edit romance novels," I continue, meeting his eyes again. Liam nods at the memory. "And the answer is hope." I smile sheepishly. "They give me hope. They let me feel love. Before I went to Hudson Hollow, not even my favorite romance novels were bringing me joy anymore. I couldn't find inspiration anywhere because life was just beating me down." Liam frowns at my statement, but I don't want him to feel bad for me. I want him to understand why I'm here, and how I got here.

"But romance has always been *it* for me. Because there is always a happy ending. And I have to believe that we have one too. Because you," I say, placing my hand on his chest. "Hudson Hollow, my trip, has done more than make me believe in love again. It made me believe in myself. It's made me believe that I could impulsively run off upstate because I had to tell you I love you." I chuckle and Liam's smile grows wider on his face. "So, I'm in. I don't want to scare you or commit too much too soon, but I can't go back to my life as it was before I came to Hudson Hollow. Too much has changed. I've changed."

Liam inhales, letting out a slow exhale that is visible on his chest. He lays his hand on the back of the couch and plays with the ends of my hair. "So, what does it look like for you? I know the planning side of your brain has thought about it." I smile at the way he talks about me like he knows me so well. "What could our options be?"

I blow out a loud breath. "Well, I don't think I want to live in the city anymore, but my lease isn't up until January. Of course, I would have to talk to Elle about that. Even though she was somewhat of a ringleader in getting me back to you, I don't think she'll be too thrilled about having to take on our rent alone."

"And then you'd move to Hudson Hollow?" Liam asks, and my chest clenches, wondering if I've scared him.

"I don't want to freak either of us out, since we've been together for a total of two hours," I say with a chuckle. "But I want to give us a shot. And I may have sort of quit my job before going to find you—"

"You did?" he asks, raising his brows.

"Kind of. I'll have to work out the particulars with Anne, but I want to be a writer. And maybe that means freelance editing or being a commissioning editor, or something like that to bring in some income. Maybe working remotely, I don't know yet. But I know that this is right for me. My life has been a bit upended this summer—with being in

Hudson Hollow, meeting you, writing a book, and Josie..." My voice trails off.

Liam watches me carefully, letting the tone of my voice sink in. "Lucy..." he starts.

I smile, pressing down the knot in my throat. "She wanted me to chase my own dream. She wanted—" I take a deep breath before continuing.

"Going to Hudson Hollow caused so much change in my life, and not just giving me the opportunity to fall in love with you," I say with a surprisingly confident tone. "It made me realize that publishing as I'm in it right now, isn't a dream. And a wise man once told me that I might need a new dream."

Liam grins. "And you've found it? Your new dream?"

"I'm looking at him."

We lean in together, the gravity of the moment so strong that we're pulled together by forces out of our control. Liam gathers me in his arms and pulls me onto his lap, and I feel his forearms clench around my back. I moan into his mouth as he pulls me tighter to him. The feeling of disbelief is caught in my chest, like at any moment I could say something wrong or snap back into reality where I don't have a man kissing me like his life depends on it, holding me like he may never let me go.

So naturally, I start laughing.

My awkward laugh breaks our kiss, and I immediately hide myself in Liam's chest. "What are you doing, you weirdo?" he says, a rumble of laughter emanating from his throat.

I can't believe I'm doing this. I can't believe I'm ruining this perfect moment. Why am I like this?

"Lucy, talk to me."

I lift my head, trying to shake the smile from my face, but when I look at his perfectly swollen lips, I run my fingers across them, and let another giggle escape my lips. "Is there something on my face, or something?" I laugh even harder at his question.

"I'm sorry," I say, my voice high like I'm on helium. "No, I'm sorry," I say, cupping his face. "You're perfect. I'm just the worst."

"What?" he asks, confusion and a hint of amusement on his face.

"I'm sorry," I repeat, trying to control myself. I hope the laughing fit has finally passed and I can focus on trying to form coherent words. "I just—you're *so* perfect." He continues to look at me cluelessly. "You're romance-novel-perfect."

Liam shakes his head, his blonde waves swaying back and forth. "You know, I think I've been told that before. Something about my eyebrows," he says, gesturing to his face. I cackle.

"When I met you that day I got to Hudson Hollow, I literally thought you were some actor Anne hired to mess with me. I couldn't believe that I had come to a small town and you were standing there," I say, sitting back on his lap. "And never, in a million years, would I have thought my summer would end up like this. And now, I don't know, I'm just wondering if I deserve it."

Liam traces a finger down my cheek and cups his thumb under my chin to lift my head. I slowly lift my lids and let his gaze absorb me. His face is solemn, like he is about to make the most serious confession of his life. "When I was in middle school, I had the worst acne."

Yes, of course, I let out the loudest, most obnoxious laugh ever.

"What?" I say, looking at him like he's crazy. "Where did that come from?"

"I was the dorkiest of the dorks. And I don't mean to put labels on anything, but I played the clarinet. I loved reading. I would blow through fifty books throughout the school year, nagging my teachers for more until the rest of the class dubbed me the teacher's pet. I wasn't competitive. The list goes on and on."

"Why are you telling me this?" I ask, all laughter disappearing from my voice.

"Because you have me pegged as this ideal romance hero, like I came out of the womb ready to be Fabio on the cover of a mass market—"

"Fabio? Mass market?" I interrupt, stunned by his industry terminology.

"Yeah, I did research. That Julia Quinn knows her shit," he says matter-of-factly. I laugh. "I'm just a guy who grew up in a small town. Maybe I remind you of some stereotype that you've read about, but that's not me. I'm real. I have a history and a family, and flaws up the wahzoo—"

"Including the fact that you say wahzoo," I mutter. When he looks at me knowingly, I roll my eyes at myself. "I'm sorry, it just came out."

"I'm not perfect. I'm just me. And I hope you can wrap your head around the fact that you're not getting your fictional lines blurred here. I'm in love with you, Lucy Bowen. Not some character in a book loosely based on you. *You*."

I smile sheepishly, but then scrunch my nose at him. "So, acne, huh?"

"Cystic," he mutters, pursing his lips and nodding his head.

I giggle before I lean in and cover his mouth with mine, pouring everything I have into him. Liam's grip on my hips tightens and I feel a change in the energy between us. When our kiss breaks, Liam's eyes don't move from my lips, and we can both sense that we are heading somewhere.

"Hey," I say softly, running my fingers through his hair and brushing it out of his face. I scrunch my brows at him, trying to gauge his hesitation. Am I reading him wrong? Is this going too fast? My heart jolts at the possibility of rejection, especially with everything we've said to each other tonight. But then Liam reaches for my face, cupping the back of my head in his hand.

"I'm sure there's something cool and sexy to say in this moment, but I've got nothing," he says, not a hint of laughter in his voice. "Except to say that I've pretty much been waiting for this moment since I met you."

"You should give yourself some credit, because that was pretty good," I say with a smile. Liam lifts one corner of his mouth up and embraces me again, wrapping his arms around my back and kissing me fervently. Liam brings his large hands to my bottom and wraps my legs around his waist. I grab on to his neck and feel weightless as he carries us to my bed, never once losing the connection between our lips.

When he lays me down on the bed, he takes his time exploring every inch of my body with his fingers. I do the same, running my hands up and down the flexed muscles of his torso once he lifts his shirt over his head. Whenever I've done this in the past, my concentration has been on making sure my partner knows I am enjoying myself. I focus on making all the right noises and trying to do what I think I should do, rather than just being in the moment. In all the times I imagined this happening with Liam, I could never imagine it being this comfortable. So natural that I'm only focusing on him, and the way he makes my body feel. I think back to all our subtle moments—brushing hands while we hiked up to The Point, nudging each other's knees when we fished from his dock, the tingle I felt when he fitted me with a life jacket on his boat. It was all leading to this. And it feels like we finally make sense.

Our noses brush one another and now, there is more urgency to our kiss. While he kisses me, Liam's hands skim down my body, one cupping in between my legs. When I gasp in response, his mouth crashes into mine harder, more passionately than before. His lips never lose their rhythm while his fingers slide beneath my panties and find the warmth beneath. My grip on his neck tightens as he massages me gently with his thumb, pressing first one, and then two fingers inside. To no surprise, Liam knows exactly what to do to make me shudder. I'm moaning, breathlessly pleading for his pace to quicken, grabbing his shoulders so tightly as he watches me fall apart beneath him.

When finally, the quaking within me settles, Liam traces my face with his hand, pressing his lips to mine gently. "I thought I couldn't love you anymore than I already did, but then I watched you do that," he whispers, brushing my hair off my face.

My brain can't form words at the moment, so I return the

sentiment with a slow, tender kiss. I don't think I ever want to stop kissing Liam. Ever. It is my new favorite pastime.

Liam lifts me up, readjusting our position and placing my head on the pillow. I watch as he retrieves a condom from his wallet. Desire stirs as he slips out of his jeans, and I take a deep breath.

Thumb-to-pointer-finger theory: proven.

Liam slides the condom on in one smooth motion and then moves on top of me. A wide smile spreads across my face as Liam's blue eyes gaze into mine, and I feel like I am home.

He presses himself into me slowly, gauging my reaction to each of his movements. He moves his hips gently, and with each movement, I feel the pleasure building. Liam breaks our kiss and slows his motions, and I see his face is strained. I nudge Liam's shoulder until he slows and I can use his weight to help us flip over.

A knowing smile spreads across my face as his surprise registers. Shifting atop him, I adjust my position, rolling my hips until I align perfectly with the exact spot I want. Liam's gaze tracks my every movement, his hands steadying on my hips. Leaning forward, I kiss him, then quicken my rhythm, my muscles tightening as I pinpoint the sensation that sends waves of pleasure coursing through me. The intensity builds as I lose control, crying out with each thrust. I collapse against him, warmth flooding through my body as release overtakes me.

I roll onto my side and let one leg drape over Liam as we both catch our breaths. I lay my head on his chest and listen to the sound of his racing heart, letting its rhythm soothe my own, drifting off to the feeling of his fingers tracing the lines of my back.

"I've dreamt of his moment," Liam murmurs against my forehead. When I look up at him from my position on his chest, he cups my chin in his hand. "You were my new dream, too," he says. "And I'm never going to let you go again."

I admire the beautiful man beside me. Before I met him, I'm not sure I knew exactly who I was. I'm not sure I knew that there was a happily-ever-after out there for me. When I met him, even though I worked every day to bring HEAs to readers, I think I truly had lost the magic in them. But every time I look at him, I can't help but feel it, not just my love for him, but my love for our story.

He is the hero of my story. My small-town romance. My happily-ever-now.

Acknowledgements

FIRST AND FOREMOST, I have to thank you, the person holding this book. If you are someone who has ever doubted that dreams can come true, this collection of bound pages in your hands is proof that they can. Thank you for picking up this book and reading Lucy and Liam's story. Thank you for making my author dreams come true.

To my agent, Sian, for being an absolute rockstar. Publishing is all about finding one person who likes your work. Just one. One who really hears you. And I am so eternally grateful that Sian picked me. Thank you, Sian, for hearing me and for being everything I could ever ask for in an agent. Thank you also to everyone at Blake Friedmann Literary Agency for all the support along the way. I am so grateful to have such a strong team on my side!

At first, publishing is about finding one person. Then, you have to find another…and another. Aubrie and the Aria Fiction team—thank you for taking a chance on Lucy and me. What an honor to have such a talented team of brilliant women on my side. (Plus, they're some of the coolest people

I've ever met.) And thank you to Simone for the gorgeous cover!

Thank you to Kate Marope (@theribbonmarker) for tearing the first draft of this book to absolute shreds. I wouldn't have been able to revise it, and revise it again, and again, without your expert guidance.

I'm a teacher, so I can't help but throw a shoutout to every English teacher and professor I've had. Thank you for fostering a love of language so deeply within me that helped me make it to this point. From Mrs. Johnston in middle school to Tommy Z at Marist, thank you for being a part of my writing journey.

Lastly, to my family, who are just reading this book for the first time upon publication (#awkward). Thank you for your love and support on this and every path I choose to take in life (and there have been a few!). Skip the sex scenes–please and thank you.

About the Author

CRISTINA WOLF wrote her first book in the third grade. It was an adventure book about her beagle, Abby, complete with hand-drawn illustrations and top-notch handwriting. Needless to say, writing and reading has been a passion of Cristina's from the beginning. After graduating from Marist College with a double major in Business and English, Cristina pursued a career in the publishing industry while earning her Master of Science in Publishing from New York University. Cristina has experience working at literary agencies and as an editorial assistant at a publishing house. Finding life in NYC a bit different than she expected, Cristina returned to her native New Jersey where she earned her Master in Teaching from Monmouth University. She now shares her love of books with her students as a middle school English teacher. Other than working or writing, Cristina loves spending time with her dogs, Zoey, Winnie, and Mabel, exercising on her Peloton, laying on her hammock with a good book, and planning her next trip to Disney World.

Thanks for reading!

Want to receive exclusive author content, news on the latest Aria books and updates on offers and giveaways?

Follow us on X @AriaFiction and on Facebook and Instagram @HeadofZeus, and join our mailing list.